Trust Me With Your Love

SYNITHIA WILLIAMS

Copyright © June 2017 by Synithia Williams
ISBN: 978-0-9975729-2-6
Edited by: Katherine Locke
Cover Art by: Mae Phillips at Cover Fresh Designs

Synithia Williams
Columbia, SC

DEDICATION

To my friends and family who've supported me from the very first book.
Your encouragement and support keeps me motivated. To the readers
who've taken a chance with my novels, thank you!! Finally, to my personal
hero, I love you more than words can express.

CHAPTER 1

Whoever said, "winning isn't everything" never found himself losing a multi-million-dollar contract.

Isaac Caldwell leaned forward on his desk and pinched the bridge of his nose. Steadily, he sucked in air then let it out slowly, counting to seven. His body didn't buy the relaxation method. Tension pierced and twisted in his shoulders like a corkscrew in a vintage bottle of wine.

After spending thirty minutes on the phone with Rudy Knopp, the City of Atlanta's Public Works Commissioner, Isaac couldn't convince him to renew the city's waste hauling contract with Caldwell Environmental Solutions. A contract with a city that large had not been easy to come by and wouldn't be easily replaced.

"Is there anything I can do to keep your business?" Isaac asked Rudy in a calm tone that didn't betray his growing frustration. No matter how much he wanted—needed—to keep this account, he wouldn't beg. He wouldn't give away the fact that he was desperate to find a way to save C.E.S. Losing Atlanta's business would be a blow they'd struggle to recover from.

"I'll be honest, Isaac, your service is good, but your father's threats aren't," Rudy said. "His influence has diminished. We've gotten rid of the old program director and did a triple background check on the new one. The mayor won't put up with threats from vendors. I'm getting pressure to look elsewhere."

Isaac bit his lower lip to keep the curse ricocheting through his brain from coming out of his mouth. "Rudy, you won't have to deal with my father. I'll personally handle all of the City's concerns."

He'd promise to answer every damn customer service call if that would keep Atlanta on the books. If only he could also promise his father wouldn't continue to try and influence business. Curtis Caldwell had built C.E.S. with blackmail, threats, and dirty dealings he'd been lucky enough to get away with due to exceptional service. Exceptional not because the employees were committed, but because Curtis didn't hesitate to threaten employees for anything less than the best.

"That's all well and good," Rudy said in his thick Southern accent. "But that doesn't take your father completely out of the equation. The mayor hasn't forgotten your father asked how much it would take to ensure we signed the next contract. He doesn't trust your father, and, honestly, I can't blame him. If you were running things, then I might be able to work some magic. I'm not sure if I can convince the mayor to keep your contract with your father around."

"Come on, Rudy, you know I'm basically running things. Curtis is nothing more than a figurehead."

The words were the truth. Ever since Isaac's brother Andre had left C.E.S. to work for himself, Curtis had been obsessed with trying to find a way to get back at his son for turning his back on the family. Curtis's need for revenge had diverted his attention from C.E.S. Isaac had picked up the slack. Not that he minded. With Curtis out of the picture, he could work toward reworking the company image and convincing clients they were no longer the C.E.S. of the past as he and Andre had originally planned.

"He's still there, and he's still a problem. I know you're trying to do this right, but he called the mayor just a month ago asking for his selling point."

Isaac's head fell back, and he gritted his teeth. Frustration over that fiasco hadn't lessened in the four weeks since Rudy had called him, furious about Curtis's "offer."

"I apologize that happened."

"I accept your apology, but apologies mean nothing if it can happen again. You know what needs to be done to fix all your problems."

"I won't kick him out of the company he built."

"That may be the only thing that will keep you in business. C.E.S. has a bad reputation. People want to work with you, but they don't want to work with your dad. I get that you're trying to be loyal, but sometimes family doesn't deserve loyalty."

The finality in Rudy's tone was clear. There was no need to argue further. "Rudy, I want your business. Let me talk to Curtis before you drop us completely."

Rudy sighed. "I'll do what I can on my end to get the mayor to at least accept any proposals you send our way, but only because I respect you."

"I appreciate that." Even though it wasn't enough.

They said goodbye and Isaac hung up the phone. He dropped his head in his hands. He'd expected that Curtis's underhanded dealings would one day bite them in the ass. After his brother jumped ship and Isaac had been left to take over, he'd hoped his efforts to steer the company in the right direction would prevent disaster. Instead, things had gotten worse in the past year. Curtis Caldwell may not give the company his undivided attention anymore, but he didn't hesitate to step in and make tenuous partnerships even worse. They'd already lost three other contracts in the past year. The loss of the Atlanta contract was the bitter icing on the cake. How could he win them back without completely overhauling the company's image or removing Curtis?

You can't.

Three short taps came from his closed office door. He glanced at the clock. The weekly staff meeting was in twenty minutes. The door opened, and his administrative assistant Kimberly Griffin strolled in wearing her typical pants suit. The tension in his body tightened even more as sexual awareness joined the party. Kim had that effect on him. Today's pantsuit was tan and complemented the golden undertones in her light brown complexion. The severe cut of the suit would be unflattering on a woman with lesser curves. Not on Kim. She could wear a pillowcase, and it would hug her eye-catching figure like a glove.

Her thick dark hair was pulled back into a ponytail. She wore no makeup except for a hint of lip gloss. Not that she needed more. Her lips were full and distracting, her lashes thick and long, her skin clear and flawless. Back before he'd left Isaac high and dry, Andre hadn't wanted Isaac to hire Kim. Isaac's tendency was to hire administrative assistants more for their looks than their brains. More than one had ended up in his bed. Kim broke that habit.

They'd almost gone there. One night in his office after hours. He'd kissed those lips. Touched her soft skin. When his fingers found the waistband of her panties, she'd spouted off about wanting everything: love, a relationship, and commitment. His reply, a shocked laugh, hadn't been his finest comeback. That had effectively ruined the mood and ended their interlude. Thankfully, they'd gotten past that awkward night and were now comfortable with one another. She'd turned out to be the perfect administrative assistant and an indispensable colleague. Which meant, even if she didn't want a relationship, he couldn't have sex with her now and ruin their tenuous rapport.

If only the memory of her soft skin and lush curves would stop taking up residence in his brain like an unwanted houseguest.

"I've finished putting together the budget numbers for the staff meeting." Kim's voice was always professional, but just husky enough to spike his testosterone. She looked up from the papers in her hand. "Uh oh, what's wrong?"

He dropped his hand from his head and looked into sexy hazel eyes that scattered his thoughts more than she'd ever guess. Drumming his fingers on the desk, he forced his thoughts back to business and off of Kim's eyes, lips and curves. "I just got off the phone with Atlanta. They aren't renewing with us."

The barest of winces crossed her face before her lips lifted in what he guessed was supposed to be a reassuring smile. "That doesn't mean we can't submit a proposal when they put out a new request for service."

"That would be a waste of time and paper."

Kim's full lips pressed together in a tight line. She hugged the reports in her hand close to her chest. Dread filled Isaac.

"How bad are they?"

Kim took a deep breath before slipping out one and holding it out toward him. "Not as bad as last month's."

Isaac glanced at the numbers and cringed. "Not as bad because they've flatlined. We can't afford to keep losing contracts."

Something she would already know. She collected the information from finance and helped put together the reports. She'd heard him complain about Curtis's lack of interest in the company and the fact that they were losing clients because she was the only person he trusted to actually show his growing concerns with the business. C.E.S. was bleeding. The cuts hadn't been life threatening, but if they lost more clients, they would hemorrhage.

Concern filled her eyes. "What are you going to do?"

"Try again to convince Curtis to let me take over. His way of doing things doesn't work anymore." Isaac stood and logged off his computer. "He's no longer interested, but he won't give me the full ability to lead us in the direction we need to take. He can't ignore this anymore."

"I agree."

Isaac pulled his suit jacket off the back of his chair. Kim pulled her lower lip between her teeth. The movement meant she was trying not to say what was on her mind and made him think about kissing her.

"But?" He slipped on his jacket and ignored memories of the one time he'd had Kim's lips on his.

Her eyes widened innocently. "But what?"

He didn't buy it for a second. "Spill it, Kim. You agree, but?"

Any pretense of holding back dropped. She squared her shoulders and gave him her prepare yourself side eye that typically preceded bad news. "The employees in finance are talking. They know C.E.S. is struggling and they're worried that we can't remain stable. It's causing some people to feel nervous."

"How nervous?"

"Greg in Finance turned in his resignation this morning. I heard a few of the ladies in accounting talk about a job fair."

Isaac's headache returned full force. "Shit. Greg is one of the best guys down there. What can I do to make him stay? How much?"

Kim shrugged, but her brows drew together as she thought about it.

This was part of what made her so invaluable to him. Her body was distracting, but her brains were damned sexy. She had a finger on the pulse of the employees with whom Isaac never came in contact. He could often diffuse a situation before it became a larger issue because Kim would come to him ahead of time.

"More money may keep him," she said thoughtfully. She cupped her chin and tapped her lips. The kissing memories ramped up again. Isaac looked away, focused on locking down his computer.

"But not for long," she continued in a thoughtful tone that didn't hint she realized her effect on him. "Greg sees the books. He'll know it'll just be a short-term fix."

"I'll take short term before I take losing one of my best employees," Isaac replied. "I'll talk with Katherine and see about getting Greg a raise."

"What about long term?" Kim asked.

"I'm going to convince my dad that it's time to turn over the reins of C.E.S. to me."

"Then I should warn you."

Isaac went still. "About what?"

"Your dad is already here, and he's telling everyone about his new plan to save C.E.S."

"What? He hasn't said anything to me about a new plan." Unease spread through Isaac.

Lately, every conversation he had with Curtis had been about ruining Andre. His dad's preoccupation with getting back at the son who'd betrayed him had increased in the last few weeks. There was little Curtis could really do to Andre, who'd moved to North Carolina with his wife Mikayla and had no business connections Curtis could easily manipulate. Isaac had hoped that eventually, Curtis's inability to get at Andre would lessen his need for revenge.

Isaac walked around his desk to the door and held it open for Kim. "Any idea what this new plan is?"

Her left shoulder nearly bumped the doorjamb in her haste to get through the door without touching him. That was another reason their comradery worked. They didn't touch. Ever. They *couldn't*. Their partnership was too valuable. That was the excuse he kept using whenever he wanted to relive that night in his office.

He leaned forward just a little and inhaled deeply. She smelled like strawberries and silk. That was the name on the bottle of lotion he'd seen her use. The damn manufacturer probably deliberately made the smell and title provocative.

She took several steps to increase the distance between them. Isaac bit back a satisfied smile. Even though they were going to be adults about things and not ruin their working relationship, he liked knowing a part of

Kim remembered the heat that had flared between them.

She avoided his gaze when she answered his question. "He only said that he had a great idea and everyone is going to love it."

That was highly unlikely. He followed her out. His office, Curtis's and the one that used to house his brother were part of a suite on the top floor of a building in downtown Greenville. Kim's desk sat just outside his door. The other two doors in the suite were closed. Isaac never looked at Andre's door. He didn't need the reminder that his brother had moved on.

The other staff members were all in the conference room when he and Kim arrived. The Monday meeting included the heads of finance, accounting, public relations, collection services, and personnel.

"Isaac, it's about time. Get over here and let's start this meeting." Curtis boomed from where he sat at the head of the table.

Isaac greeted the other managers as he sat opposite of Curtis at the other end of the table.

"I didn't realize I was late," Isaac said easily. He didn't have to glance at his watch to know he'd arrived in the boardroom with five minutes to spare.

"This meeting is important," Curtis said, as if all of the other meetings weren't.

Curtis wore a dark gray suit tailored to fit his wide shoulders and widening waistline. Small lines framed his dark eyes, and his hair was just beginning to show more gray than black. He clasped his hands, still rough despite weekly manicures, in front of him on the table. The light shone off the gaudy gold rings on both ring fingers. He would still be considered handsome if it weren't for the condescending smirk that seemed to remain on his face. Right now, that smirk was directed at Isaac.

Kim handed out the copies of the financial report to the other staff members. Curtis frowned at the paper and slid it away with enough force to send it sailing half way down the table.

"I don't care about the numbers. I know exactly what we need to do to fix these numbers."

"You should care," Isaac kept his tone easy in an effort to hide the irritation bubbling inside him. "Fixing these numbers isn't going to be easy."

Curtis flicked his wrist. "That's your problem. Always worrying and overthinking. I know what we need to do and I say we're doing it."

Isaac leaned back in his chair and cocked a brow. "What are we doing?"

"We're going to buy out a small composting business and expand our market." Curtis grinned and looked around at each of the employees.

Stiff smiles and nervous shuffles were what he got in return. Isaac took a deep breath instead of rolling his eyes like he wanted.

"C.E.S. isn't in a position to buy out anyone," Isaac said calmly. Arguing with Curtis wouldn't get him anywhere. "Instead of trying to purchase another company we need to make up the losses we suffered. Newer, smaller companies like Southern Sanitation have underbid us in three key markets just this year alone. We need to figure out why we're losing clients and focus on getting clients in new markets."

"To hell with Southern Sanitation. They're a small collector and no threat."

Isaac straightened in his chair but kept his movements relaxed even though he wanted to lash out. "You said that two years ago and look what happened. We can't afford to continue to ignore what's happening."

"Expanding into composting will bring in the additional revenue." Curtis sounded so sure of himself. Confident in his decision, but the flare of a predator ready to kill lit his eyes.

Isaac tried to reason with him again. "There are other companies already farther ahead of us in that market."

Curtis nodded and held out a hand toward Isaac. "Which is why we need to buy one of them now."

"Not when we're losing money." His frustration leaked through.

Curtis threw up his hands in exasperation. "We wouldn't be having this argument if your brother was still here. He knew how to get things done."

That wasn't the first time Curtis threw out that jab. Just like any other punch taking the hit wasn't easier just because Isaac was used to it. He compartmentalized the damage. He knew Curtis preferred Andre to him. Andre was more like Curtis. More cutthroat, ruthless and shrewd in business. Or at least he had been before he'd changed in the name of love. Isaac was the backup son. The one who filled in when Andre wasn't available. He doubted Curtis ever expected the son he'd given the least attention to would be the one he'd be stuck with.

Isaac straightened his cuffs and mirrored his father's earlier stance by clasping his hands together before him on the table. "Andre isn't here, I am. Any move to buy out another company would only hurt C.E.S."

Curtis's eyes narrowed. "Are you trying to tell me what to do with my company?"

Scott Morrison from accounting cleared his throat. Curtis and Isaac both glanced at him. "Isaac makes a valid point. The accounts we've lost have had an impact on our revenue. Trying to stem the flow of cash lost should be the priority."

Scott wasn't one of Isaac's favorite people because he tended to take Curtis's side in most arguments. Isaac suspected Scott wanted to be the next in line to take over Andre's empty COO position. Curtis refused to fill the spot. He foolishly thought Andre was coming back.

Curtis's dark eyes traveled between the two. "Oh, I see how it is. You two are working against me."

"No one is working against you," Isaac said with barely veiled annoyance. "We are all trying to save this company. I just got off the phone with Atlanta. We've lost that one too."

A series of groans and gasps came from the other managers. He definitely hadn't wanted to make the announcement this way, but Curtis was delusional. He needed to understand what was going on.

"I suggest we table the idea of purchasing a composting operation until we are more financially stable," Isaac said before Curtis could start again.

Curtis's nostrils flared. The fire in his eyes would have turned Isaac to ash if it had been real. Isaac didn't back down. Curtis had shown on numerous occasions that he'd do anything to prove he was right, even humiliate his own son, but Isaac loved this company. He would not let Curtis drive it into the ground.

He held Curtis's stare for several tense seconds. Curtis finally looked away. Isaac glanced at Kim in the corner. Her lips lifted in a small, reassuring smile. Some of the tension left his shoulders. Her reassurances when he wanted to lash out always kept him calm. His relationship with Kim was good as is. He couldn't mess things up by sleeping with her. She wanted love, which was one of life's biggest cons. He responded with a curt nod and focused back on the meeting.

CHAPTER 2

Kim held her breath and watched Isaac and Curtis. The vein at Curtis's temple beat erratically. That usually preceded him blowing up and kicking everyone out of the boardroom so he could yell at Isaac in perceived privacy. Curtis fought Isaac on everything. As much as Kim wished she didn't care, she did. She worked here, and she saw how much Isaac tried to turn things around. Add to that a two-year crush she'd tried to suppress, and she was emotionally involved.

Curtis looked away first. She exhaled slowly. Isaac's dark gaze met hers, and her heart did a cartwheel. She smiled instinctively and was grateful he was far enough away to not see how much her breathing had quickened. He nodded and looked away. As always. That particular romantic ship had sailed, crashed, and sunk.

"You know what," Curtis said in a falsely calm voice. "We'll table this for later."

Isaac's face didn't change, but his absolute stillness told her he was surprised Curtis dropped the argument. In every situation, he always remained calm. Calm, cold and calculating. Just like the street hustlers she'd grown up around. That was exactly what made her want him so much.

Idiotic, maybe, but her hormones always jumped for an unavailable man. Isaac was the worst kind. Skin like polished mahogany, intense dark eyes, a body honed to swoon-worthy perfection thanks to boxing workouts, and an attitude and swagger she'd rarely seen shaken. With a quirk of his lips, panties flew off. Something Kim had forced herself to remember on numerous occasions. She wasn't a plaything for men. Not anymore.

Isaac turned to the head of Finance. "Then we can move on to the financial reports."

Kim let out a silent prayer that the tense situation was diffused for now. She'd be sure to get the aspirin ready. He always had a headache after a run-in with his father.

Her phone vibrated in her pocket. She kept her phone on her at all times in case her mother or grandmother needed her. Kim, her mom, and younger sister had moved in with her grandmother right after their grandfather died Kim's senior year of high school. The move had brought stability to their grandmother, whose gambling habit spiraled out of control after her husband died, and to Kim and her sister who'd watched their mother struggle to keep the bills paid.

Between her grandmother's gambling and her mom struggling to find a job, things had been rough, but in the past year, their lives had stabilized. Kim's mom landed a good job at a local manufacturer, and her grandmother had stopped visiting internet "cafes" set up for illegal online gambling and spent her days at the senior center. Things were finally stable enough for Kim to get her own place.

The text message was from her grandmother. *Mr. Jackson is selling the house.*

Kim's mouth fell open in a silent gasp. Mr. Jackson owned the house her grandmother had rented for the past fifteen years. She glanced at Isaac. He was still in deep conversation with Curtis. She bit her lower lip and gripped her phone. Her grandmother didn't like text message conversations. Kim stood, and Isaac immediately looked her way. She held up her phone and pointed to the door. He frowned but nodded.

Kim slipped out of the conference room and called her grandmother. Ruby answered after the second ring.

"Why are you calling me?"

"Why do you think? You can't text information like that. Mr. Jackson is selling the house?"

Ruby's annoyed sigh came through the phone. "Yeah, he says he's ready to retire to Florida or some mess."

"Is he kicking you out?"

"He says he isn't. Offered to sell the house to me. He says he'll give me four months to see if I can come up with the down payment before he puts it on the market. As if that's some type of favor."

Kim pressed her hand to her temple. "It is a favor. He could have said nothing. We could have woken up to a for sale sign in the front yard."

Her grandmother grunted. "He didn't have to sell the house at all. All the work I did making the house look nice, and now he's about to profit from it."

"This could be a good thing," Kim said. "You said you wanted the house. Do you have the down payment?"

"What do you think, Kim? My social security only pays so much. Mr. Jackson rattled on something about the neighborhood being trendy. I asked him how much he wanted for the place."

"How much does he want?" Kim asked hesitantly. Her grandmother told her the amount and Kim flinched.

"How am I supposed to come up with that?" Ruby sounded defeated.

Her grandmother's place was in an older neighborhood that, thanks to its proximity to downtown, was being revitalized and considered desirable. Her grandmother was on a fixed income. Her mother's job paid decent enough, but she'd only been in the position for a few months and had bounced around before that.

"We'll find a way. We've got four months."

"I can go to the cafe." Excitement filled Ruby's voice. "I've been pretty lucky playing BINGO at the senior center. I know that luck will pass over on the games."

"No," Kim said forcefully. Ruby's sharp inhale made Kim soften her tone. "Come on, Grandma, you know that's not a sure way."

"Then what way do we have? I know you want to move out of the house, Kimmie. Nakita holds down a job about as well as your momma," Ruby said, referring to Kim's younger sister. "I can't keep the house. I might as well find some retirement home that takes social security checks."

Kim shook her head. Dozens of ideas ran through her head. None of them very good. Her grandmother's home had been the only place of security after her father died when she was ten. Roland Griffin had worked two jobs to take care of his wife and daughters. The stress of both probably led to the heart attack that had taken him. Kim's mother, Jackie, had gone from her parent's house to her husband's home. She'd always been taken care of, and Roland's sudden death had left her floundering. Jackie had tried to be a provider, but in the end, her inability to keep stable work led Kim to find other ways to supplement the family's struggling finances. Ways Jackie pretended not to notice.

Kim pushed those thoughts aside. Her life was different now. She didn't have to hustle in the streets anymore. She wouldn't have to hustle again. There was always another way.

"You're not going into a retirement home, Grandma. I've got some savings." Savings she'd built up for her own place. Savings that weren't quite enough for a down payment.

"I knew you'd find a way to fix this," Ruby's relief was palpable. "Do you have enough?"

"No."

"Oh," Ruby said deflated. "Maybe you can work some overtime."

Overtime wasn't really an option in her position. Kim was a salaried employee, which meant she got paid her salary regardless of the time she worked. Granted, she had a decent salary as an administrative assistant to Isaac Caldwell, but between handling most of the household bills for herself, her mom, grandmother, and Nakita on her random stints of moving back home she wasn't swimming in tons of extra income.

"I'll see what I can do. We'll cut some corners, too. Mom's working and she can also help out. Don't worry. We'll find a way to buy the house."

"Are you sure you don't want me to try to win the money online?"

"I'm sure. Promise me you won't go." Gambling nearly cost Ruby everything. Kim didn't want this threat to cause her grandmother to backslide.

"Fine. Oh, wait, I think I hear the mailman coming. You know I gotta run out there 'cause Coretta is stealing my mail."

Coretta, their neighbor, was in a battle with Ruby to see who could be the most petty. After Ruby not only won yard of the month and the affections of Smoky Davis, a widower in their neighborhood both ladies had flirted with, Ruby insisted Coretta had decided to steal her mail.

"She's not stealing your mail, but I know you won't feel better unless you go out there and watch. I've got to get back in this meeting. We'll talk more when I get home."

"Say what you want, I know she's stealing my mail. I'm going to catch her ass, too. Bye Kimmie."

The line went dead, and despite the bad news about the house, Kim smiled at her grandmother's silly rivalry with her neighbor. The humor didn't last long. How were they going to come up with the down payment? The answer came immediately. She'd have to do it. Tap into her savings, put off her own plans to get her own place, stretch her credit, which she was already struggling to repair. She loved her mother and grandmother, but at the moment she wanted to be selfish and tell the two adults in her life to find a way to fix their own problem. But she wouldn't. Guilt wouldn't let her see her grandmother kicked out in the street.

Kim slipped back into the conference room. Curtis threw her an annoyed glance. Isaac's gaze asked if everything was okay. Kim averting her eyes and went back into the corner. She checked the recorder she brought to the meetings to make sure it was still on. She'd refer to that when she put together the minutes for the meeting.

Just as she focused on the meeting again, her phone buzzed. Another text from Ruby.

Rebecca's out. She came by here looking for you.

Kim's blood turned to ice water in her veins. The sounds of the room faded into the background, and her heart thudded. She did a quick mental count of the years. Not that she really needed to. She'd known the six years were coming up.

Her hands shook as she texted back. *That's cool. I'll call her.*

Kim had no intentions of calling Rebecca. Not until she was ready to actually face what could have easily been her fate.

She turned her phone off and put it back in her pocket. Kim hadn't spoken to Rebecca in years. The first year after Rebecca went to jail Kim had visited her once. Guilt had gnawed away at Kim in the years since. Rebecca had taken the job meant for Kim, and because of that, she'd been the one caught. For six years, Kim fluctuated between feeling grateful she'd gotten out of the life and hating that Rebecca took the fall.

She owed Rebecca, but what form of payment would Rebecca demand?

I'm gonna be working with Benji when I'm out. He wants you to work with us. Think about it. The words in the only letter Rebecca had written Kim a few months ago. She wouldn't go back to that life.

"Kim, can you get that together?" Isaac's voice broke into her thoughts.

Her head jerked up. Isaac and the rest of the managers were watching her. Heat prickled her cheeks. "I'm sorry, can you repeat that?"

Isaac's brows drew together. "Can you get a list of the new waste haulers that have come on the scene in the past six months?"

Her nod was jerky. Her smile felt tight. She'd been caught off-guard and being caught off-guard wouldn't help her get the money they needed, and it wouldn't help with Rebecca. "Of course. When do you need it?"

The confusion in his gaze intensified. "End of the day tomorrow," he said as if he was repeating the instructions.

"I'm on it." She looked at her iPad and wrote the reminder in her notes.

Rebecca was out. Cool, she'd known the day was coming. She was out of the game, but she wasn't anyone's punk. Kim straightened her spine and took a deep breath. She'd deal with whatever Rebecca, Benji or anyone else in the old crew might try to throw her way.

The meeting continued, but she felt Isaac's probing gaze through the rest of the meeting. She'd never not paid attention before. She had to get her mind on work.

*

Isaac called Kim into his office immediately after the meeting. She went without question. They typically met after staff meetings to review the notes she'd taken and make any plans for new initiatives discussed. Today was no different, except she could barely keep her mind on their discussion.

"Even though Curtis let the issue slide, I still need to know what he's thinking," Isaac said. He sat behind his desk scrolling through the emails on his computer. Kim sat across from him taking notes on her tablet. "Update the list of companies providing composting services not only in South Carolina but North Carolina and Georgia. If Curtis wants to do this, then he already knows which ones are the best to try and buy out."

She nodded and typed a few more lines. "That list will probably include Andre's company."

Isaac nodded grimly. "I know. I'd like to believe he's not trying to take over Andre's company, but I've learned not to underestimate him. Some people are driven by revenge."

Kim's fingers froze over the tablet. The memory of Benji's hard grip on her arms surfaced. *You think we're going to forget this? Oh, no. You owe me for all this shit.* "He'd blamed her for breaking up his plans to use girls, drugs, and gambling to become a big-time hustler. That's when Kim stopped visiting Rebecca and broken her ties with the old crew.

"Kim?"

She snapped her head up. "Yes, sorry. When do you need this?"

"Do you think you can have it together by the end of the week?"

"I'll have it ready by then."

Instead of looking satisfied, Isaac studied her intently. "What's bothering you?"

She shook her head and tried to appear relaxed. "Nothing is bothering me." She met his eyes. Most people believed her when she looked them in the eye.

Isaac wasn't most people. "You're lying. You're distracted and not listening."

"It's nothing. I apologize." She stood.

Isaac stood and came around the desk. "I can help. Is there anything, you need?"

Brushing him off wouldn't work. He insisted on solving problems. He became methodical and ticked out every step to a resolution. That's how he resolved any challenge brought to him. Her problem would be no exception. They hadn't worked out as lovers, a good thing even if sometimes she wished otherwise. Their pseudo-comfortable working relationship functioned because they kept personal issues out of their discussions. Kim told him nothing of her personal life. The little she knew of his was because she kept his calendar and saw the dates he had with various women.

"This is a personal issue," she said. "I won't let it interfere with my job anymore." She turned toward the door, fully expecting him to drop the subject.

"Is your family okay?" he asked. "No one is hurt or anything?" He stepped closer. His cologne and the prickle of awareness across her skin whenever he was close added to her frayed nerves.

She turned and met his eyes and was surprised to see the concern in them. Isaac didn't show emotion. If anything, he became even more robotic when confronted with others' feelings. His interest made her want to confide her troubles. She had no one to talk to. Her mom, grandmother, and sister wouldn't want to know she was worried. Her friends in the office were colleagues who knew nothing of her troubled past. She'd left the old life because she'd wanted to have a real relationship with a man who would be there for her.

Except Isaac had laughed after she had admitted she wanted a relationship. His laughter had hurt, but knowing he could have lied, slept with her, and broken her heart later had eased the pain.

Kim stepped back. She needed space, but an ocean of space wouldn't be enough to make her not want Isaac. "No one is hurt. Just a minor annoyance. Everything is cool."

"If there is anything you need, I'm willing to take care of it."

Of course, he would. That's what he'd offered that night. To take care of her like a prized poodle. "Thank you, Isaac, but I don't need to be taken care of."

CHAPTER 3

"I don't need to be taken care of."

The words irritated Isaac for the rest of the day. Through lunch with a client, an afternoon meeting with his human resources director, and conference call with an operations manager in Georgia. They scratched at him like a tag in the back of a cheap shirt. He shouldn't be annoyed. Their relationship was built on not getting personal. But something had shattered her unwavering focus, and he wanted to know what.

Typically working out helped rid him of any annoyances from the day. He'd always been active but picked up boxing after Andre left the company. The urge to hit something had grown stronger around that time. He practiced at The Arena, a warehouse converted into a boxing gym. What the place lacked in aesthetics was more than made up for with excellent training. Isaac knew the owner, Cal Sandler, from the old gym where Cal, a former cop, and MMA fighter, had been one of the trainers. When Cal opened his own boxing studio, Isaac joined Cal's location.

Isaac got through Cal's crazy definition of a warm-up, which included four hundred reps with the jump rope followed by a sprint down the street before they sparred in the ring. He never planned to fight professionally, but he trained with the professional fighters under Cal's tutelage and attended some of their fights to show his support.

"You're distracted!" Cal's booming baritone was the only warning Isaac got before Cal's right hook aimed at Isaac's head.

Isaac bobbed to avoid the hit. "I'm not distracted."

Cal didn't reply. Isaac focused back on Cal to avoid a left jab that would knock out a few teeth. He could image the crazy look Kim would throw his way if he came in with his front teeth missing.

That is if he could get a smile out of her. She'd been more withdrawn after telling him, in her own way, to back off and stay out of her business. Sure, they'd avoided personal situations since the incident in his office two years ago, but that didn't mean he couldn't take an interest if something bothered her. He was being a good boss. There was nothing wrong with that. He'd read that in a book on leadership. Show an interest, talk to your employees, and empathize with their problems. She didn't have to get so closed off.

Pain shot through the left side of Isaac's jaw. His sight blurred. Ringing buzzed in his ears. He shook his head to clear his mind and his vision.

"Not distracted, huh." Cal voice was pure sarcasm. He wore the evil smile that warned pain-and-or-death was coming. A smirk taught to trainers everywhere.

To think he paid for this torture.

"I didn't expect the left hook." Isaac shook his head again before lifting his hands to the guard position.

Cal matched Isaac's position, and they circled each other. "Distractions don't belong in the ring."

"I know that."

"If you know it—" Two quick jabs. Isaac avoided both, but not as quickly has he would have if he hadn't been cold-cocked because of thoughts of Kim. "—then why is it in here with you?"

Good damn question. "I pay you to train me. Not for therapy."

Cal laughed. "You pay me to turn you into a machine. Leave those human emotions aside. Don't cry in my ring." Cal followed the word with a jab hook jab combination in a quick succession that would have had Isaac flat on his back if he hadn't been focused.

Frustration tightened his muscles. He concentrated on the fight and attacked back. Cal's evil trainer grin didn't go away, and he met Isaac with just as much gusto. Some of the other people in the gym stood along the outside of the ring to watch. Cal got the most hits, but only by a slim margin.

Afterward, every muscle in Isaac's body screamed "mercy" while his lungs worked overdrive to supply oxygen. Exhilaration simmered just beneath the surface. He wanted to roll out of the ring but forced himself to hop down even though is body protested. He accepted the compliments on holding his own against Cal from the others before making his way to one of the benches along the wall where he'd tossed his gym bag.

Cal followed him over. He pulled two clean towels from a shelf near the bench and tossed one to Isaac. "When am I going to get you to represent my gym in a fight?"

"Never," Isaac said between gulping breaths. "I do this for fun." Though, at the moment, his pounding heart didn't agree with his brain's definition of fun.

"Fun?" One of Cal's brows lifted nearly to his hairline. If he'd had a hairline. His head was shaved. "Someone collects stamps for fun. You train that hard in the ring for a reason." Cal sounded almost as breathless as Isaac. Which gave Isaac a modicum of comfort that he hadn't been totally distracted in the ring.

"For fun and my health." He sucked water from his plastic bottle then took a few more deep breaths. "That's the only reason I'm here."

Calvin sat on the end of the bench. "Something else had you fighting hard just now. Why don't you tell me what's really going on?"

Isaac glared at Calvin. "I thought you gave ass beatings, not therapy."

"You were one of my first clients. I have to listen to you whine occasionally." Calvin said with a teasing smile.

Isaac wheezed out a laugh. He took several more deep breaths and finally his heart and breathing slowed to not-gonna-kill-you levels. "Work trouble," he said then thought of the worry on Kim's face. "Women trouble."

"Women?" Calvin's tone was disbelieving. "Hell, half the women that see you are ready to give you some ass."

Isaac shook his head. "Not like that. An employee. I think she's in trouble but won't say what."

"Let me ask a question," Cal said. "Is she your woman?"

The urge to claim Kim was as real as the sweat pouring down his brow. Hell, no. He'd fought that need a long time ago with near-embarrassing consequences. They both wanted what the other refused to give. He would never claim her because he refused to be in a relationship. "Nah. It's not like that."

"Then, unless her problems affect your business, leave it alone."

"That's the thing. I've got a feeling it might." Okay, maybe her being distracted in the staff meeting wasn't really affecting the business, but Kim was rarely distracted. She was the best damn administrative assistant he'd ever had because she was always focused. She anticipated his needs before he could even vocalize them, knew every appointment he had during the day even when she wasn't in front of the calendar and could whip up a report on anything he needed more information on in less than forty-eight hours. She didn't tune out in meetings and ask him to repeat himself constantly.

"Then deal with the problems that are related to the job," Cal said. "Don't get into her personal business. You get personal with a woman and before you know it she's your woman."

Isaac shook his head. That's exactly what he didn't need. Emotions, relationships, and commitments were distractions that he'd watched lead others to bad decisions. He didn't have time for distractions. He had a business to save.

Isaac took a deep breath. "I damn sure don't want a relationship."

"That's good to hear," Calvin said.

Isaac cocked his head and peered at Cal. "Why?"

Calvin looked toward the front of the gym. "It'll keep Zaria away from you." Cal's sister Zaria, who was also a trainer, sat at the front desk.

Isaac had wondered if Zaria was interested in him, but out of respect for

Cal, he'd never followed her up. She was attractive, long legs, decent breasts, and even though her muscles were cut better than some men Isaac knew, she was sexy, but he wasn't interested.

"Even if I were in the market, I wouldn't touch your sister. I've felt your punch." Isaac rubbed his jaw.

Cal laughed. "Glad you know it. On the real, don't let the woman at your job distract you. Get her out of your mind. Have a little fun. Not with my sister, but with someone. Look, next time you come to a fight come hang out at the club with us afterward. You need to get out more, and there are plenty of women to get your mind of this one."

Isaac drank more water and considered Cal's suggestion. What the hell would it hurt to go to a nightclub with Calvin? Find a woman interested in having sex instead of making love. He stood but nodded. "I'll think about it."

CHAPTER 4

Nakita's car sat in the driveway when Kim got home. Not surprising. Even though Nakita had gotten an apartment with one of her co-workers six months ago, neither Nakita nor her roommate cooked. Her sister often popped in during the week for dinner. Kim would probably do the same when she moved out.

If she ever moved out.

Their grandmother's house had always felt more like home than the cheap apartment they'd lived in after their father died.

Kim entered the side door. A multitude of delicious smells hit her when she walked into the kitchen. Her stomach growled. Her mouth watered as her grandmother pulled a ham out of the oven.

"What in the world are you cooking?" Kim asked and shut the side door.

Ruby placed the ham on the counter. Kim dropped her purse on the kitchen table and walked over to the stove. Her eyes widened as she took in the selection of food. Not only was there ham, but macaroni and cheese, collard greens, candied yams.

"Is that a pot roast?" Kim pointed to the roast in a baking pan on the stove.

Ruby's hazel eyes sparkled with excitement. "Just making a nice dinner for my family."

The heat from the oven caused a small sheen of sweat to cover Ruby's face. Laugh lines framed her mouth and eyes, the only signs of age on her golden skin. An apron imprinted with a baby picture of Nakita and Kim protected her white crew neck shirt and jeans.

"This is more than a nice dinner, Grandma. This is special occasion cooking." Kim looked over her grandmother's shoulder and grinned. "Is that a pound cake?"

"Yep."

"What got into you?"

Ruby shrugged and used the towel draped over her shoulder to blot her brow. "I won a little bit at BINGO last night at the senior center and decided to spend the money saying thank you to my family."

Kim's smile faded. "Grandma, you aren't supposed to be gambling."

Ruby grunted and turned off the stove. "BINGO isn't gambling. Besides, it was at the senior center. The game started right after the book club. When everyone asked me to stay what was I supposed to say? That I have to leave because I *had* a gambling problem? I don't think so."

"You could have made any number of excuses. You don't have to announce that you have a gambling problem."

"I don't have a problem," Ruby said with an eye roll. "Why can't I enjoy BINGO without feeling guilty? I haven't played video poker in almost a year. I'm not buying lottery tickets. Even though both could help come up with the down payment for this house."

Kim bit her tongue. If she pushed too hard about avoiding triggers, her grandmother might go to one of the houses with illegal video poker machines in them just to prove a point. "BINGO's fine. We'll figure out the down payment without going to one of those gaming houses, okay?"

Ruby grunted and waved a hand. Kim sighed quietly. "Did you tell Mom about the house?"

Ruby turned and leaned her back against the counter. "Not yet. She's worried enough with them talking layoffs at her job."

"I thought her job was safe."

"She did too, but when she called on her lunch break, she said they'd just sent home some people in her section."

"You know what? We can't worry about that unless it happens," Kim said more to try and calm her own rising concern. Her mother's income could help get the rest of the down payment together.

"That's what I said. I'll tell her about the house later after we find out a little more."

"Is that the real reason for the special dinner?" Kim glanced around at the food.

Ruby's shoulders relaxed. "A little surprise never hurt anyone."

"What about Ms. Corrine and the mail?"

Ruby scowled. "I got out there before she could take it. I'm telling you if I catch her stealing my mail I'm going over there, and she's not going to like it."

Kim shook her head. "She's not stealing the mail, Grandma." Though going over there and talking to Ms. Corrine to make sure she wasn't messing with the mail to get on Ruby's nerves wouldn't hurt. "Where's Nakita?" Kim shrugged out of her suit jacket and untucked her shirt.

"The den." Ruby motioned with her head to another door off the kitchen toward the back of the house.

"I'll go say hey before I change."

Kim kissed Ruby on the cheek then crossed the kitchen to the den. She stepped down into the room Mr. Jackson had added to the house. Since there were only three bedrooms, one bath, and a living area, the den had previously served as Nakita's room.

Nakita lounged on the couch in front of the television. Her head rested on the arm of the chair, and she swiped through her cell phone.

Kim walked over and pulled her sister's hair. "Get up."

Nakita swatted at Kim's hand. "Heifa, quit pulling my hair. You know how much I paid for this?"

Nakita sat up and scooted over on the couch. She ran her hand over her short blonde tipped tresses. Nakita had their mother's dark brown eyes. She was curvy, like Kim, with a small waist and the same honey brown skin. She must have gone to her apartment before coming over because she wore a pair of cutoff shorts and a white tank top instead of the curve-hugging slacks and blouses she wore to her job at a call center.

"You shouldn't spend so much on your hair," Kim joked.

Nakita raised a brow and gave Kim's ponytail a critical look. "Maybe you should spend a little more on yours."

Kim pulled the band off her ponytail. The relief of pressure was heavenly, and she sighed. "I've got other things to spend my money on." She ran her fingers through her hair.

"What, your clothes?" Nakita teased. "We really need to take you shopping."

Kim kicked off her shoes then nudged Nakita's leg with the foot. "Really? Is it pick on Kim's fashion day?"

Nakita laughed. "Every day I see you in those ugly suits is pick on Kim's fashion day. Thank God you don't dress like that when I drag you out. Otherwise, I'd have to pretend you weren't my sister."

Kim flipped Nakita the bird, but her sister only grinned. "You staying for dinner?"

Nakita gave Kim an isn't-it-obvious look. "Uh, yeah. Deana is on some tofu replaces everything meat kick." Deana was Nakita's roommate. "I need real food. I didn't know grandma was cooking enough to feed the neighborhood." A hint of concern filled Nakita's voice.

Kim sighed and nodded. "She says the money came from BINGO."

"You believe her?"

"It's been over a year. Let's give her the benefit of the doubt."

Nakita raised her hands in a "whatever" motion. Kim doubted Nakita wanted to go down the road of their grandmother's gambling problem any more than Kim did.

"So, how was work? More importantly, how is that fine ass boss of yours? Have you decided to finally give him some?" Nakita said with a sly grin.

Kim nudged Nakita with her foot a little harder. "I'm not sleeping with my boss."

"I don't see why not."

"I told you why."

Nakita cocked her head to the side. "Because he's rich and wants to spend all his money on you. Yeah, and I told you you're stupid."

Kim rested her elbow on the arm of the couch and rubbed her temple. No matter how many times Kim explained her reasons to Nakita, her sister didn't understand. "It's not stupid. I want a real relationship."

She wanted someone who cared about her. Who wouldn't laugh at the idea of a relationship? A man to actually cherish her, not celebrate a victory after getting her in bed.

"Heifa, please. You're always talking about wanting a relationship, but you're afraid to give a man a chance."

Kim lowered her voice and glanced at the door even though it was unlikely that Ruby would overhear them. "I know how bad men can be, remember. Even the good ones used to try and pick me up when I was barely seventeen."

Kim and Rebecca had started making extra money picking up men in the bar where Benji's older brother worked. He'd let Kim and Rebecca in and point out the guys with money. Rebecca and Kim flirted and made the promise of doing whatever they liked. The men never cared about their ages, which is why Kim hadn't had any qualms about stealing their money after the men inevitably took them to a hotel or back to their place. Benji and his boys would follow in case things got rough, but typically Kim and Rebecca could get in and out before the guys realized they'd been tied to the bed not to be freaky but to snatch their wallets. The hustle had worked for years. So well, they'd started picking up gullible men at grocery stores, gas stations, and outside of gyms. Then Benji'd gotten the bright idea there were other ways the girls could make money.

"Not all guys are like the creeps you used to hustle," Nakita said. "For the ones who are, you can get yours and move on. Since you don't really believe there are good men out there, quit waiting to fall in love and use men the same way they want to use you."

Kim stiffened and stared. Usually, her sister told her to stop thinking all men were dogs. This was the first time she'd even hinted that Kim should start using men. "Hold up, you were the main one who hated when I went out and worked with Rebecca. Now you're telling me to stop looking for a good man and go back to it. What gives?"

Nakita shifted her position on the couch. "This gives." She pointed around the room. "You're still living with *grandma*. Working for chump change. Do you remember how much money you used to make?"

She remembered. She'd remembered when she'd had to bail her grandmother out of gambling debt. Whenever Jackie said she couldn't contribute to that month's bills. Each time Nakita reminded her that her wardrobe was woefully neglected. She also remembered how scary hustling had been. That wasn't worth any amount of money.

"I make a decent salary," Kim said defensively. "Decent enough not to risk my life. I remember how dangerous, stupid and crazy cheating men out of their money was. I remember how that led to worse things. The money isn't worth it."

Nakita smirked. "Yeah, well, to live the life I want, it may be worth it. I hear Rebecca and Benji are going big time. They've got someone backing them. Really turning what they were trying to do into a legitimate business."

Kim shot up. "No. Nakita, don't get involved with her." When Nakita looked like she was going to wave her off, Kim grabbed her hand. "Promise me you won't get involved with anything Rebecca is starting up."

"Girls, your momma's here. Let's get ready to eat," Ruby called.

"Come on, let's eat." Nakita tried to move, but Kim tightened her hold on Nakita's hand.

"I'm serious, Nakita."

Nakita rubbed Kim's hand and smiled. "Don't worry. I won't get involved in anything stupid." She crossed her heart with her free hand. "I promise." She pulled away, jumped off the couch and hurried to the kitchen before Kim could reply.

Kim frowned and followed at a slower pace. Not getting involved in anything stupid wasn't the same as not getting involved in any scheme Rebecca had.

CHAPTER 5

Isaac went to his father's house the next morning before going into the office. Curtis didn't come in early, if at all some days, but he was an early riser. He'd called Kim to let her know he would be in late. She'd sounded just a professional and pleasant as always. Of course, she would. When all he wanted to do was to find out if she was as worried as she'd been the day before.

Isaac rang the bell, and his dad's butler answered. He had nothing against butlers, but his dad didn't need anyone so formal. Just like he didn't need the huge estate he'd purchased in northern Greenville. Curtis Caldwell liked to flaunt that he'd built an empire off of other people's trash. Everything he did was extravagant.

"Good morning, Robert. Is my dad up and about?"

Robert shook his thin head. His expression was congenial but cool. His blue eyes revealing nothing but vague interest. His simple black suit impeccable even at eight a.m. "Yes, sir. He's in the media room."

"I'll go there."

Isaac walked through the marble foyer and up the stairs. The inside of his father's house was filled with extravagant art and expensive furniture. All to demonstrate his financial strength when he invited politicians and business tycoons over to plot his latest scheme. The only thing Curtis knew about the décor in his home was the cost of each piece.

He found Curtis sitting on a leather couch before a huge television with a morning news show on screen instead of preparing to come into the office. No surprise there.

Curtis glanced at Isaac and held up one hand, while the other was on the phone against his ear. "Let me call you back later. I'll check her out later." Curtis nodded a few times as he listened to whoever was on the phone before hanging up.

He tossed the phone on the coffee table and pulled the gaping edges of his dark blue bathrobe closed. "What are you doing here?"

Isaac crossed the room to stand next to the couch. "I've been thinking about your suggestion. Please tell me you aren't trying to buy Andre's company."

Curtis leaned back into the corner of the couch and spread one arm over the back. "What if I am? We need your brother back here."

"Andre is happy where he is. He's not coming back here."

"Happy," Curtis snorted. "He won't be happy for long. After a few months married to that girl, he'll realize happily ever after is some bullshit women spout off at men."

Isaac slipped his hand into the pocket of the pants of his dark gray suit to keep from balling them into fists. "He and Mikayla have been together for over a year now. Married for six months."

"That's nothing. Still honeymooning and fucking in every corner they can find. Once that wears off, he'll be back."

"He loves her," Isaac said flatly.

"What? You believe in love now? I thought you realized that emotion didn't exist." Curtis said in an oily tone.

Anger punched him harder than Calvin's hit the night before. He knew well enough to not give a hint of a reaction. Of course, he knew love didn't exist.

"I thought you loved us." Isaac glared at Curtis from the floor after Curtis broke up Isaac's fight with Andre.

Curtis's laugh was caustic. "Love you? Boy, quick acting like a bitch. You're worse than a female."

Isaac had been thirteen. Curtis manipulated Andre and Isaac into the fistfight. Isaac couldn't remember what they'd fought over, just that it involved getting Curtis's approval and ended with his dad laughing at them. That day he and Andre vowed to always stick together no matter what Curtis threw at them. Isaac watched Curtis manipulate everyone who cared, saw friends and colleagues get screwed over by cheating spouses and business partners they'd believed cared for them. He'd scoffed at their stupidity. Then Andre fell in love and bailed on him. Love was just an excuse to get what you want out of people, control them. He preferred being upfront than using the guise of *love* to get what he wanted.

"I believe in letting Andre be happy. For however long it lasts," Isaac said calmly.

Curtis's laugh was deep and heavy. "You know just as well as I do they won't last. Why are you fighting me on this? The sooner we buy him out, the faster he's back here, and things are the way they're supposed to be."

"If Andre wants to do his own thing, let him. We don't need to mess up his life and plant the seed of resentment by destroying his plans. I am handling things. We don't have time for petty revenge. We need to worry about the contracts we're losing."

"We wouldn't be losing contracts if your brother hadn't left."

Isaac agreed, but not for the reasons Curtis believed. After Andre had left, ideas of how to get back at Andre for "betraying" him had consumed

Curtis. This wasn't the first time Isaac had to try and stop his father's efforts to ruin his brother's newly found happiness.

"He's gone. It's time to move on. We need to focus on C.E.S. and regain our contracts."

Curtis sat up abruptly. He pounded a fist against his thigh. "I told him he was either with me or against me. He chose the latter."

"Choosing to do his own thing isn't going against you."

"Yes, the hell it is," Curtis snapped. "He chose to be a competitor. He knows how we treat competitors. I will get him back here. One way or the other."

"Will it be worth it to have him hate you?"

The frustration left Curtis's face. Replaced by a look of smug assurance. "He won't hate me. Once he's tired of that girl, he'll thank me for getting him back."

"I wouldn't be so sure about that."

"Don't doubt me, boy. My brother doubted I could build an empire and look at what I did." He spread his hands and looked around with pride. "Your mother thought I wouldn't leave her for slacking off just because we had kids, and I found a better wife. Every time you and your brother think you know better and try to get out of line, I pull you back in. Andre is just out of line right now."

"You expect loyalty but refuse to give it in return," Isaac said, his anger barely restrained. Every point reinforced Curtis's selfishness. His inability to care for anyone except for how he could manipulate and use them to his advantage.

"Building an empire takes ruthlessness. We're stronger together. Don't you ever forget that." He nailed Isaac with a hard glare.

That was the only thing keeping Isaac loyal to Curtis. When they were all working together, him, Andre and Curtis, they had made C.E.S. the most profitable it had ever been. Whenever he'd considered walking away, Andre convinced him to stay. He'd put everything he had into C.E.S. Giving it all up because of Curtis wasn't a win for him, it was only a win for Curtis.

Then maybe it's time for Curtis to walk away.

"I haven't forgotten who's responsible for the company." Responsible for the recent failures.

Curtis nodded. "Good. I'll be in after lunch."

"Take your time. I'm handling things."

Curtis didn't answer, and Isaac had nothing left to say. He turned and walked out of the room.

"Robert told me you were here," his stepmother said from his left.

Isaac turned and smiled at Cynthia Caldwell. Cynthia's smooth dark skin was barely touched by age, and affection filled her dark brown eyes when she looked at him. She was tall, thin but curvy. This early he wasn't surprised to see her in a lavender silk bathrobe, and matching pajamas with her thick hair pulled up into a messy twist.

When Curtis left Isaac's mother to marry his best friend's wife, Isaac never would have imagined one day he'd like his stepmom. Andre had never forgiven Cynthia for her part in the breakup of their parents' marriage. Isaac had a begrudging sort of respect for her. Cynthia was smart, knew she was the trophy wife and played the part to her advantage after realizing love would never be part of the deal. She hadn't even batted an eye when Curtis started sleeping with Isaac and Andre's mother again.

"I'm just leaving," he said.

"You've figured out that he's trying to buy out Andre to get him back here?"

"I had an idea. Today confirmed it."

Cynthia's lips twisted into a rueful smile, and she crossed her arms over her chest. "Don't argue with him. It'll only make things worse."

"I can't let him do this. C.E.S. isn't in a position for a hostile takeover."

"That may be true, but your dad doesn't listen to reason. Don't argue with him. Stop him." The last words were hard as concrete.

"How am I supposed to do that?"

"You're a smart boy. A lot smarter than Curtis gives you credit for. You'll figure out a way to stop this madness. Plus, Andre is happy. Let him be," she said with a wave of her hand.

"I'm surprised you care about Andre's happiness. We both know his feelings about you." Andre refused to acknowledge Cynthia.

"I'm not the best stepmother, but I do want you both to be happy. Besides, I like to think happiness will work out for someone in this family." She strolled over and patted him on the chest. "Think about what I said, okay? You'll never get love from him." She nodded toward the closed door. "But you deserve what he owes you. He promised you C.E.S."

Isaac nodded, and Cynthia patted his chest again before continuing down the hall toward her bedroom. She and Curtis hadn't shared one for several years. He didn't need to analyze her words. C.E.S. was his. The time for Curtis to accept that had come.

CHAPTER 6

Kim started the morning working on the projects Isaac assigned her. He'd called to say he would be in late. Not a hint of concern from the day before had filled his voice. He'd been direct and to the point. Fine with her since she felt a little guilty for snapping at him and considered apologizing. She tended to automatically assume the negative when a guy did something nice. She didn't need to be taken care of, but she didn't have to get so sensitive about his offer for help. Most friendly co-workers would ask if they could help. They had spent the past two years ignoring the attraction simmering between them and acting the part of friendly colleagues. His offer to help hadn't been an offer to turn her into his mistress.

Isaac's blasé tone this morning, and the fact that his dating life hadn't suffered in the two years since that night was more rock-solid evidence that she was way more invested in Isaac than he was in her.

The door to the executive suite opened, and Kim turned her chair to the door to greet Isaac. Curtis Caldwell rarely, if ever, came in before noon. Neither were at the door.

"Good morning, Kim," Rodney Green said.

Rodney worked in the collection services division. He'd started as a driver of one of the trucks, worked his way up to shift supervisor, and was now an assistant manager. He'd also shown an interest in her a few weeks ago when he'd come to the main office for a meeting.

Kim rarely made it down to his division. The trucks and the people in collections worked at a garage on the edge of town. She'd heard the stories of all the fine men who worked in the division. Rodney was a prime example. In his mid-thirties, Rodney stood about six feet, had reddish-brown skin, sleepy brown eyes, and a perfectly manicured beard. He didn't wear the dark gray jumpsuits most guys in collections wore. Every time she saw him, he was in a dark green C.E.S. polo shirt and khakis. Both fit just enough to indicate there was plenty of muscle beneath.

"What are you doing up here?" Kim asked.

Rodney strolled over and stood in front of her desk. "I had a meeting in customer service. Since I was here, I figured I'd come on up and say hey."

Rodney was handsome, and he was interested. Kim was still trying to figure out if she was interested, too. Nakita's words from the night before indicated she needed to become interested. From what she'd heard, Rodney was a nice guy.

"What was the meeting about?"

"Some changes to the routes. People are angry at the schedule changes. They're blaming us when marketing handled the announcement," he said in a tired voice and shook his head.

Kim leaned back in her chair and smiled. "That's why you're the assistant manager."

"Man, if I'd known all of the headaches that came with this job, I would have stayed on the back of the truck." He leaned a hip on the end of her desk. "I can't wait for the weekend."

"You and me both," Kim said in solidarity.

"Big plans?"

"No, just hanging with my baby sister Friday night. We always hang out on the third Friday of the month."

"Why the third Friday?"

Kim shrugged and looked down at her nails. "We've always done that."

Back when Nakita worried about Kim working with Rebecca, Kim promised not to go out one Friday of every month. Rodney didn't need to know all that.

She looked back up at Rodney. "What about you? You've got big plans?"

"My boy is having his first amateur fight on Friday. You like boxing?"

"I've been to a fight or two." Illegal underground fights, but that had been years ago.

Rodney shifted his stance until he fully faced her. "Oh, you've got to come to one of his other fights. He's got another one next week. I think you'll like it."

Kim lifted a brow and cocked her head to the side. "You think I'll like watching your boy get beat up?"

"He ain't gonna get beat up," Rodney said with a chuckle. "He's decent. Since you're busy with your sister on Friday, what about having dinner with me on Saturday?"

There it was. The official offer for a date. She glanced at Isaac's closed office door then immediately wanted to kick herself. If she wanted all the things she said she did, then she had to stop thinking about Isaac. Rodney seemed like a nice guy. The least she could do was give him a chance. Isaac, on the other hand, had laughed when she'd told him she wanted a relationship and had no problems moving on after their close call while she spent way too much time comparing every other man to him.

"Sure," she said a bit too brightly. She wanted to glance at Isaac's door again but forced eye contact with Rodney. Would Isaac care about her dating someone in the company? Does it matter?

Let's be honest. You kinda want him to care.

The door to the office suite opened. Isaac froze at the door. His dark gaze swung to Rodney, then to her. Her body buzzed as if she'd just taken three shots of espresso. She always got that feeling after her first glance of Isaac in the morning. A quick flash of displeasure crossed his face. Kim sat up and hoped she didn't look as guilty as she felt.

He's not your man. You don't have to feel guilty.

She gave him her practiced, professional, you-don't-make-my-heart-stutter smile. "Good morning, Mr. Caldwell."

Rodney straightened and watched Isaac with barely veiled admiration. "Mr. Caldwell, how are you doing?"

"Tired," Isaac said, his voice flat, but not cold. "Rodney Green, right? New assistant manager in collection services."

Rodney nodded. He took several steps toward Isaac and held out his hand. "It's a pleasure to officially meet you."

Isaac shook his hand. "Congratulations on the promotion. Your area is the most visible area of the company. I'll be watching your department's performance closely." His tone held a hint of warning.

A few fast blinks were the only indication Isaac's words affected Rodney. "Then I'll be sure to do a good job."

Isaac's nodded and dropped Rodney's hand. "Are you here to see me?"

Rodney shuffled his stance. "Actually, I came up to speak to Kim." He sounded almost apologetic.

Isaac lifted his chin. "Ahh, I see." He glanced at Kim, eyes expressionless, but tension coated his face and stance. "Any messages?"

Kim picked up the notepad on her desk and skimmed her notes. "A few. I've already emailed the most important things to you and set up any necessary meetings."

"Good. I'll take the others." He held out his hand.

Kim tore out the small sheet and handed them to him. His fingertips brushed hers. The shock of his touch after they avoided touching for so long flared like lightening. Electric sparks danced across her skin. She sucked in a breath. Isaac held her gaze and slid the notes out of her hand.

"Thank you." There was no hint their touch affected him in his tone. "I'll only be in for a few minutes. I've got a meeting to discuss new disposal options in about forty-five minutes." He glanced at Rodney. "Do you need anything else?"

The words were blunt but clear. He wanted Rodney to leave. Isaac was always blunt though rarely rude. Was this because Rodney was here to see her? Had he touched her on purpose? They didn't touch. Or, was she the one avoiding touching him and he hadn't given brushing against her a single thought?

Stop it, Kim! Stop looking for mirages in a desert. Isaac does not care about you.

She would drive herself crazy. He didn't play games. There were no hidden emotional meanings in his words and actions.

Rodney looked back at Kim. "I just need to settle a few things with Kim. Give me your number. I'll call you later to set up the details for Saturday night."

Isaac walked to the door of his office. He didn't appear the least bit phased by Rodney asking her out. She was dumb as hell for thinking he'd have any interest.

"Sure." Kim gave Rodney her number as Isaac strolled into his office.

Kim ignored her accelerated heart rate and the left-over tingles from the brief touch of Isaac's hand. She pushed aside any weird feeling that she was doing something wrong setting up a date with Rodney. Isaac Caldwell wasn't her man. She'd better remember that.

*

Isaac was prepared for the frustration dogging him after his visit with Curtis to dissipate when he saw Kim sitting at her desk. Instead, he was greeted with Rodney grinning at Kim like a schoolboy with a crush on the hot teacher. He didn't close his office door. The murmur of their voices as they finalized their date scraped his nerves like nails on a chalkboard.

"She's not yours," he whispered to himself.

Then why did you touch her?

Because he couldn't help himself. She wasn't his, but seeing her with Rodney made him want to see if his touch affected her the way it affected him. She'd pulled away so quickly he wasn't sure if the reaction was good or bad. Which meant he was losing his mind obsessing about something so small.

Closing his eyes and taking a deep breath he acknowledged the frustration, and hint of jealousy for what they were. A haze of emotion clouding his vision. He mentally blew the haze away. There was no time for distractions and irritation. He had too much to really focus on.

By the time Kim came into his office to give him the mail, he'd pushed aside the reaction. "I made coffee." Her warm voice interrupted his reading of an email. "If you want a cup."

Isaac turned away from the computer. Her long, thick hair was pulled back in a tight ponytail, and a navy pantsuit tried to hide her curves. There was a cup of coffee already in one hand, a folder in the other. Full lips raised in the easy, professional smile she always gave. Completely oblivious to how quickly his emotions had gone into a tailspin seeing her with Rodney.

Damn, her smiles did something to him. He wanted to smile back. Stand up, pull her close and press a kiss to her forehead. Maybe not her forehead.

His reaction to her date had to be a result of them never sleeping together. His curiosity would forever be unsatisfied which meant he'd always react to her. That had to be why he had difficulty shaking this thing for her.

"Thank you," he said, making his voice easy.

She took a coaster out of the wooden case on his desk and set the coffee mug on it. He waited to see if she would turn and walk out. He'd upset her yesterday with his offer for help. He wouldn't ask again. He'd find out what was wrong. He couldn't let anything threaten the company, but he wouldn't approach her unless he needed to.

Kim clasped her hands in front of her. "How did the visit go with Mr. Caldwell?"

"I confirmed what I suspected. He's trying to buy out Andre's company." Isaac hid his relief that she hadn't left by turning the coffee mug so the handle faced him and took a sip.

"How are you going to stop him?" she asked.

She placed the folder on his desk. The seductive strawberries and silk scent she wore whispered against his senses. He thought of feeding her strawberries while she lay on silk sheets.

His silk sheets.

He brought his thoughts back to the conversation. "Not by arguing with him."

Cynthia was right. Arguing with Curtis would only lead to more headaches. He had to stop his dad another way.

Kim nodded. "I agree fighting him head on won't work, but he can still go around you and make a call. You should be running the company."

"I'd have to kick my father out in order to run this company the way it needs."

That was the second time in two days the ultimate solution to his problem came up.

Kim didn't respond. When he met her gaze, her head tilted to the side, and she cocked her brows. She was so damn cute when she gave him her you're-not-giving-me-a-good-explanation look.

"The fight might tear this company apart," he spoke his concerns aloud. "Curtis doesn't care who he hurts to get what he wants. Including the very people who work here. If he got any hint that I was trying to boot him, he'd tear this place apart brick by brick to stop me from doing so. Trying to minimize the damage he can cause as head of this company is better than watching it implode because I tested his authority."

"You know him best. I trust your judgment," she said in her cool, professional tone. Which meant she thought he was full of shit.

Maybe he was. He'd watched others fight Curtis and fail. Andre only "*won*" because he'd left the company and the state. Isaac was not leaving.

He didn't want to start over, and he refused to let what he'd worked hard to save, disintegrate into nothing.

Kim turned and walked toward the door. His gaze dipped to the sexy sway of her hips. His fingers flexed. He'd held those hips in his hands. Pulled her soft ass against him. Heard the sharp inhale of her breath right before her head fell back against his shoulder. She'd been so responsive, not coy or hesitant. Passion had burned like wildfire in her.

"Tell me what you want, Kim," he'd murmured between kisses along her neck. "I'll give you anything you want. Just name it."

"I want everything. I want love."

The words had broken through his lust. He'd thought she was joking and laughed. She'd stiffened and pulled away.

He hadn't pursued her since, but his need for her had clutched him tight afterward. After an embarrassing encounter with a previous lover in Kansas City, he'd been afraid no woman would arouse him again. Thank God, he'd overcome that. He wasn't proud of the number of women he'd slept with after Kim to prove she wouldn't possess his dick forever, but he never wanted a repeat of Kansas City again.

"You and Rodney," he said before she walked out.

Kim stopped with her hand on the door. Her shoulders rose and fell with a deep breath, but when she turned her face revealed nothing.

"Are you two seeing each other?" Did Rodney have the right to hold her, touch her?

"Would you have a problem if we were?" Her tone was even but screamed her relationship status was none of his business.

He'd have a big problem with that. But he couldn't say that without giving her what she wanted. "Only if it'll interfere with your performance. He can't make unnecessary trips to the main office just to see you. We can't afford distractions, especially from the managers."

She winced as if his words had hurt. He wanted to take them back, but she quickly recovered and nodded. "I'll relay the message."

Her quick recovery iced over his lingering emotions. This was for the best. "Be sure that you do." Isaac turned to his computer. He felt the heat of her glare right before she left the office and shut the door with a solid thud.

CHAPTER 7

The one good thing about being busy all day was the required focus on her work kept Kim from obsessing about Isaac's question about her and Rodney. She didn't need to obsess about why Isaac asked. He had the future of C.E.S. to worry about. He didn't need anyone not focusing on the job. That's why he asked, not because he actually cared about whom was she dating.

Or did he?

See, this was exactly why she needed to go out with Rodney on Saturday. She needed to drown herself in some type of distraction. If she didn't, she'd continue wondering if Isaac actually cared if she dated someone or not.

The elevator stopped on the fifth floor. Fanta Young from accounting stood on the other side. Fanta's brown eyes lit up, and she grinned at Kim.

"Hey, girl, you're just now leaving?" She got onto the elevator and pushed the long bang of her dark hair out of her face.

Kim and Fanta had bonded shortly after Kim started with C.E.S. over their mutual love of the bagel shop that delivered to the C.E.S. headquarters every morning. Fanta was fun and upbeat, with cinnamon brown skin, curves she didn't try to hide beneath ugly suits the way Kim did and a ready smile. Kim couldn't help but like her.

"Yes, I had to work on a report for Mr. Caldwell. I promised to get it to him by the end of the week."

"The old one or the young one?" Fanta asked.

Kim cocked her head to the side. "Which one do you think?"

Fanta laughed and waved a hand. "You right. I know Isaac Caldwell is the one always working. Damn, girl, I don't know how you do it."

"Do what?"

The elevator stopped on the ground floor, and the two of them walked toward the door.

"Work with that fine ass man every day," Fanta said. "I heard the stories from Tanya, and they are juicy as hell."

Tanya worked in marketing. She'd been a former administrative assistant to Isaac. One he'd slept with then moved to another department when the affair was over. Not that Tanya minded. She loved to tell everyone about how great Isaac was in the sack. Kim thought he and Tanya had started up again a few months ago. Not that Isaac would say anything to her about who he was seeing. Tanya was the one with the extra skip in her step and suggestive remarks about him.

Kim tried not to care. Isaac could sleep with whomever he wanted. He'd laughed at her when she said what she wanted. Still, wanting him was dumb. She wasn't supposed to be dumb anymore.

"Mr. Caldwell and I have a good working dynamic," Kim said casually.

"That doesn't mean you can't notice he's fine. I mean, for real, for real, if I were up there with him, I'd be trying to find ways for him to bend me over the desk."

Fanta laughed, and Kim joined in half-heartedly. She tried not to think of how close she'd come to letting him do just that. Another fun plaything for a man with money to spend. She was never going back to that.

She waved bye to Fanta with a promise to call her later and walked toward her car in the side parking lot. She reached into her purse for keys when the door to the car next to hers opened. The last person she expected to see got out.

"Hello, Kim," Rebecca said. The years in jail had taken their toll. Rebecca still looked good, but the lines around her eyes and mouth made her appear older than her twenty-seven years. The curvaceous figure she'd used to get whatever she wanted was thinner. She dressed the way they had back in their teens: skintight pants and a fitted shirt with maximum cleavage exposure.

Ice ran down Kim's spine. The last time they'd talked was in the visiting area of a correctional facility. She'd expected to run into Rebecca in the old neighborhood, where she'd planned to hunt her down this weekend to get the confrontation over with and tell her to stay away from Nakita. Not in the parking lot of her job.

Despite suddenly slick hands and pounding heart, Kim squared her shoulders and looked Rebecca in the eye. "I heard you were out."

"From who?"

Kim shrugged. "I hear things."

"Asking around because you're worried I'd come back and ask you to pay up?"

Kim's heartbeat tripled in tempo. Guess that answered the question about Rebecca expecting payback. Kim crossed her arms and leaned against her car door. "How are you, Rebecca?"

"How are you, Rebecca?" Her former friend's voice was mocking. "How do you think I've been? I went to jail for you."

"You went to jail because you were caught."

"You were supposed to be in that room."

"I told you I couldn't do it. I wasn't going the extra step."

Rebecca smirked and eyed Kim as if she were inspecting a car she wanted to purchase. "Didn't like it the first time, huh." She walked over and ran a finger down Kim's arm. "You were a natural."

Disgust sent a shiver down Kim's spine. She kicked out her elbow, and Rebecca's hand fell away. "I didn't want that for my life."

"You always thought you were better than me."

"Not better than you. I wanted better for me."

"That's why you let me go to jail."

"I'm sorry about what happened to you, but I told you and Benji I couldn't do it. Now that you're out if you need a reference for a job or anything…"

Rebecca let out a caustic laugh. "What will your reference say? I used to hustle horny-ass men with her? The reason she went to jail was because I got scared and ran out on her?"

Kim gritted her teeth as the guilt from the past tried to tangle her up. "I can be a personal reference. I'll say we grew up together and that you're a hard worker."

"Yeah, hard worker." Rebecca took a step back and waved her hand. The afternoon sun reflected off the rhinestones on her nails. "Look, I didn't come here for a reference, but I did come to ask you for help. We were friends once. Best friends, and despite what happened, I hope that because we were friends, you'd be willing to help me out."

"What do you need?" Kim asked cautiously. She doubted Rebecca wanted any type of easy help.

"Benji is doing big things now. He's making a shit ton of money, and we need girls that know how to play the game. Sexy girls." Rebecca tilted her head to the side and let her gaze roam over Kim again. "He wants you to come work with us."

Hell no. That idea wasn't even worth her consideration, but she didn't want to outright piss Rebecca off. "You just got out, and you're going back to the same thing that put you in?"

"What the hell else am I supposed to do, Kim? Wear ugly-ass suits and sit at a desk in some fancy office? They're not going to hire me. Not with a record."

"That's not true. I got a job."

"You didn't get caught. I did."

Kim touched her forehead and took a calming breath. When she dropped her hand, she tried to sound rational. "And I'm sorry you got caught, but I can't go back. I won't go back."

Rebecca's lips twisted into a derisive frown. "Figures. You only wanted the easy money. Never wanted to put in any work."

Kim pushed away from the car and stepped toward Rebecca. "Easy?

How many times did we almost get beaten because the guy we scammed realized we were more interested in his wallet than him? That was hard enough. I wasn't signing up for more."

"You said you would help me."

"I can help you get a job. I can give you a reference. I can give you a few bucks to get back on your feet. I won't work with you again. I damn sure won't work for Benji."

Benji got off on making women cater to his demands. Kim hadn't liked it when she was seventeen, and she was damn sure she wouldn't like it ten years later. Plus, he'd always looked at her like he couldn't wait to turn her out.

"Fine."

Rebecca's quick agreement startled Kim. "Fine?"

"I'll take money."

She should have known that was all Rebecca wanted. She'd always been about making money. "How much?"

"A million."

"Are you crazy?" Kim nearly yelled. "I don't have a million dollars."

"I know. You're just a glorified secretary. But you work for a company that is worth millions."

"The *company* is worth that. I don't have access to that type of money."

"You're smart, Kim. I'm sure you can figure out how to skim some of that money off the top. I won't even ask for the million all at once. As long as it takes for you to get it to me," Rebecca said as if she were asking to borrow a cup of sugar.

"I won't." She moved to walk toward the driver's door.

Rebecca's hand shot out and grabbed Kim's arm tightly. The strength of the grip had increased. Kim looked down, noticed the sculpted biceps of lean muscle beneath Rebecca's arm.

"Spend your time in the weight room?" Kim said.

"I spent my time figuring out how to survive. You owe me."

"Not a million dollars."

Rebecca jerked Kim's arm. "A million, or I'll get my payback another way."

Kim pushed Rebecca back with her elbow then faced her. "Don't threaten me."

"I'm not just threatening you." Rebecca grinned slyly. "Word on the street is Nakita is looking to make some money."

Kim's hands clenched into fists. She took a step toward Rebecca. "If you go near my sister…"

"Kim." Isaac's voice cracked like a whip. "Is everything okay?"

Kim and Rebecca spun his way. Kim tried to calm her breathing. Rebecca eyed Isaac from head to toe with a shrewd grin on her face. "You always have the handsome ones stepping in." She looked back at Kim. "You know what I want. Pick which direction I take."

Rebecca glanced back at Isaac before she got into her car. As soon as she drove away, Isaac came over and placed his hand on Kim's arm. "What was that about?"

The shock of the touch, his body so close to hers, and the concern in his eyes shot her pulse to the moon. The urge to lean into him and confess her problems drowned her good judgment. She met his dark gaze. Struggled to suck in air. She leaned closer. Isaac eased forward.

No! She jerked away from his touch and took a few steps away. She couldn't believe leaning on Isaac would make things better. That wasn't what Isaac Caldwell would provide. He wanted her in his bed. He didn't want her personal life drama.

"I'm sorry, Mr. Caldwell. It won't happen again." She avoided his gaze and ignored him when he called her name as she jumped into her car and drove off.

CHAPTER 8

Isaac scheduled a meeting with Bob Livingston the next morning. Bob was one of the longest-serving members on the board. Before making any moves, he needed to gauge the likelihood of the board working with him, and he needed to know sooner rather than later. Meeting with Bob before being sure he was ready to force Curtis out was risky, but if he had any chance, Bob was the best person to let him know. Bob swayed most of the board decisions and knew more about Curtis than the rest.

Bob could also go straight to Curtis and reveal Isaac's plans. That would unleash every vindictive trait in Curtis before Isaac had the chance to prepare.

He found a parking space downtown and walked the few blocks to Coffee Underground. The locally-owned coffee shop worked well for business meetings during the day and catered to a more relaxed crowd on weekends with poetry, Improv, and comedy open mic nights.

Isaac entered Coffee Underground and spotted Bob at a table in one of the back corners. He waved before going to the counter and ordering. After getting his coffee, Isaac joined Bob and shook his hand. "Thanks for meeting with me."

Sharp, dark eyes in a dark brown face met Isaac's. "You said it was important." Bob was around the same age as Curtis. He was several inches shorter than Isaac and ran marathons which kept his build slim.

"It is. I want to talk to you about Curtis."

Bob unbuttoned the jacket of his trendy gray suit and leaned back in his chair. "Funny, I need to talk to you about him, too."

Isaac cocked his head to the side. That was surprising. "You first."

Bob rotated his cup of coffee on the table. "I'm not good at beating around the bush, so I'll be blunt. Are you involved in any of your father's activities outside of the company?"

Isaac tensed and frowned. "Activities? What activities?"

"We both know Curtis doesn't always work on the right side of the law when he's trying to make money."

"Unfortunately, yes. He's the reason we've lost a few accounts."

"Are you working with him?" Bob watched him closely.

"I work with him at C.E.S., but I don't believe in blackmail or intimidation."

Bob's sharp gaze didn't soften. "Is that all? I need to be sure before we move forward."

Unease settled over Isaac. "What are you implying? My main goal has been, and always will be, making C.E.S. successful. I'm ready to push him out and take over if necessary."

A flicker of surprise crossed Bob's face. "Strong words."

Isaac didn't back down. "I think you agree with me."

Bob drummed his fingers along the coffee cup. "Your dad wouldn't like to hear what you're saying."

"Yet, I'm trusting you to hear me out," Isaac said. "I knew his ways eventually would catch up to him. That time is here. We're losing contracts, and the ones we do have aren't guaranteed renewal. My dad's inability to move forward with the times will run C.E.S. to the ground along with all the people attached to it. I won't let that happen."

Bob leaned forward and rested his elbows on the table. "How do you plan to stop him?"

"By convincing you and the rest of the board to vote him out then vote me in as the new head of the company."

If Curtis found out, he would do everything in his power to take Isaac down. Isaac hoped he was right in trusting his plans with Bob.

"You really think you're going to oust Curtis Caldwell from his own company?" Bob didn't look or sound convinced. At least he didn't outright reject Isaac's plan.

"It's what's for the best."

"It's going to take more than getting rid of Curtis to rebuild people's trust in C.E.S. You're not your father, but you're similar enough to him to make people leery."

The idea of anyone comparing him to Curtis and finding similarities made Isaac's stomach twist. "How so?"

"You're smart, Isaac. Everyone believes you know what needs to be done and that you care about the company more than your father, but that's all you care about. You're cold."

"I didn't realize being warm and fuzzy was part of a CEO's job description."

"Don't get angry about the truth. You need to show you have a human side. You want to save C.E.S., but do you care about the employees?"

Isaac opened his mouth to interrupt, but Bob raised a hand. "I know you do, but how do you show it? You don't interact with them. You know their names, and their business statistics, but that's about all. Then there's your personal life."

He actually cracked a disbelieving smile at that. "My personal life?"

"Yes. It's pretty well known you're a playboy. You've slept with a few women at C.E.S., and the ones you've been seen with outside of C.E.S. have been arm candy that lasts as long as a cheap peppermint. People trust a family man."

"Are you saying people won't trust me until I get married?"

"I don't think you'd have to go that far, but you could at least be seen to have something of a heart. Show some emotion. If you can get the employees to buy into your vision, and make people think you care about more than the bottom line, then you've got a good chance of turning this company around. And believe me, you need to get a hold of C.E.S. now before your dad completely ruins it."

Isaac sipped his coffee. He understood Bob's logic but pretending he was capable of trusting someone enough to consider marriage meant he'd have to pretend to be in a relationship. The only thing more annoying than a real relationship was pretending to be in one. He'd focus on the employee part. That was easy. He already knew who worked for him. Kim would know a good way to get the employees excited about working for C.E.S.

Kim could help you with the relationship part, too.

Hell. No.

Kim wanted a man who'd give her everything. He respected her too much to pretend like he was giving her that. Even if it meant watching her get closer to Rodney.

"What do you think?" Bob asked.

"I'll work on softening my image, but my personal life will remain that, personal."

"I think finding a good woman to settle down with will help, but I understand."

"Does that mean you're still willing to help me convince enough board members to put me in charge of C.E.S.?

Bob held out his hand. "If you're taking him down and saving this company, I'm with you."

CHAPTER 9

Curtis Caldwell coming to work before noon was surprising. Curtis coming in at ten forty-five was damn near astonishing. Kim tried to give him the same friendly smile she gave Isaac every morning, but Curtis's nasty character made her skin prickle with warning.

Curtis stopped at the door and frowned at her. "Why aren't you at lunch?"

Kim fought not to look at him as if he'd lost his mind. "I don't take my lunch break until twelve thirty."

Curtis waved his hand in a motion indicating she should get up. "Go on. Take your break now. You can have longer. I've got an important meeting in my office in a few minutes."

Kim pointed to her computer. "I've got to finish this report."

"Damn, girl, I'm trying to give you a benefit here. Now go on." Curtis smiled, but his voice burned like acid.

Kim gritted her teeth. Suddenly the idea of getting out of the office while Curtis was there wasn't so bad. "Do you need me to do anything for your meeting?" She quickly saved the report to her cloud account and picked up her tablet. She could work somewhere else.

"The only thing I need is for you to be gone in five minutes. Got it?"

She stood and collected her things. "Isaac isn't in. I'll be back around one if either of you needs anything."

Curtis just waved her words off and crossed to his office. A second later he'd unlocked the door and was inside. The slam of the door was his final word on the matter.

He was such a jerk. Why Isaac hesitated to push Curtis out was beyond her. Isaac was a cold-hearted businessman, but he was loyal to his family. She doubted Curtis would give Isaac the same loyalty.

She considered hiding out in someone else's department, but then she'd be constantly interrupted. The sun was out, and the sky was clear. Falls Park wasn't too far from the office, and she'd worked there a few times before when she needed to clear her head. Several minutes later, she crossed the Liberty Bridge over the rocky waterfalls in the park to sit on a bench at one of the overlooks. The day was bright and comfortable, and there were plenty of people milling around enjoying the beauty of the park.

Kim leaned back on the bench and soaked up the warmth of the sun. A few years ago, she wouldn't have put up with a man like Curtis. She would have cursed him out the first time he talked to her like an idiot. Then stole as much as she could from him before walking out the door. She wasn't that person anymore, but, damn, sometimes she missed that life. Not the stealing…or what came after, but the take no shit personality she'd once worn like armor. She'd said, done, and gone for what she wanted.

Now she hid behind pantsuits and the rules of being "good." Nakita was right. She was boring. She hadn't gone to jail, but she'd put herself in her own prison. What the hell was she punishing herself for?

A shadow covered her. "Kim, what are you doing out here?" Isaac's deep voice startled her.

Her eyes popped open. Their gazes locked. Her body hummed and heated. She straightened and looked away. "Isaac. Hey, just taking my lunch break."

"Lunch break?" He said with confusion.

This time when she met his gaze she was ready for the jolt and could smile normally. "Curtis came into the office and told me to get lost. He has a meeting. I brought my tablet so that I can keep working on the list of companies you need."

"I didn't know about a meeting." His tone mirrored the frown on his face. "No telling what he's up to." He took a deep breath and sat next to her on the bench.

His nearness made her pulse flutter. She resisted the urge to scoot away and reveal his effect on her. "What are you doing here?"

He stared out over the falls. A line formed between his brows and his lips were curved down. "Thinking."

He looked so troubled she couldn't help but ask. "About?"

Isaac leaned forward and rested his arms on his legs. "I met with Bob Livingston this morning. He'll support my effort to take over the company."

Her eyes widened. Kim faced him more. "You're going to do it."

"I am. To do so, I'll need Bob and a majority of the board to support the decision."

"How are you going to do that?"

"See who all agree with me taking over and convince them to vote Curtis out."

"Sounds simple."

"If only it were."

He continued to stare at the falls. She should be focused on his problem. Instead, she couldn't take her eyes off the strong set of his jaw or the tight line of his lips. The urge to reach over and brush her hand across his cheek nearly consumed her. Rub his neck until the concern evaporated. She ran her hand over her arm instead and chose to focus on his problem. As she should.

"What's the problem?"

Isaac rubbed his jaw. "My image. Apparently, I'm too cold."

Kim looked away. She couldn't really argue with that.

He scoffed. "You agree?"

Well, he asked. Plus, she knew he could handle her honesty. "To a certain extent, yes. You rarely interact with anyone other than the directors sitting in your weekly meetings. When you do talk to the other employees, you're blunt and impersonal. You don't have friends."

"I have friends." He sounded affronted.

"That we see," she added. "You work, workout, then work some more. Your social life is business dinners and a string of lovers that don't last more than a few weeks." She tried to keep her voice even on the last part, even though the idea of his various lovers made her chest ache.

"How do you know about my personal life?"

"I keep your calendar." She let her tone imply the duh. "Don't worry, I'm not discussing your personal life with co-workers, but remember you have three former lovers working at C.E.S. They're more than happy to discuss how you treat them like fun toys and easily move along when you're done."

The biggest reason why she hadn't slept with Isaac that night. She'd played the whore once. Didn't like it. Didn't plan to do so again.

"Emotions don't have a place in business," he said. He didn't appear the least bit concerned by the way his former lovers described him.

"Which makes you sound like your father." His body stiffened, and he glared at her. Kim shrugged apologetically even though the look made her tremble, and not with fear. When Isaac got angry and focused, he also got sexy. But he needed to hear this. She was probably the only person willing to be honest with him. "I know you don't like the comparison, but you need to know what you're facing. People want to feel appreciated and wanted. They want to feel like the company is vested in their well-being."

The tension slowly drained from his body. He ran a hand over his face. "My response to that would make me sound even more like Curtis," he said wryly. "Point taken."

"I know you want the people at C.E.S. to succeed. If anyone has a concern or a question, they come to me for information."

"Information like what?"

She thought about the last possible change that had many of her co-workers skittish. "The possible health care change. You and H.R. were debating raising the cost for employees. That had many people afraid and ready to leave."

Isaac frowned and tilted his head to the side. "You researched the company we switched to. Showed me their ability to meet our needs without raising costs. I met with them, and we made the switch."

She nodded. "It's one of the reasons I like my job. I can be the voice of the employees to the CEO, a voice they never had before."

"I knew you were in tune with the employees but didn't realize how much."

Kim shrugged. "You never asked either."

"You make me sound like a terrible boss." He didn't sound upset, just thoughtful.

"You're not a very in tune boss, but you're not terrible. I know you care about the success of C.E.S., including the employees."

"To change the company image, I can't just do that from the top. I need the employees to be happy." His dark gaze studied her. "You'll know how to do that."

The confidence in his voice made her smile. "I do, and I'd be more than happy to help."

"You already have ideas to improve employee morale?"

"I do. I've been tossing this idea around for a few months. An employee appreciation week. That way you can show gratitude for what they do, get to know them, and they can know you."

His brows drew together. He sat back and looked out over the falls. "Why didn't you say something sooner?"

"I didn't think your father would go for it."

"Exactly the problem. Go ahead and plan it."

"Do you want to be involved?"

"I trust you," he said easily. "set a date for a few weeks out. Let me know what you come up with and where I need to be."

Kim's jaw dropped. "In a few weeks? Are you serious?"

His lips tilted up in a half smile, and her heart flipped a little. "Are you saying there's something you can't handle?"

There was no way she would back down from that challenge. "Of course not."

He nodded. "Good, a few weeks then."

They sat in silence for another several beats. Kim's mind raced with all of the ideas she'd had for an employee appreciation week and all of the work that came with planning one.

Her cell phone buzzed. She pulled it out and frowned at the text icon from an unfamiliar number before reading the text.

We aren't done talking. I want my million.

Kim gripped the phone and gritted her teeth. The roar in her ears was louder than the falls in the park. Rebecca.

She had to handle that. She barely had a down payment for the house how was she supposed to come up with a million dollars? Worse, what would Rebecca do when she realized Kim wasn't paying her?

Isaac shifted slightly. "The woman you were about to fight the other day? Everything cool there?"

Kim's spine turned to cement. She glanced at Isaac to see if he was looking at her cell, but he still gazed at the falls. Kim sucked in a deep breath and stuffed the phone back in her purse. She didn't want to tell him about Rebecca.

She crossed her arms. "It was an argument, not a fight."

"What was the argument about?"

Kim shook her head. "Nothing."

Isaac gave her a *try that lie with another fool* look. He did deserve a partial explanation. "She wants money. I'm not giving it to her."

"Do you owe her money?"

"I owe her a debt," she said forcefully. "Not money."

"Hmph." He grunted and frowned. She waited for more, but he turned away.

"What's the hmph for?"

"Owing someone a debt is as bad as owing them money. Get out of her debt."

Kim sat forward until she was nearly on the edge of the bench. "Pay her off?"

He didn't back off or bat an eye. Instead, he looked at her as if what he said made perfect sense. "Yes. Don't let anyone hold something over you. That puts them in the position of power. If you get her off your back, she can't use your debt against you."

Kim lifted a hand. She couldn't do this right now. The more he pressed, the more she wanted to confide, and before she knew it, she'd end up telling him all of her sordid secrets. Rebecca was her problem. She'd figure out something. "Can we talk about something else, please?"

"Fine." He glanced at his watch. "I need to get back to the office. I only came here to think about what Bob said."

She wanted to get back to the office, too. Focusing on work and problems she might actually be able to solve. "Curtis told me to stay out for a while."

"What Curtis wants has nothing to do with what I do. We both have work to do. Wouldn't you prefer to work at your desk than here at a park bench?"

Kim gathered her stuff and stood. The stylus to her tablet fell. Isaac quickly picked it up. He held it out to her, and when she tried to take it, he didn't let go.

"Bob also suggested I start a serious relationship. He thinks showing I'm capable of commitment will help soften my image and set me apart from

Curtis."

His dark gaze bound hers. With the barest hint of a pull on the stylus, he tugged her slightly closer. Kim's skin tingled. A rush of excitement saturated her blood.

"What did you say?"

"I could only think of one person."

Her pulse fluttered. She tried to swallow, but her mouth was dry as toast. "Who did you think of?"

"Someone who wants what I can't give." He let go of the stylus. "I couldn't ask her to do that."

She blinked serval times. Opened her mouth to respond only to snap it shut again. Her? He couldn't possibly mean…her? Only being swept over the falls would have made her feel more shaken. A multitude of emotions washed and churned over her. The most frightening realization: she wouldn't have immediately said no. "Maybe she would have considered helping you."

Something flashed in his eyes. His lips parted as if he were going to say something, then he licked his lips and looked away. "Arrangements like that never work. Emotions make things complicated. Things are good." He made eye contact. "Let's not make them complicated."

Kim bit her lower lip. Disappointment and relief both wrestled within her. She knew saying yes to an offer like that would be idiotic. So why did she wonder if that was the only reason he hadn't asked?

"Let's get back," she said.

For a second he appeared just as disappointed as her before he nodded and they left the park. His unspoken question a heavy weight between them, and Kim's uncertainty that she would have refused an even heavier burden on her heart.

CHAPTER 10

Isaac knocked once before entering his dad's office and immediately regretted the decision. Curtis glared at him. The unfamiliar woman kneeling between his legs turned ten shades redder than her hair.

Isaac quickly turned his back. A headache grew with his anger. "Shit, can't you lock your door?"

"I shouldn't be bothered before noon."

Isaac gritted his teeth. "You're the owner of a major corporation. You can't ignore business until after lunch."

The sound of clothes rustling and grunts made Isaac hope Curtis and the redhead were getting dressed.

"Why the hell do we pay all these damn people?" Curtis said.

Tension gripped Isaac's shoulders. This is why Curtis needed to be pushed out. "You're still the head. Decisions need to be made."

The redhead slipped into Isaac's peripheral vision. She wiggled her fingers at Curtis and tucked a few folded bills into the cleavage of her low-cut blouse. "Call me."

"Yeah, sure," Curtis said with all the sincerity of con artist.

The woman slipped through the door. Hopefully, Kim was still in accounting where she'd made a stop when they'd returned to the office. He had no idea how he'd explain this. He needed a clear head to get through the next few minutes without yelling this behavior was exactly why he decided to kick Curtis out of his own company. Isaac visualized his anger. Blew the cloud of emotion away. After a few deep breaths, he faced his father.

Curtis grinned and snorted. "I found her on a website this morning. What the hell would I call her again for?"

"You what?"

"A friend mentioned this website where women offer up anything. I didn't believe it but what do you know? One phone call and bam." He slapped his fist into the palm of his other hand. "A morning blowjob for fifty bucks."

"Since when do you need cheap whores?"

"I don't. Just wanted to see if she would come." Curtis glared at Isaac. "Too bad I didn't." He sank heavily into his chair.

His temple throbbed. "You can't bring random women you find online to the office. You shouldn't be doing this in your office," Isaac said with barely suppressed anger.

Curtis smirked. "Don't tell me you haven't had a little fun in the office. I think Tanya would disagree with that."

Isaac's spine stiffened. Tanya had been his administrative assistant before Kim, and she'd been very happy to give Isaac similar attention at the end of a long day. She'd moved on to marketing after realizing their affair would go nowhere. She'd also been the one to snap him out of his obsession with Kim two years ago. He'd never considered how his interactions with Tanya made him resemble Curtis. Never again.

"I'm not married. Your actions are disrespectful to Cynthia." The claim was his only defense.

Curtis snorted, reached for the bottle of lotion he always kept on his desk and squirted some into his hands. Despite years of no longer being behind a truck, the roughness of his hands never went away.

"Cynthia knows what she married. That's how she got me away from your mom in the first damn place." He vigorously rubbed the lotion into his skin.

"You should still keep up appearances in public. It'll go a long way toward helping to improve the image of C.E.S."

Curtis's hand slowed, and his eyes narrowed. "Improving the image? We don't need to improve our image. We're a powerhouse."

"We were on the way to becoming a powerhouse two years ago. Now we've lost one of our biggest CEOs, several clients and are on the verge of losing more."

"Which is why we have to show our strength by stealing Andre's company," Curtis said with greedy enthusiasm.

"I've told you trying to take over Andre's business will only cause further problems for us. I've got a better idea."

"What could be better than adding a new side to our business?"

Isaac shifted his stance and slipped a hand into his pocket. "Getting back the businesses we lost. Avoid losing any contracts that are on the brink."

"Who's on the brink? I can make sure they go nowhere." A gleam lit Curtis's eye. One that only came when he was ready to strike at someone.

"That's what I'm talking about. We can't be sustainable if the only way we keep our clients is through pressure and blackmail." Isaac strode forward and clutched the chair across from the desk. "We need to rebrand."

"Rebrand?" Curtis said as if the word was distasteful.

Isaac gripped the back of the chair and suppressed the need to physically shake sense into Curtis. "Yes. Our customers need to know we're a company they can trust. Before Andre left, that's exactly where he wanted to take us. We got the Kansas account by proving our abilities. We can continue to do that. Externally and internally."

"Internally?"

"The employees fear us."

"As they should." Curtis's forefinger tapped the desk with every word. "It's my way or the highway. If they don't know that, then they need to go work somewhere else."

Anger clouded his vision. The need to snap prodded. Inhale deeply, exhale slowly. Focus on making valid points not arguing. "That's not what's going to help us keep and retain good people."

"It has so far."

"Times have changed. We've got to change with them. I'm doing this so we can protect C.E.S., and I'm doing it with or without you."

"Are you threatening me?" Curtis's voice lowered to a menacing tone.

Isaac pushed away from the chair and met his dad's stare head on. "This is no threat. I'm telling you quite clearly that I will not let you run our company into the ground. Andre is gone. Get over it. Let him do his thing and work with me to make C.E.S. prosperous."

Curtis watched Isaac with narrowed eyes. A cold-blooded crocodile ready to attack. "Are you trying to take over?"

The truthfulness of the statement didn't bother Isaac. Of course, Curtis would automatically think any ideas contrary to his were an attempt to overthrow him. He'd flung that accusation out a number of times over the years. The really hard part would be doing exactly what his father feared without getting caught. He really hoped trusting Bob had been smart.

"You are still the head of this company," he said calmly.

"And don't you forget it."

"Neither should you. Help me save what you're so happy to remind everyone you're the head of."

Curtis sneered and stood. "You do things your way, and I'll do things mine. We'll see whose methods work best." He picked up the set of keys on his desk and his jacket off the back of the chair. "I've completed my in-office work for the day. Now I'll go secure some of our accounts." He strolled to the door.

"Curtis—"

Curtis spun and pointed a finger at Isaac. "I'm your damn father. You're going to address me with respect."

"When you act like a father, I'll do that." The bitter retort was out before Isaac could think about his reply.

"What are you trying to say, boy?"

Now that he'd started, the rest spilled out. "Fathers teach, nurture and build up their children. You demand loyalty through threats, intimidation, and blackmail. You taught me how to make money, you taught me how to build an empire out of nothing. I respect you for that, and I'm loyal to the company you built for Andre and me. I will address you as I would any other colleague. Not like a loving son to his father."

Isaac and Andre were just pieces in Curtis's game of life. Curtis wanted kids to carry on his legacy. Demanded their loyalty because his own brother betrayed him. Gave them money and power only so they'd be indebted to them. Any love he had for Curtis withered and died long ago.

"Fine, but don't ever forget I'm in charge of all of this. Challenge me, and I'll ruin you just like I'm going to ruin your brother."

"Whatever you say, Curtis."

Curtis's nostrils flared. He sucked his teeth before wrenching open the door and storming out of the office. Isaac rubbed his pounding head. If he wasn't sure before he was dead certain now. He would do everything in his power to push Curtis out.

CHAPTER 11

Kim read the email and immediately wanted to shove the monitor onto the floor. The email was the fifth one today from a coworker regretfully informing her they were too busy to help plan the employee week. Add today's five with the four she received yesterday, and her employee week committee consisted of her and Fanta.

Isaac strolled out of his office. His thumb swiped over his smartphone, and he didn't look up as he walked to her desk. "Kim, are you busy? I need you to come with me to this meeting."

Now she wanted to shove the monitor off the desk directly onto his foot. Of course, she was busy. "I happen to be in the middle of planning the employee appreciation week. I'm trying to figure out the best location for the picnic, decide who will handle the catering, pick out all the decorations, and come up with a fun activity that most will enjoy."

Isaac looked up with a confused frown on his face. "Why are you doing all of that?"

"Because I can't get help from the other departments."

"Why not?"

"Officially, everyone is busy." She made air quotes with her fingers. "Unofficially, your dad told the various department directors that employee appreciation week is not happening."

Isaac stilled. The line between his brows deepened. "I would ask where you heard that, but there's no need. I should have suspected Curtis would try something like this." He glared at his phone, thumbs flying over the keyboard.

In the week since he'd revealed his plans to rebrand the company, Curtis had been curiously silent. He may not know about his son's plans to take over, but he typically fought any changes Isaac suggested. She'd hoped Curtis finally agreed with one of Isaac's decisions until the enthusiasm of everyone who'd liked the idea of an employee appreciation week evaporated faster than a water drop in the Sahara Desert.

Isaac finished typing with a few hard taps to the screen. "There," he said with a satisfied glint in his eye.

"What?"

He nodded toward her computer. "Check your email."

A new email popped up on the monitor. Kim glanced at him. "What's this?"

He shrugged. Kim clicked on the email.

Seeking volunteers to help with employee appreciation week, which will be held four weeks from now. All departments are encouraged to participate. See Kim Griffin to volunteer.

Her entire body breathed a sigh of relief. "Thank you."

"You're welcome." He slid the phone into the pocket of his slacks. Kim's gaze involuntarily followed the movement. Isaac's suits were tailored which meant he perfectly filled a pair of pants. "That should get you some help, which means you can go to this meeting."

Kim jerked her gaze from his crotch to his face. He stared directly at her. Heat spread through her cheeks. This wasn't the first time he'd caught her ogling him, but now the unasked question from the week before lingered between them. The good thing was Isaac never gave her a smug, I-know-you-want-this, look when he caught her guard slipping. The bad thing was the absence of a smug look didn't take away from the desire that flared in his sultry eyes.

She glanced away first and looked at the planner on her desk. "Go where?"

"I'm meeting with Scott Kelly in accounting and a few of his managers. I've asked for their suggestions to reduce our tax liability. My dad's idea of charitable giving is to fund cocktail parties of people who've lined his pockets. I'm not completely convinced they're all legitimate non-profits. Changing how we give back can help our image and clean up the books."

Kim saved the work on her computer. "Okay, now it makes sense."

"What makes sense?"

"His assistant manager, Fanta, worked over the weekend on that project. We talked about her ideas at lunch on Monday. She's got some good suggestions, but she doesn't think Scott will listen."

"Did she say Scott was also working on the project?"

Kim shook her head and stood. "No. He tends to assign his projects to her and then turns in the work with his name on it. It's one of the reasons she's looking for another job."

Isaac's head cocked to one side, and his eyes narrowed. "How long has he been doing this?"

"A lot more after Andre left the company. Your brother typically handled the financials and oversaw Scott's work."

"I'm glad you told me. I'm ready to fill the CFO position. I don't like Scott, but I thought he was at least competent at his job."

"I'm not saying he's incompetent, just don't overlook the other managers on his team. They pretty much run the department." She picked up her tablet and followed Isaac to the door.

He held it open for her and gave her an approving look. "You keep reminding me why I can trust you with the employees. I'll keep what you told me in mind."

Kim's face heated and appreciation swelled in her chest. Her phone chimed before she could give a reply. A welcome distraction when his praise had left her a little speechless.

She checked her email as they walked to the elevator. "I've got two volunteers already." She slipped the phone back into her pocket. "Your word has been accepted. Now I can really get into planning."

Isaac pressed the down button by the elevator. "Why didn't you tell me Curtis was making things difficult?"

"I didn't know yesterday," she replied. She hadn't realized Curtis was the reason for the decline in enthusiasm until Fanta said something the day before. She'd planned to tell him about the issue later today. From now on she'd be sure to let him know if he heard of anything else Curtis was doing behind his back as soon as she realized what was going on.

His shoulders tightened with the last statement. "I'm sorry he hindered the process."

"We've got it worked out." She tried to sound cheerful. Hopefully, Curtis wouldn't do anything else to sabotage the project. "Is there a reason he's so against this?"

The elevator door opened and they stepped inside. "He thinks he can win back clients his way. Therefore, we don't need to rebrand. As for the employees, they should just comply without question."

Kim grimaced. "What happened to him? I mean, he was always unpleasant, but in the past year or so he's gotten more difficult."

Isaac pressed the button for the floor below. "You know why."

Andre's defection. Curtis's spiral began after Andre left the company. "But you're still here. You work just as much as Andre did. I don't understand why he doesn't work harder to keep you here."

"Because I'll never leave. He knows that. C.E.S. is my life. My legacy. It's the one thing I can depend on." Determination filled his voice and his face.

The ride was quick, and they stepped off the elevator. Kim stopped Isaac with a hand on his arm. The muscles beneath the fine material of his suit flexed. His power and strength subtle but enticing. Her fingertips tingled with the need to squeeze, explore. Isaac's dark gaze collided with hers then lowered to her hand on his arm and lifted again. Desire lit his eyes. His nostrils flared. The air thickened with the awareness that hovered between them.

Kim snatched her hand away but didn't drop her gaze. Her thoughts were muddled, but she remembered what drove her to break their unspoken no-touching rule. "Is C.E.S. really the only thing you can depend on?"

"People can be fickle." His voice was deeper, rougher. He cleared his throat and licked his lips. "I've seen that every day in my own family. I can't put my trust in others, but if I do everything I can to make C.E.S. successful, then I know I can count on it to thrive. I put my trust in that. Curtis knows how I feel. He knows I wouldn't leave."

"I would have said the same about Andre. Maybe you'll find a reason to leave the way he did."

Andre left for love. The thought of Isaac doing the same was bittersweet. She wanted him to be happy. He was too robotic, too unfeeling, but knowing him, if he did fall in love it wouldn't be with his administrative assistant. Sure, he wanted to sleep with her, but he was big on legacy. If Isaac married, it would be to someone who could help his reputation. Not a former street hustler and half-ass whore turned good girl.

"I'm definitely not leaving for love," he said the words slowly and with confidence. His gaze grew more intense. She had the feeling he wanted her to really listen and understand his stance on this. "Curtis created C. E. S. out of nothing. He built this business to spite his brother and prove that he could. Now that he's done that, he doesn't care about his shitty reputation, possibly destroying the business or disgruntled employees. I do. Fixing what he ruined, making sure every employee who's stuck with us through good and bad doesn't lose their job and making this a company they can be proud to work for is my legacy."

The conviction in his voice convinced her he believed that wholeheartedly. She believed in him, even though she disliked the idea that he was so against trusting another person enough to care for them. "You'll succeed. Andre cared, but he was tired of being here."

"What makes you say that?"

"I could see his weariness. He tried to be like your father, and the effort began to wear him down. You're not trying to be Curtis. You're only interested in saving the company."

Isaac half smiled. He leaned forward just a bit. "You really do pay attention." His tone said he was impressed.

"A good assistant should pay attention to her boss."

"Is that the only reason?" Isaac's stance shifted. The movement brought him nearer. The essence of him mingled with the faint scent of his cologne. Kim leaned closer, drawn in by the lingering excitement of touching him. The craving to touch him more.

"Should there be another reason?" She knew her tone was flirty. That if she licked her lips, which she did, that his gaze might drop. It did, and the one emotion he couldn't hide, desire, heightened his scrutiny.

Footsteps sounded right before a throat cleared to her right. Isaac blinked and stepped back. Kim jumped and spun to face the newcomer. Fanta watched them with a raised brow.

"Um, hello Mr. Caldwell. I was on my way to the meeting room." Fanta sounded slightly unsure and a whole lot curious.

Isaac, ever cool, didn't appear the least bit phased to have been caught leaning in and melting Kim's bones with his sexy eyes and rumbling voice. "So were we."

He held out a hand in the direction of the conference room. Fanta smiled and the three of them walked toward the meeting room. Isaac fell in step with Fanta. Kim followed.

"Kim was telling me about your ideas to improve our charitable giving," Isaac said. "I'd like to hear more about that during the meeting."

Surprise flitted across Fanta's face before a huge grin took its place. "Of course. I wasn't sure if Scott put my suggestions in his proposal."

"Even if he didn't, we'll discuss them," Isaac said and entered the room.

Fanta held back at the door and took Kim's arm. "You told him my ideas?"

"Yes, he's really trying to turn things around here."

Fanta gave Kim a quick shoulder bump. "Thanks for having my back."

Kim grinned and was immediately glad she'd told Isaac about Fanta's involvement. "I love your ideas, and so will he."

Fanta winked. "From the looks of things, he loves your ideas, too."

Kim didn't have a quick response. Reading more into Isaac's interest in her ideas would be easy. If she didn't get a grip, she'd begin to think because he valued her mind as well as her body he'd one day wake up and realize they belonged together. She had to get her shit together. Focus on the guy who actually wanted a relationship: Rodney. Their date Saturday had been nice, and he hadn't pushed for more than a hug when he'd dropped her off. That was who she should be obsessed with.

The elevator dinged and Kim automatically glanced down the hall. A group of people were on, and a few got off. She smiled at her colleagues as they strolled to their offices. A dark-haired woman in tight black leggings and a white top quickly slid to the side in the elevator out of her view. Kim's stomach dropped. Was that Rebecca? What the hell was she doing here?

She took a step in that direction. Then noticed Curtis was also on the elevator. He grinned at the woman Kim prayed wasn't Rebecca before the door closed again. She glanced back into the conference room at Isaac, but he was focused on a conversation with Scott.

Okay, if that was Rebecca with Curtis then she couldn't rush upstairs and confront her. Why would she even be with Curtis?

Curtis was older, rich, and slimy. Of course, he would be the perfect

TRUST ME WITH YOUR LOVE

man for Rebecca to try and hustle. Kim stepped completely out of the conference room, glanced around to make sure the hall was now empty, it was and dialed Rebecca's number.

"Are you calling about my money?" Rebecca snapped.

Kim gripped the phone. Her other hand balled into a fist. "Are you in my office?"

"What? Is that why you're calling me? To ask me where I'm at?"

"I'm not playing, Rebecca. Stay away from my job."

"Or what?" Rebecca challenged.

"Or I'm going to make you wish you were still in jail." Kim lowered her voice to a near snarl.

"Are you threatening me?" Rebecca asked incredulously.

"Threat, promise, whatever the hell you want to call it. This is between you and me. My family and my job are off limits. So back off."

"Then pay me, and I'll leave you, your sexy ass boss, and his horny old daddy alone." The line went silent.

Kim's entire body shook with rage. She wanted to yell. Kick something. Punch Rebecca in the face.

Isaac's voice came from inside the conference room. "Are we ready to get started? Where's Kim?"

Kim placed her hands on her face and took a deep breath. She lowered them, straightened her shoulders and walked back into the conference room. She smiled her practiced smile at Isaac and held up her phone. "Sorry, I had to step out a second."

She quickly looked away and sat as far away from him as she could at the table. She felt his direct stare. Knew he must have seen through her calm façade. Luckily, Scott started the meeting. Kim's hand trembled as she took notes. She had to do something about Rebecca.

CHAPTER 12

The afternoon sun warmed Isaac as he stood on the balcony of his condo. He'd just gotten home, hadn't bothered to change out of his suit, though he had tossed the jacket on the back of the couch. Isaac leaned on the railing and watched the people walking along the sidewalk below. He took a sip of the beer in his hand before setting it on the rail. The sunshine, the beer, neither soothed him. Something had upset Kim again today. The idea of something bothering her and not being able to do anything about it made him feel inadequate. A feeling he had little familiarity with.

He pulled out his phone and called Andre. Now that he'd confirmed Curtis was coming for his brother's company, he wanted to give Andre a heads up. He could at least do something about that.

"I've decided to force Curtis out," Isaac said after he and Andre greeted each other.

"You're ready to fight him," Andre's deep voice replied.

"I gave him a chance to prove he had an interest in trying to save the company. He's set against a rebrand or doing anything to recruit and retain good employees."

"My way or the highway, huh?"

"His words exactly." All of his exhaustion from hearing those words for years filled his voice.

"Are you surprised?"

"Nothing Curtis does surprises me. I'd hoped he would understand salvaging client relationships is important. He prefers intimidation and bribery."

"That's all he knows. He doesn't like listening to reason," Andre said bitterly.

"He doesn't like listening to me. He would listen if you were here." Isaac pushed away from the railing and paced the length of the balcony.

"Not necessarily." Andre didn't sound convinced.

"We both know it's the truth. He fought us on all changes, but you would eventually convince him."

"He listened because we were a united front."

"Some united front. I'm the only one trying to salvage what's left of our legacy. No, wait. My legacy. You're building a new one with Mikayla. I've got to fix the company and stop Curtis from destroying yours." Isaac heard the frustration and resentment in his tone. He didn't care. He and Andre had been united once. They'd agreed to prove they were better businessmen. They'd agreed to erase the taint their father had spread while building the company. They'd agreed to stick together. Then Andre walked away.

Isaac wouldn't turn his back on his brother or start a bitter feud like Curtis had with his own brother Philip, but when Andre abandoned C.E.S., Isaac had understood some of the betrayal Curtis must have felt.

"Just because I'm not there doesn't mean I don't care about C.E.S." Andre's tone was even but hard. "I will help you any way that I can. My relationship with Mikayla doesn't change that."

Isaac stopped pacing. "Your relationship changed everything. You're there, not here. You have your own company to worry about. I know you'll help me figure this out, but let's be real. Pushing him out and getting the company on track is on me."

"You aren't in this alone. I'm serious, Isaac. Whatever you need, let me know."

He needed Andre here. He needed his brother to have stuck to their plan. "I appreciate the offer." He took a deep breath and crossed the balcony to where his beer sat on the rail. "Kim is helping me. She's planning an employee appreciation week. She thinks it'll be a good way for me to get to know the employees and for them to get to know management."

"Kim? She's still working for you?"

"Why do you sound surprised?" Isaac grabbed the beer and left the warm sunshine for the cool interior of his condo.

"When I left, you were trying to sleep with her. The administrative assistants who end up in your bed don't work for you much longer."

Isaac gritted his teeth. Damn, he wasn't that bad. "We haven't slept together."

"Why not?"

Isaac crossed the polished hardwood floors toward his kitchen. "Because we haven't. She's a good employee, I don't want to lose her."

"She turned you down?" A hint of surprise entered Andre's voice.

No need denying. "At the time, I couldn't give her what she wanted."

"Let me guess, a relationship? I don't understand why you're so against commitment."

"Because commitment is bullshit. People lie to get in a relationship. When they're tired of the relationship, they lie to get out of it or they find what they're missing somewhere else and lie about that. Relationships are distractions. My focus is on rebuilding C.E.S."

"Relationships aren't distractions and commitment isn't bullshit. The right woman can make getting through the day to day crap easier."

Isaac snorted. "Look, I get that you and Mikayla are now some power couple ready to conquer the world together, but I didn't call for your newfound romantic view of the world. If anything, I'm trying to avoid the trap of false commitment. C.E.S. already lost you. It can't afford to lose me just because I *fell in love.*"

He'd meant what he said to Kim earlier. He wouldn't abandon the company because of an emotion he didn't trust or believe in.

Andre didn't immediately respond. "I didn't want to believe it because I thought you were happy for me. You don't believe in my relationship with Mikayla. You think it's part of the reason C.E.S. is suffering."

"You left because of your emotions," Isaac stated flatly.

"I left because of Dad," Andre countered.

"Because he didn't like Mikayla. You could have stayed. We could have pushed him out together."

"No, I couldn't. He wouldn't have let us be. You know this. He would have dragged us back into his petty fight with Uncle Philip."

"Only if you'd let him. Curtis was only against you and Mikayla because of her connection to Uncle Philip. You'd made it very clear that she was off limits. You didn't have to quit. You chose to because you didn't want to be here anymore. I know you were tired of fighting with him and you hated the reputation he'd built. Don't use the excuse of needing to make things work with Mikayla as the reason you left C.E.S. You left because you wanted to." Resentment snuck back into his tone with each long, withheld word.

"Is that what you really think? That I decided to abandon you and the business?"

"That's not what I think. That's what happened."

"Isaac, my choice didn't have anything to do with wanting to turn my back on you or the family. I love Mikayla. We needed to get all of the negative influences out of our lives. We've been happier for it."

"And I wish you all of the happiness you can stand," Isaac said, his tone mocking. "I prefer to focus on saving the only thing I can rely on from ruin."

"Are you saying you can't rely on me?"

"When's the last time you've been to Greenville?" The question was answered with silence. Isaac grunted and shook his head. "Exactly. You left and haven't looked back. For the first time, I understand why Curtis was so angry when Uncle Phillip didn't go into business with him."

"I didn't turn my back on you," Andre said defensively. "I wanted something different for my life."

"Yeah, well you got what you wanted. Now I'm going after what I want for my life." He glanced at the time on the microwave mounted above the stove. He'd come home to grab his gym bag. After this conversation, he couldn't wait to take one of Calvin's hits in the ring and give a few of his own. "I've got to go."

"Isaac, wait. We need to talk about this."

"There's nothing to talk about. You're my brother. I'm not going to hold a grudge. I'm not Curtis."

"That's not what this sounds like."

"I'm stopping him from taking over your company. What does that sound like?" Isaac ended the call. Andre could leave, Curtis could challenge him, and Kim could tempt him, but he wouldn't let anyone stop him.

CHAPTER 13

Kim took a deep breath and forced herself to smile pleasantly at Tanya, who was sitting across from her in the committee meeting for the employee picnic. With everything going on in her life Kim was in no mood for playing power struggle with Isaac's former lover over the planning of employee appreciation. She'd gone looking for Rebecca yesterday to confront her about coming to C.E.S, but her old friend was nowhere to be found. Kim didn't like bringing personal frustration to work and had done a decent job of being calm today until Tanya decided to challenge every decision Kim made.

"I don't think renting out a banquet hall is what Mr. Caldwell had in mind for an employee luncheon," Kim said. The effort it took to keep her voice calm was monumental. "The point of a picnic is to have a relaxed, informal event."

Tanya flicked her wrist in Kim's direction. "Please. A banquet hall can be relaxed."

Any attempt at smiling evaporated. Kim glared at Tanya. "It's over our budget."

"Over budget? I know Isaac can afford it. He wants this to be a success."

Tanya's voice glided over Isaac's name with a familiarity that grated Kim's nerves. She had no claim on Isaac, but she really hated Tanya's implied possessiveness toward him. The rest of the committee members, Rodney included, threw their expectant gazes back to Kim. Kim had no issue with Tanya personally, but her blatant attempt to disregard every idea Kim brought to the committee proved she obviously had an issue with Kim.

The urge to snatch away the shaky foundation of entitlement Tanya felt she had by being Isaac's on again and off again lover was strong. Tanya was convenient, not important.

Or maybe that's what you want to believe.

"The picnic can be a success without costing a fortune or feeling too formal," Kim said. "I believe—"

"I know Isaac," Tanya said and pressed her hand to her chest. "You may know how he likes his coffee, but I'm *very* familiar with his likes and dislikes."

A few uncomfortable coughs and shuffles of the people around the conference room table greeted *that* statement. This woman really made being professional by not slapping her into next week very difficult.

As if he sensed impending doom and had come to rescue them, Isaac strolled into the room. He looked delicious in a dark suit and gray tie. He glanced at all of his employees and gave his usual cool smile. "How is everything coming?"

Kim straightened the notes in front of her. "Things are going...well. We're discussing the location of the employee picnic."

Tanya sat forward. "I think we should rent a banquet hall. It would be a great way to show employees we spare no expense when it comes to celebrating them."

Isaac's eyebrows drew together. "That doesn't seem like the best location for a picnic. I was thinking something more informal. A way for the employees to get to know the other executives without feeling uncomfortable."

He glanced at Kim. "Do you agree with her?"

Kim knew her smile was smug and didn't give a damn. "My recommendation is something at Flour Field," Kim said referring to the baseball stadium downtown. "The guys in collections have a recreational league baseball team, and other departments have shown an interest in doing the same. A baseball game is family friendly, informal, and a lot of fun."

Satisfaction replaced the concern in Isaac's gaze. He nodded at Kim. "I like that idea. That's why I put you in charge of this event. You know what my goals are." He looked at the rest of the committee. "I don't want anyone to feel uncomfortable during this picnic. I just want the employees to have a good time."

"We'll be sure to keep that in mind," Kim said.

He nodded and turned to leave. Tanya perked up in her chair. "Isaac," she called.

Kim gritted her teeth. Once again hating the familiarity between Isaac and Tanya.

Isaac raised a brow at Tanya.

"I have a redraft of the profits report," Tanya said. "Is it okay for me to drop it off in your office after this meeting?"

Kim gripped the pen in her hand and looked at her notepad to hide her eye roll.

He glanced at his watch then nodded. "I'll be here for about another hour or so. Otherwise, leave it with Kim."

He left without another glance at either of them. Despite having lost the battle for location, Tanya didn't back down on trying to get her ideas pushed. Eventually, they found compromises and ended the meeting. Kim packed up the laptop and various handouts she'd brought.

"Let me help you with some of that," Rodney said taking the laptop bag from her.

Kim gave him a smile of thanks and picked up the rest of her items. A few other committee members left the conference room and got on the elevator with them. The conversation flowed about the plans for the employee week. Everyone was excited, and Kim would be sure to let Isaac know.

She and Rodney got off on the top floor, and he followed her to the executive suite. The sound of Tanya's voice came from Isaac's office. The door was partially closed. Kim's stomach twisted.

"You can just set the laptop next to my desk," she said.

He did then leaned a hip against her desk. "My cousin has another fight this weekend. Saturday night. Want to come?"

Isaac's voice was a low murmur followed by Tanya's sultry giggle. Kim met Rodney's gaze. His smile was confident and hopeful at the same time. He liked her. He had a great job. He was the kind of man she should want.

He wasn't in another room giggling with Tanya.

"I'd love to," Kim said with forced excitement.

Rodney stepped forward and took her hand in his. "This makes our third date. I think we're getting serious."

His thumb rubbed the back of her hand. Her heart sped up, but not from the touch. Had it been three? They'd had dinner, then there was that quick lunch when he'd been downtown. Yep, Saturday would make three.

"Uh oh, you look upset." Rodney tried to sound lighthearted, but Kim heard the concern in his voice.

She shook her head. "Not upset, just surprised. I didn't really think we were…that you wanted."

Rodney gently squeezed her hand. "I don't play around when it comes to what I want. I like you, Kim. I want to see where this can go."

"You're always talking about wanting a relationship, but you're afraid to give a man a chance."

Nakita's words. Her thoughts drifted to Isaac. She jerked them back. Met Rodney's gaze. "I do, too."

Rodney grinned then leaned forward and pressed a kiss to her lips. Kim stiffened. He'd hugged her after dinner, and she'd rushed off after lunch. This was their first kiss. She should be excited. All she could think about was how to end it before Isaac saw.

The sound of Isaac clearing his throat filled the space. Kim jerked back. Rodney didn't let go of her hand. Tanya looked at them both with a satisfied smirk.

"You two make a cute couple," Tanya said with false cheer. She glanced at Isaac. "I'm working late tonight if you want to go over those reports."

She winked at Kim before sauntering out of the office. Rodney squeezed Kim's hand, jerking her attention back to him.

"I need to get back. I'll call you tonight. We'll make plans for Saturday."

She ignored the insistent pressure of Isaac's gaze. "Sure. Talk with you later."

He let her hand go, nodded at Isaac. "Have a good day, Mr. Caldwell." He waved and walked out.

She and Isaac stared at each other in silence. She saw it, right there in his hard expression. He was jealous. Some sort of explanation tried to form in her mind. Then she saw something else. The stain of lipstick on his collar. Apparently, he and Tanya were on again. She wished he would fling some sort of accusation about Rodney kissing her in the office with that damn stain on his collar. Isaac didn't care about her. He only wanted to possess her.

"Can I get you anything?" she asked.

Isaac sucked in a breath, let it out slowly. The emotion in his expression dissipated with the long exhale. "I have meetings all afternoon. Call my cell if something important comes up."

"I will."

He turned on his heel, went into the office, and shut the door with a solid thud.

CHAPTER 14

Kim's bravado about making things work with Rodney diminished by Saturday. Which was why she dragged Nakita with her to the fight. They stood just outside of the small auditorium where the fight was happening.

"Who is this guy again?" Nakita asked. She tugged on the short hemline of the sage green sleeveless dress clinging to her curves, then flipped her bang out of her face.

"Rodney. We've been to dinner once and lunch last week. This is the third date." Kim didn't bother to hide her exasperation. She'd told Nakita his name at least four times. "Why won't you remember his name?"

"Until I know he's worth remembering, why bother? You'll either dump him because he's for real, or he's sorry and I'll tell you to kick him to the side."

"He's not sorry. He's a nice guy."

Nakita rolled her eyes. "Ugh! Nice guys are the worst. They fall in love quickly and follow you around like sad puppy dogs."

Kim pushed her sister's arms. "Seriously? Every woman wants a nice guy."

"Nah, every woman wants a man who can screw her brains out, beat up any dude that threatens her, and spends money like it grows on trees." She gave Kim a knowing look. "I know that's the type of man you always went crazy for."

"When I was young and silly."

"Yeah, yeah…you want love and all that jazz. Okay, we'll see if Mr. *Rodney* can stick around long enough to get through your tough defenses."

"He will." She ignored Nakita's disbelieving grunt and pulled her phone out of her purse to text Rodney. He said he'd be here by now.

"Hey, Kim!" Rodney's voice rang out before she could send the message.

Kim turned in his direction, smiled and waved. She gave him props for always being on time. Rodney grinned bigger than a kid on the last day of school as he approached through the crowd. A light gray three-button shirt fitted well over his defined upper body. Dark jeans accented long legs and were paired with dark gray casual slip on shoes. His faded haircut appeared fresh, and a diamond stud glinted in his ear.

"Damn, Kim, you didn't tell me he was fine," Nakita leaned in and whispered. "Okay, plus one for him."

He does clean up nice. If she were going to move on, Rodney wasn't a bad choice. A look of appreciation filled his gaze sweeping over her. No boring business suit and tight ponytail tonight. Her hair brushed her bare shoulders. A black romper showed off the curves she hid at work and stopped high on her thighs.

A man with pecan brown skin and tattoos on his arms walked over with Rodney. The white button up shirt and black shorts he wore screamed preppy sophistication, but the tattoos, stylish high top fade, and swagger hinted at underlying toughness.

Rodney leaned in and hugged Kim. "You look fantastic."

Kim hugged him back. He smelled nice. "Thank you. This is my sister, Nakita."

Nakita wiggled her fingers. Her lips curved up in a flirtatious smile. "Hey."

Rodney shook her hand. "Nice meeting you. This is my boy, Derrick."

Derrick took Nakita's hand in his and brought it to his lips. "It's a pleasure to meet you."

Nakita giggled and stepped closer. Kim barely stopped from rolling her eyes. Of course, Derrick was right up her sister's alley. Derrick kept Nakita occupied in conversation while they entered the auditorium.

Hundreds of people moved around, and a buzz of excited conversation filled the air. Rodney led them to the second row of seats from the boxing ring. Nakita continued being absorbed in Derrick, which meant Kim felt no guilt for dragging her sister on this date.

The buzz and excitement in the crowd sent a rush of anticipation through her veins. She rubbed her hands together. She was glad she'd agreed to come. She needed a night out. She'd tried to hunt down Rebecca again the day before but heard she was out of town. At least she wouldn't have to worry about her popping up at C.E.S. No worrying about the house or Rebecca tonight.

No thoughts of Isaac.

She pushed that thought aside.

Rodney shifted in his seat to face her. "Nervous?"

She shook her head. "Kind of excited, actually. I haven't been to a professional fight."

"Oh, been just hanging out at the underground ones?"

She'd gone to a lot of illegal underground fights back when she'd hung out with Rebecca. The strength and power of the fighters used to excite her. She'd forgotten how much she enjoyed those fights until tonight.

She let out a breath and a nervous laugh. "Not any of those either." She was still easing into this thing with Rodney, no need to dump her rocky past on him on the third date.

"This one should be good. My boy has been training for over a year. He won his first fight the other week. He's favored to win tonight."

The lights changed, and the announcer came out to introduce the first fighter, a black guy in red trunks with dreads pulled into a ponytail.

Kim looked at Rodney and pointed to the fighter. "Is this your friend?"

Rodney grinned and nodded. "That's my boy, Bobby. He trains at this gym that opened a few years ago. The fighters coming out of the place are making a name for themselves." Rodney leaned in close and wrapped his arm around Kim's shoulder. "He's shorter, but he's quick. I've got my money on him."

The arm around the shoulder was unexpected, but she didn't pull away. "Maybe I should have put some money on him."

Rodney lightly squeezed her shoulder and scooted closer. If she was going to do this, then she had to try. Kim leaned just a little into his side.

Her skin prickled. For a second she wondered if her response was due to Rodney's nearness before realizing she wouldn't have to wonder if that were the case. Whenever Isaac was near or watched her, she felt the same prickly excitement. She looked around at the people near them. She was crazy. Isaac Caldwell wouldn't be at an amateur boxing match.

She focused on Bobby's corner again. Her gaze collided with the exact person she hadn't expected to be there. Her stomach plummeted, and her lips parted with a silent gasp. Her back straightened. Isaac raised a brow, his only form of acknowledgment.

"You good?" Rodney asked.

She jerked her gaze from Isaac to the man beside her. "Uhh…yeah. Is that Mr. Caldwell up there?"

Rodney squinted at the corner of the ring. His eyes lit up. "It is. He does work out at the gym. I saw him one or two times when I went there with Bobby. I'm surprised he's not in the amateur fight. He's good."

"He is?"

"Yeah. Bobby says he doesn't want to fight, though. Still, that's cool as hell."

And hot as hell! Just the thought of Isaac in a pair of boxing shorts, sweaty and pumped full of adrenaline, sent a thrill of desire straight to her core.

She shook her head. The image didn't disappear. "Yeah…pretty cool."

The announcer introduced the second fighter. Kim's gaze was pulled back to Isaac's. His focus on her turned the desire in her to a smoldering fire. She couldn't force herself to look away. He always commanded her attention. This was the first time she'd seen him in casual clothes. His red shirt matched the fighter's colors and accentuated his wide shoulders. Dark pants framed muscular legs. Even with the distance between them, need sparked as the seconds stretched. Her nipples tightened. She squeezed her thighs together, tried not to fidget in her seat.

The bell announcing the start of the fight rang and jerked Kim to reality. Rodney gave her a questioning look. She gave him an *I'm good* nod before turning away. He tugged her a little closer into his side. She wanted to pull away. The force of Isaac's gaze on her was the only thing that kept her from doing so. That and the memory of Tanya's lipstick on his collar.

*

She should have avoided the after party. The thought orbited Kim's mind with lightning speed every time she caught Isaac's eye across the club. Isaac was actually in a club! Drinking beer, talking and joking with the fighters from the gym like a normal guy. This revelation was not doing good things for her plans to ignore her attraction.

Rodney's friend had won his amateur fight which meant The Arena's fighters, which she'd learned was the name of the boxing gym, were still undefeated. The group had a VIP section of the club, which Rodney obviously wanted to hang in and celebrate with his boy and—to Rodney's utter excitement—Isaac Caldwell. Kim half expected him to do a fangirl squeal when he'd heard their boss was hanging with the fighters at the after party.

Kim had managed to drag Rodney to the bar and kept him either there or on the dance floor since their arrival. Yes, it was a sorry attempt at avoiding really hanging out with Isaac, but she didn't care. She'd perfected staying distant and professionally friendly at the office. She didn't think her emotional preservation defense would stand away from the office.

"Hey, let's dance again," Kim said when Rodney indicated they should go back to VIP.

"Again? You are really trying to wear me out, girl."

Kim laughed as if she were having a good time instead of stalling. "I'm just making sure you can hang."

Rodney's gaze turned subtly sly. He took a step closer and placed his hand on her hip. "Oh really?" His voice dropped an octave.

Poor choice of words, Kim! She was attracted to him, but it was much too soon to bring up the idea of sex in their relationship.

Kim lifted her drink to take a sip. Her bent arm also required him to move back. "If you can't keep up with me on the dance floor, then I need to know early."

The knowing look in his gaze didn't change. "I may not be able to dance forever, but believe me, my stamina is more than adequate."

He wasn't going to make getting out of her slip-up easy. "You know what? Go sit for a little bit. I'm going to get some water. I'm thirsty."

"You've got a drink."

"Also trying to avoid a hangover. Water helps."

A chorus of "Ooh" loud enough to be heard over the music in the club came from the VIP section. They both looked that way. Rodney's friend waved him over. Thank heaven for small miracles.

Rodney grinned at her. "Let me go see what he wants."

"Sure. I'll be right there." She forced cheer into her voice.

She glanced around and found Nakita huddled up in a corner talking to Derrick. Well, she wouldn't get any help from her in rushing from the party. She turned back to the bartender and asked for water.

Her neck prickled a second before strong hands clasped the bar on either side of her. A current of awareness penetrated her immediately. Isaac. The strength and the heat of him made her body hum.

"Dance with me."

His voice was a warm caress against her ear. He hadn't even touched her, and she wanted to lean back and press her body into his. She lifted her glass to her lips to down the last of her cocktail. Her heart beat like crazy, but her hands remained steady. The bartender placed a glass of water in front of her and Kim smiled her thanks before she slowly turned to Isaac. She met his gaze, and her breath caught. He looked at her as if she were air and he couldn't breathe.

She leaned back against the bar and tried to pretend as if his proximity hadn't turned her knees into jelly. "Sorry, I don't dance with the creepy guy who stares at me all night."

"I'm creepy?" His lip curved into a sinful smile. He eased forward, wrapping her in his scent, trapping her with his gaze. "What does that make you? I've caught your stare several times." His voice was a rumble of temptation she felt deep in her midsection. Maybe a little lower.

She licked her dry lips. Wrong move, because he focused on her mouth and his intense stare sharpened. "Why are you here?" Her voice came out easy, the barest of tremble she hoped the music hid.

"You know I take boxing lessons. Calvin, the gym owner, asked me to come. Why are you here?"

Again, the vision of Isaac, sweaty and sculpted, in nothing but a pair of boxing shorts filled her brain. What did he ask? Oh, yeah, the reason she was here. "Rodney asked me."

He shifted and glanced away. Tightness covered his jaw a second before he looked back at her. "And are you enjoying yourself?"

Not as much as she enjoyed standing with Isaac so close. "I am. Rodney is nice." *He won't break my heart.*

He leaned even closer. They didn't touch which made her yearn for his touch. Between the bar and his arms on either side, she couldn't move away. The thing was, she didn't want to. She couldn't blame the drinks. Isaac's blatantly possessive stance sent sparks across her skin.

"Is that what you like? Nice guys?"

Isaac was a decent guy, but he wasn't a nice guy. He would take everything she had to give and not give anything in return except toe-curling sex and a few meaningless gifts. She knew she'd heard the stories. *What's wrong with that, exactly?*

"I do."

"Does being on a date with a nice guy mean you can't dance with me?"

He was flirting with her. Which only made her want to do the same. That was definitely the rum's fault. Rum and an underutilized sex drive were the perfect tag team to ruin good intentions.

"Depends. Are you a nice guy?"

"No. I'm the guy you wish you didn't want."

The heat in his eyes was more exciting and tempting than any thoughts of long term with Rodney. Her nipples puckered into hard points. Heat throbbed between her legs.

"Then I should say no."

He took her hand in his. With the other, he pulled cash from his pocket and tossed the bills onto the bar. "What you should do and what you want to do don't always have to line up."

Her mind gave one last weak attempt to remind her she shouldn't go on the dance floor with the man she'd strictly avoided getting close to. The promise in his dark eyes as he slowly led her to the edge of the dance floor steamrolled that weak attempt.

The DJ was also to blame. Couples on the floor were pressed together while the provocative beat of Beyoncé's *Partition* played. The beat fast enough to keep people on the dance floor, but slow enough for Isaac to pull her flush against him and move to the music.

She sucked in a breath, lightly held his shoulders and moved her hips with his. Isaac's hands held her waist, guided her movements to the sensual beat. Their gazes never disconnected. The eye contact linking them until nothing mattered but the music, their touch, getting closer. Her limbs loosened. One of her hands slid from his shoulder to the back of his neck. His fingers tightened on her waist. Desire flooded every cell. The tight points of her nipples brushed his hard chest. Pleasure erupted from the intimate contact. She couldn't hear him groan, but she felt a rumble go through him. She watched as the intensity of his gaze grew, and he drew his lower lip into his mouth. He glanced down at her mouth. His lip slid out and need pounded in her sex.

Isaac pulled her closer. His head lowered. Kim twisted in his arms until her back pressed against his front. She didn't want out of his arms, but if he kissed her, she'd be completely lost.

His hand spread over her stomach, the other gripped her hip and pulled her back. The rigid press of his dick cradled in her backside. A low moan vibrated through her chest. Wrapped in his strong arms, surrounded by the strength of him, everything she pretended she didn't feel for him when they touched broke free. She breathed in his masculine scent, let her mind go, and let the surge of emotions infuse her.

Isaac's hand slid lower until his fingertips grazed the top of her thong through the material of her romper. An image of his hands there with her wearing nothing but the thong filled her mind. He'd held her like this that night. Reached down and touched her from this position.

His head lowered and his lips lightly brushed her neck. Kim sucked in a breath. Her nipples ached, and shivers danced across her skin. "Come home with me."

Yes, sat on the tip of her tongue. Every bone in her body wanted to leave now. The problem was what would happen after. She wanted to be held. Wanted him to look at her like he couldn't imagine waking up with anyone else. Wanted him to kiss her softly then slowly make love to her after they got the initial passionate wild and crazy energy out of the way.

She wanted them to be a couple, and he would laugh at her again if she said that.

Kim slowly lowered her hand from his head. "I can't."

She waited for his body to stiffen. For him to push her away and call her a tease. Or, for him to continue kissing and touching her. God knew if he kept that up her sex-starved brain may win out over self-preservation. He did neither.

His body continued to move to the sensual music. "Why?"

"I still want everything."

His body stiffened with that. The smart part of her brain overpowered the desire. She pulled out of his arms and faced him. "I deserve everything."

His eyes were dark, his expression unreadable in the lights of the club. Kim didn't wait around to see if he eventually laughed or sneered. She walked around him and off the dance floor. When she reached the VIP lounge, Rodney was part of a group huddled around one of the fighters watching a video. If he was angry about her dance with Isaac or had noticed anything, she couldn't tell. He grinned at her, took her hand and pushed the guys out of the way so she could sit next to him.

Kim smiled and tried to ignore that every time her heart beat, it sent an answering pulse of unsatisfied need to her breasts and core. She watched the video, laughed with Rodney, and tried to remember that she wanted and deserved a guy who would give her everything.

CHAPTER 15

When Bob called Isaac on Sunday to say he believed Doug Campbell would be interested in helping push out Curtis and wanted to meet first thing on Monday, Isaac had immediately emailed Kim and asked her to clear his schedule. He couldn't force himself to call her. Not after making a fool of himself on Saturday.

Jealousy and possessiveness were two emotions that encouraged dumb decisions. Two emotions that brewed the second he'd seen Rodney kiss Kim in the office. Two emotions he'd spent all weekend trying to clear from his mind. Despite the effort to overcome the feelings, he would have been fine avoiding her all day if he didn't need someone he could trust at the meeting. If Curtis found out Isaac was meeting with multiple board members, his suspicions would skyrocket. Isaac could bring Kim under the pretense of taking notes, and there was no one else he trusted to take with him.

He entered the office. Kim's fingers hesitated on the keyboard. She didn't greet him with her usual smile. Her hazel eyes met his briefly before she gave a quick nod and turned back to her computer.

They should talk about what happened. That's what most people would do. Get all of their feelings out in the open and move forward with the air clear. They could also move on without having a deep, emotional discussion. He preferred the latter.

"Kim, I'd like you to come with me to meet Doug this morning."

Some of the tension in her posture eased. Obviously, she didn't want to talk about Saturday any more than he did. "Shouldn't you take another executive?"

"Right now, I don't know which executive I can trust. Swaying the board is on me, but I don't like being the only person at meetings like this. I need someone else there who can vouch for what was said. Andre used to be that person. Now, you're the only one I trust."

She watched him for a second. He wondered what was going through her mind. He hoped she understood what it meant for him to admit to trusting her. He believed Kim wanted the company to succeed just as much as he did.

"Sure," she said.

A few minutes later, they left the building. He'd asked Doug to meet him outside of the office at the same coffee house he'd met Bob to limit the possibility, no matter how slim, for Curtis to come in and interrupt.

"Why Doug versus another board member?" Kim asked after they were settled in the car.

The tension from Saturday night vibrated between them like a low-frequency beat. If she could ignore the pulse, so could he. For all he knew she'd left the club and spent the night with Rodney. His grip on the steering wheel tightened.

"My father's blackmailed Doug in the past. It's the reason he gave Curtis money to start C.E.S. in the first place. Doug was conning a rich older woman. Telling her he loved her and planning a wedding. He told her he was a businessman and had her convinced if she bought into his plans they'd be set."

"He's not married."

"He married her, invested all her money in some scheme and when she lost the money, divorced her. Except he was involved in the scheme and actually got her money. His mistake was also scamming a few influential people in the area. Curtis knew about it and threatened to go to the police. They struck a deal, and Doug's been on the board ever since."

He'd never told anyone that story. Never trusted anyone not to take the story and use it for their own purposes. He believed Kim wouldn't betray his trust.

She sucked in a breath. "They sound a lot alike." Her concerned gaze swung to him. "Why would he side with you?"

"Because Curtis slept with Doug's wife last year. Not to mention all the shady schemes Curtis has roped him into over the years. Bob thinks Doug is ready to get out of Curtis's debt."

"This is some mess," Kim mumbled. She crossed her arms and looked out the window.

He agreed but chose to remain silent. They didn't talk anymore for the rest of the ride.

Isaac shook Doug's hand when he approached his table. "Doug, I appreciate you meeting me so early," Isaac said once they were seated at a table. He gestured to Kim. "You know Kimberly Griffin, my admin assistant. She's helping me with my plans to improve C.E.S and I asked her to be here."

Doug glanced at Kim, his dark eyes sharp and assessing. "What type of plans?"

"Plans to get Curtis out as the head of C.E.S."

Doug shot forward in his chair. "Are you trying to set me up?" His forefinger pressed into the table. "I know your dad likes to test the loyalty of his people."

Isaac assumed Doug would be suspicious which is why he'd been straightforward about his plans. Whenever someone criticized Curtis, the words always got back to him, and Curtis always found a way to get even. In order to get Doug to trust him, he couldn't speak in innuendos.

"I'm not setting you up," Isaac said calmly. "I'm here because we both know his focus isn't on making money. It's on getting revenge on my brother. He's ready to drag us into a fight to buy out Andre's company that we can't win. We don't have the capital, and we're losing clients."

"I'm sure Curtis is already working to get them back," Doug said with a disgusted smirk.

"That's not the way we can keep our clients," Isaac countered. "I'm going to push him out. I need you to help me."

Doug's sharp gaze landed on Isaac. A second later he laughed and slapped the table. Kim jumped. Isaac nearly reached over to soothe her.

"You can't be serious." Doug wiped a tear from his eye. "You're funny. Dumb as hell, but funny."

Tension squeezed Isaac like a python. "This isn't a joke."

Kim gently touched his thigh. The shock of the touch snapped through his anger. He darted a look her way. She shook her head slightly. She was right. He didn't need to attack.

Isaac took a deep breath, blew away the anger, forced his shoulders to relax. Doug wouldn't easily agree with Isaac. He'd been double-crossed by Curtis too many times in the past. Isaac needed to be patient and hope he wasn't making a mistake trusting him.

"I know it's not a joke," Doug said, the humor not completely gone from his voice. "This is some serious shit. You do this, and he'll hate you more than Andre. More than his brother. Are you sure you know what you're in for?"

Isaac didn't care about how Curtis would feel afterward. He only cared about doing what was right. "We can do this if we're smart. Not only do we need him out, but we need to take away his leverage. Find out what he has on the key people likely to be retaliated against and clean that up."

"You're acting like that's easy. Curtis has dirt on a lot of people. Damn near everyone on the board."

"I didn't say it would be easy. I'm saying it needs to be done. You've either got the balls to do what's right with me or you run back to Curtis and tell him what I'm doing." That erased any vestiges of humor from Doug's face. Isaac leaned forward and rested his elbow on the table. "What are you going to choose?"

Doug's jaw tightened and his nostrils flared with his angry breaths. His gaze cut to Kim. "He's actually doing this, huh?"

Kim didn't bat an eye. "Absolutely. I put together the reports submitted to the board. I also smudge the numbers when Curtis doesn't like things and wants to mislead the board. The company can't sustain itself at this rate. Isaac wants to save it. Not just for his legacy, but for the people working there. This is a rebrand, inside and out. We can do it without the board behind us, but we'd rather do it with you."

Doug sighed and considered Kim's words. Isaac struggled not to stare at Kim in wonder. *We* can do it. She'd said we. Like they were a team. He hadn't been part of a team since Andre left. He trusted her to help, but for her to say we and us. The words fucked him up. He liked the sound of them too much.

"I'm sick and tired of the way Curtis thinks he can blackmail me. He's roped me into some pretty messed up stuff. His latest scheme..." Doug shook his head. "I can't do it."

"What scheme?" Isaac asked. "Is there something other than the purchase of Andre's company?"

Doug shook his head. "Your daddy does some under the table deals outside of C.E.S. Invests in some messed up schemes. If you don't know everything he's tapped into, the better. Just know I can barely show my face places. Everyone knows he's a crook and a liar. A crook and a liar with money who can make their lives miserable if they disagree with him. I remember when he started this company. He wanted to get back at his brother and show him he could be a success without him. He did that, but somewhere along the way he let his need for power corrupt him."

"Let's be honest," Isaac said. "There wasn't much to corrupt." He couldn't remember a time, even from his youth, when Curtis had shown compassion, love, or empathy for anything or anyone.

Doug's smile was sad. "No. Between him and Philip, your dad was always the worst one. If you're taking him down and saving this company, I'm with you." He held out his hand to Isaac. "I just hope you know what the hell you're doing."

CHAPTER 16

"Do you think you can trust him?" Kim asked as she and Isaac waved goodbye to Doug as he drove away.

Isaac let out a heavy breath. "I don't know. I've always suspected Doug didn't agree with Curtis's tactics. I just hope him disagreeing with Curtis means he's really willing to go up against him."

"If he's not willing..." she knew the answer. Isaac would be ousted. Curtis was hateful and took pettiness to a new level.

"I need at least three board members on my side. Otherwise, saving C.E.S. will be difficult."

His dark eyes met hers. They were hard with grim determination and something else as well. Uncertainty, maybe? Isaac looked away before she could identify if the emotion was real or imagined. She must be mistaken, Isaac was never uncertain. Confidence accompanied every move he made and each word he spoke. The bold way he'd approached her at the after party was why she'd gone with him on the dance floor. Why she'd considered going home with him. Why she'd given some excuse to Rodney when he'd asked her to his place and spent the rest of the weekend giving lame excuses to Nakita when she'd insisted Kim needed to sleep with Isaac and get it over with.

She really hated that her sister had seen them on the dance floor.

"You can do this," she said. "I know you can."

"At least someone believes in me." Isaac closed the small distance between them. "Inside you said we could do this."

She had. Only because Doug acted as if Isaac couldn't go up against his father. She believed in him and had wanted Doug to understand Isaac wasn't doing this alone.

"I didn't mean to imply anything other than you're not alone in this," she said quickly, not wanting to reveal the strength of her need to defend him.

"I'm glad you said we. I like having you on my side, Kim. I like it a lot." The words were spoken slowly almost as if he were afraid to admit how much he liked her defense.

She liked being on his side. Wanted to be the one person he could always count on if he'd let her. Which is exactly why she couldn't take Nakita's advice and just sleep with him to get it over with. She wouldn't get over him. She'd be sucked in more. He'd made it clear, yet again, that he didn't want a relationship.

None of that mattered now as he stood close to her and looked at her as if she were the key to success. Kim licked her dry lips. Isaac's eyes dipped to her mouth. The attraction bouncing between them made her feel unbalanced. As if he were the only thing steady in the world and she needed to hold onto him. Isaac leaned in. Kim's pulse beat an agitated rhythm. She eased forward.

Her phone rang. Isaac blinked, his gaze cleared and he turned away. It took Kim another ring before she snapped back to reality. Thank God for cell phones. With shaky hands, she pulled the device out of her purse. Her grandmother was calling.

"Hey, Grandma," she said in a somewhat normal voice.

"Kim, she's stealing my mail again. I know she is," Ruby sounded straight up pissed off.

Kim pressed a hand to her forehead. "Grandma, she's not stealing your mail." She tried to keep the exasperation out of her voice.

"Yes, the hell she is," Ruby said. "I know she's stealing my mail because I saw the mail truck come down our street. I went to the den to see what was happening on the stories—you know Vickie was just about to reveal she was really her sister's mother and aunt," Ruby said referring to her favorite soap opera. "Well, I heard the truck stop in front of my house, but when I checked the mail after my program went off, nothing was there."

"Maybe he stopped at the house next to us."

"No. Kimmie, I know what the truck in front of the house sounds like. That evil witch stole my mail. I bet she took it trying to commit that identity theft."

Oh good Lord! Kim took in a deep breath. She didn't know whether to laugh or cry. "Grandma, this is crazy. She's not trying to steal your identity."

"I got one better." A clicking noise that sounded like a gun being cocked came through the phone. "I'm going to get my mail."

"No, you are not going over there. Grandma, do you have a gun?"

"I got what I need to get my mail back."

Ruby and Corrine were overdue for one of their overblown arguments. The last one was three months ago. Ruby snatched Corrine's wig, and Corrine had ripped Ruby's shirt. It took both Kim and her mom to get the two ladies to calm down. Now, with her mom working, there was no one there to keep Ruby from losing her shit.

"Look, I'm coming. Just wait a few minutes. I'll check the mailbox."

"I'm old, not blind. There wasn't any mail in the box."

"Then I'll ask Ms. Corrine if she happened to accidentally take your mail."

"Accidentally, my ass," Ruby huffed. "You got twenty minutes before I go over there myself."

Kim shoved her phone in her purse. "Shit. Shit. Shit!" She didn't think her Grandma would go over there and shoot Corrine, but she would go over there waving her gun. The thing was a B.B. gun she'd gotten at Walmart, but it looked real enough. Which meant Corrine would start waving a real knife and it would be a Golden Girl war in the neighborhood.

She spun around then froze. Isaac stared at her with wide eyes. She'd forgotten he was there.

"Isaac, I'm sorry, but I need to go."

"Did I hear right? Is your grandmother about to take a gun to someone because she thinks she stole her mail?" Even when he said something as ridiculous as that, he managed to sound calm and unaffected.

"Yeah, you heard right." Kim glanced around. "I'll catch a cab, or call an Uber." She looked at her watch. Neither would get her home in twenty minutes.

"I'll take you."

"What? No, I can't drag you into my personal stuff."

"Kim, your grandmother is about to confront a neighbor with a gun. You don't need to wait around for a cab or some stranger to drive you. I'm taking you."

His voice had the don't-argue-with-me quality he used in meetings. She scowled. "Fine, but only because I'm in a hurry."

They hurried to his car. Isaac held the door open for her. "Do you really think she'll go over there with a gun?"

"I don't know. They've been fighting over the mail for a few weeks. My grandma has her faults, but violence isn't one of them." Kim slid into the car and ignored Isaac's raised eyebrow as he closed the door.

Twenty minutes later, they arrived at her home just as Ruby marched across the street to Corrinne's house, thankfully minus a gun.

"Oh, crap, what is she doing?" Kim mumbled as Isaac pulled into their driveway.

Ruby went straight to the rolled-up water hose on the side of Corrine's house. Kim jumped out of the car. "Grandma, what are you doing?" she called across the street.

Ruby held up the nozzle. "She's screwing with my mail. I'm going to screw with something of hers."

Ruby stopped at the front of the house. Twisted the nozzle then aimed a jet stream of water at the potted begonias on Corrine's front porch rail. The force of the water knocked over the pot and spread dirt and flowers all over the porch.

Corrine's front door opened. "Ruby, you evil witch, what do you think you're doing?"

Ruby stopped the spray of water. "Give me my mail."

Kim ran across the street. "Grandma, stop!"

Ruby didn't listen and aimed another jet of water at the second flower pot. Corrine ran onto the porch. "My begonias!"

"You stole my mail. I know you did." Ruby aimed at the third pot.

Kim grabbed the water hose and tried to pull it from her grandmother's grip. Ruby jerked back and a hard stream of water hit Kim in the chest. In her periphery, she saw Isaac running over. Ruby must have seen him too because she spun his way and blasted him with the hose.

"No!" Kim jumped in front of Isaac and held up her hands. She kept her back to her grandmother. The water wetted her back before it stopped.

"Kimmie, what the hell are you doing?" Ruby asked. "Who is this?"

"I'm Isaac Caldwell," Isaac answered in his no-nonsense voice.

Ruby's eyes widened. She lowered the hose. "This is Isaac?"

Kim slowly faced her grandmother. Embarrassment set her cheeks on fire. "Yes. My boss. I was with him when you called."

At least Ruby looked moderately upset. Kim wished she could hop on a magic carpet and fly out of this craziness. Her wet suit stuck to her and water dripped from the strands of hair that had escaped her ponytail.

"See," Corrine said from the porch. "You're going to get your granddaughter fired. Acting the fool and spraying people with water."

Ruby spun back towards Corrine. "I saw you shuffling back across the street when I came to get my mail. My stuff has gone missing at least twice a week. My social security check is in there. Give me my mail, Corrine."

Kim sighed heavily. "Ms. Corrine, will you please tell my grandmother that you didn't take our mail?"

Corrine crossed her arms over her chest. "I did."

Ruby yelped with victory. "I told you." She aimed and knocked over the last flower pot on the porch.

Isaac stepped forward and plucked the sprinkler out of Ruby's hands. "I think you've made your point."

Kim threw him a thankful look before focusing back on her thieving neighbor. "Why did you take our mail?"

"Because she messed with my sprinkler head. It's been turned toward the road all week. The roses I planted are all but dead in this heat. I know it was her. I was keeping the mail until she came over and confessed."

Kim glared at Ruby. "Grandma?"

Ruby shrugged. "My car might have hit the sprinkler head on the way to BINGO last week."

"You two are ridiculous," Kim snapped. "This ends today. Otherwise,

I'm calling the police my damn self and having both of you arrested."

Ruby huffed. "On what grounds?"

Isaac dropped the hose onto the ground and met Ruby's gaze. "You'll go to jail for vandalizing someone's property." He then turned his hard stare on Corrine. "Stealing mail is a federal offense. Not to mention disturbing the peace for both of you."

Kim didn't need to look around to know the other retirees in the neighborhood were out on their porches watching. Isaac's easily spoken words made both women look properly chastised.

"Fine," Corrine said. "I'll get your mail." She went into the house.

Kim, Isaac, and Ruby stood in silence for the few minutes it took for Corrine to come back out. She walked down the steps and held out a stack of mail. "Here."

Ruby snatched the mail and shifted through it quickly. When she was satisfied, she nodded. "I'll watch where the wheels of my car go on the way to BINGO."

Corrine lifted her chin. "And I'll make sure no one puts salt around your azaleas."

Ruby's eyes nearly bulged out of her head. "You what?"

She took a step toward Corrine.

Isaac quickly stepped between them and blocked Ruby's advance. "I think that's fair."

Ruby stepped left and glared at Corrine. "How do I know I can trust her?"

Isaac faced Corrine. "I've got the best private investigator in the city, and I know Bradley Roger. He'll be happy to help prosecute any further violations of the law."

Kim's gaze jumped to Isaac. Bradley Roger was the best defense attorney in the area. He took on high-profile cases. Her grandmother's petty argument with Corrine wouldn't even be on his radar. Isaac met her gaze then winked. The corner of his mouth lifted and humor flashed in his eyes before he erased any signs.

Ruby was too busy gloating at Corrine to notice. "You hear that? He's got a lawyer."

Isaac looked at Ruby. "For both of you." His tone was cold and serious. If Kim hadn't seen the laughter in his eyes earlier, she'd think he was angry. "Please shake hands to seal this deal."

He stepped out of the way. Ruby walked over to Corrine. The two women glowered before begrudgingly shaking hands.

Kim leaned over and whispered to Isaac, "I can't believe you did that."

"I'm good at diffusing tense situations. Though these two may be worse than Curtis and Andre in the boardroom."

Kim pressed a hand to her lips to try and suppress her smile. "You're actually telling a joke."

"I've been known to occasionally smile or laugh." He threw a half-smile in her direction.

She got so hot she was surprised her soggy clothes didn't steam. The laughter in Isaac's eyes made him even more irresistible. All of the craving and tension that had hit them on Saturday slammed her. Her breasts felt heavy and slick heat spread through her core. Hunger filled Isaac's dark gaze. His nostrils flared.

"Come on, you two. Let's go dry you off," Ruby's voice interrupted.

Kim jerked her gaze away from Isaac. Ruby's grinned knowingly at Kim and Isaac. Kim turned and sped walked back to the house. Ruby and Isaac followed. Her pulse hammered the entire way. Saturday night was going to continue to mess with them until they resolved the situation.

Inside, she immediately went down the hall. "I'll change. Grandma, will you get Isaac a towel?" She didn't wait for a response, just rushed down the hall to her room and shut the door.

She was pathetic. Not a hint of the bravado that once ruled her. People would laugh if they ever heard she'd once gone into bars and seduced men out of their wallets. Now she was running from Isaac. Avoiding what she really wanted. Why? Would being his lover really be that bad?

"List all of the cons," she said out loud. She jerked off her wet jacket and shirt. "He's your boss. Your co-workers will think you're just another of his playthings."

Who cares what people think?

Why did she care? She unhooked her bra, tossed it on the floor then slipped out of her pants. No one could possibly judge her harder than she'd judged herself. One night all those years ago and she'd hated and judged herself ever since.

Kim went to her drawer to pull out new underwear. The bedroom door opened. "Can you knock first, Grandma?" She put a hand over her breasts and turned to the door.

Isaac stood like a giant statue in the door. A towel in his hand. His jacket and tie missing. "Shit, sorry, your grandmother said this was the bathroom." Isaac's gaze glided over her body with the thoroughness of a lover's caress.

Every inch of her body prickled with need. "Shut the door before she comes down the hall and sees you."

She didn't think, didn't breathe as she devoured his firm muscles outlined by the wet dress shirt. His nipples were hard. From the wet shirt or seeing her didn't matter. She wanted to taste them. The arm barely covering her breasts dipped revealing one tight nipple. He stepped further into the room and closed the door. Shutting her in a bedroom, nearly naked, with the one man she was failing to talk herself out of having sex with.

CHAPTER 17

Tell him to get out. You really should tell him to get out.

The thoughts were sensible. It was the middle of the day and her grandmother was home. But Isaac's white shirt clung to the muscles of his chest and his eyes blazed ebony fire. Desire pooled in her core, and her nipples turned to hard points. Her own hunger grew until the sensible thoughts in her brain were deafened by the rush of blood in her ears. Only one thing took hold: she wanted him.

She slid her arm away from her breasts and leaned back against the chest of drawers. Isaac dropped the towel and was across the room in front of her in a second. Strong hands gripped her waist at the same time her arms wrapped around his neck. The kiss was hard, deep and full of the pent-up desire that began on the dance floor. No, from the first day she'd met him.

Isaac took her ass in a firm hold. The rigid length of his dick pressed into her. Kim moaned low and deep. Mindless to anything but the pleasure of him against her. Her fingers ran across the back of his head. The sensitive tips of her breasts brushed along his damp shirt. He lifted a hand to pull her wet ponytail. Her heart jumped with excitement. Her head fell back. Warm, confident lips kissed and sucked along her jaw and neck.

Isaac breathed in deep. "What the hell do you do to me, Kim?" His voice was gravely and urgent. "You fucking took over my brain. All I can do is think about you."

Kim slipped her knee between his legs. Her hand ran over the hard muscles of his chest. The heat of him seeping straight to her heart. "All I want is you."

The noise he made, half groan, half growl, was full of possessiveness and yearning. He kissed her again. Kim matched his fervor with her own need. Reveling in the feel, smell, and taste of him. His hand surrounded her breast. Firm fingers caressed before his thumb brushed lightly over the hard tip. Kim gasped and gripped him harder.

Isaac pushed her breast up. His head lowered and took the tip into the decadent warmth of his mouth. Pleasure popped in every corner inside Kim. His tongue danced around her nipple. Flicking until it was diamond hard then he pulled and sucked deep. Every tug of his mouth Kim felt deep in her core.

One second she was against the chest of drawers, the next he had her on her back on the bed. "This bed is too small."

"My room is small."

"I'll buy you a bigger house."

She opened her mouth to tell him he didn't need to buy her anything, but his awesome mouth went back to pay homage to the tip of one breast. Kim's back arched. She gripped his head and held him in place. Isaac shook her hands away from his head. He shifted to the other breast. His fingers pushed into her underwear. They glided across her slick outer folds, feeling her desire, and he groaned. Kim's legs widened, and he slid one long finger deep within.

A soft cry of pleasure burst from her lips. Kim pushed his shoulders and used the momentum to get him on his back. She rolled on top of him. Isaac cupped her breasts and teased her nipples. Her hips rocked back and forth over his dick. She reached for his pants and popped open the first button.

A knock on her bedroom door. "Kim, your momma's home. Something is wrong." Ruby's voice broke in. A few seconds later another knock sounded on the bathroom door next to Kim's room. "Mr. Caldwell I've got a dry t-shirt hanging on the door." Then Ruby's footsteps went back down the hall to the front of the house.

She and Isaac had frozen with the knock. The sound of their heavy breathing echoed in her room. Isaac's chest rose and fell with each deep breath. His hands were still on her breasts. Gently, he brushed the thumbs over her nipples. "Later."

Common sense whacked her brain. What the hell was she doing? She shook her head and lifted her hands away from his pants. Isaac quickly sat up and held her hips in place so she couldn't move away. He brushed his lips over hers in a soft kiss, then smoothed the loose strands of hair away from her face. Amazingly, her ponytail had withstood their activities.

"Later. I can't ignore this anymore." He sounded sweet and tender. It was enough to make her heart melt just a little, and she nodded. If he would have gone cold, she would have said no. "Go check on your mom."

Kim slipped off his lap. Isaac kissed her cheek again before opening the bedroom door. He looked left and right then snuck out the door. Kim heard the bathroom door open and close as she hurried and changed into something dry.

A few minutes later, she was dressed in a blouse and pencil skirt and headed to the kitchen. Her mother sat at the table with her head in her hands. Ruby rubbed her back.

Ruby raised a brow at Kim. "Finally finished getting dressed?" Her tone said she'd guessed Kim hadn't been alone in her room.

Kim ignored the taunt and went to her mom. "Momma, what's wrong?"

Jackie lifted her head. Her eyes were red-rimmed and bloodshot. "I got laid off. Again. Why can't I keep a job?"

Kim grimaced. When she met Ruby's gaze, her grandmother just shook her head. Kim touched her mom's shoulder. "It's not your fault. You were doing great. You'll find another job."

"In time to come up with the rest of the down payment?" Jackie asked. "We needed that money."

"Shhh." Kim rubbed her mom's back and threw a quick glance at the door of the kitchen. She didn't want Isaac to overhear this. "We'll talk about this later. Don't worry. I'll figure something out."

Jackie's bleary gaze sharpened. "I don't want you figuring things out the way you used to. You hear me. We'll live on the street first."

Isaac walked into the kitchen. He'd put on an old Budweiser t-shirt her grandmother had dug up from somewhere. Kim recognized it as one her grandfather used to wear. The shirt was a little small and looked painted onto his defined upper body. His pants were still damp and clung to his legs. "Is everything okay?"

Kim straightened and dragged her eyes away from Isaac in a tight shirt. "Yes. Everything is fine." She looked at her mom and Ruby. "We've got to get back to work. We'll talk about this later, okay? Don't worry."

Ruby nodded and gave her and Isaac a smile. "Thanks again for helping with Corrine. I'm sorry I pulled you from work."

Isaac tilted his head to the side. "Try to stay out of trouble."

Jackie looked between the two. "Trouble? What trouble? Momma, did you start up with Ms. Corrine again?"

"I'll explain everything in a second," Ruby said.

Kim squeezed her mom's shoulder and kissed her forehead. "We'll talk soon."

Kim quickly walked away before her mom could say anything else. She brushed past Isaac on her way to the front door. She heard him tell her family goodbye before his footsteps followed.

"I'll drop you off at the office then go home to change," Isaac said as they walked to the car. "I've got a few meetings this afternoon. We can talk about our next steps when I get back in the office later."

His tone was brisk and to the point. Just like when he threw out directions on what they would need to do next in a project. He was treating their relationship like another business arrangement. Her heart iced over just a little. She'd actually begun to hope his feelings had changed. One kiss, one amazing kiss, and she'd believed he'd changed.

He looked at her over the top of the car. "Does that work for you?"

She nodded tightly. "Sure." There would be no *next steps*. She wasn't going to be his plaything, but that argument wasn't for now when her emotions and body were going haywire.

CHAPTER 18

Isaac had never understood the phrase "walking on air" until today. Now he couldn't imagine not feeling that way. Kim was his. After going so long suppressing how much he wanted her, to now have her was unbelievable. And not just as a lover. For the first time in the two years since his brother left the company, he had someone on his side.

The unknown was how to keep her there. She wanted love, but he'd seen people give up a lot of things they claimed to love for something else. He'd give her something better. Loyalty, commitment, and stability. All of that was worth a lot more than love.

He strode from the elevator to the executive suite. A smile hovered at his lips. Anticipation to see her again, hold her again, quickened his steps. He opened the door and found Rodney sitting on the edge of Kim's desk.

"We're still good for tonight," Rodney said completely unaware Isaac had walked in. "I got tickets near the front. Afterward, I want to take you to this spot I know. They've got good jazz on Mondays. That cool?"

Kim didn't spare Isaac a glance. "I'm looking forward to it."

What the fuck was this? The angry thought speared through his brain. Tension seized his body, and he held the doorknob in a grip that would have choked the life out of Rodney.

"You're going to need a rain check," Isaac said in an ice-cold voice.

Rodney jumped from Kim's desk and spun to face him. Isaac didn't know what the man saw in his face, but he appreciated the unease that flashed across Rodney's. "Mr. Caldwell, good afternoon."

"Kim's busy tonight," Isaac said.

Rodney's spine straightened. "She didn't say she was busy."

"We've got work to do." He examined Kim for any indication of guilt. He saw none and his anger grew.

"I thought we were done for the day," Kim said calmly.

"Like hell we are," he said. "Rodney, get out. You—" he pointed at Kim. "—My office."

Rodney regarded first Isaac then Kim. "You can't order her around."

Isaac tucked on the sleeve of his jacket and stared down his nose at

Rodney. "You better stay out of things that don't concern you. Now get out of my office before I fire you."

Kim jumped up. "Rodney, go."

Rodney shook his head and frowned. "But he—"

Isaac crossed the room and took Rodney by the arm. He shoved Rodney out the door and locked it behind him before he could say anything else.

"My office," Isaac said through clenched teeth.

He strode into the office. Kim's footsteps followed and then his door slammed.

"What was that?" she said. "Have you lost your mind?"

He unbuttoned his suit jacket and tossed his messenger bag onto the floor. "I could ask you the same question. You were going to go out with him?"

"We're dating."

"Not anymore."

She slammed her fists on her hips and threw pitchforks with her glare. "Why? Because I kissed you earlier?"

"That was a hell of a lot more than a kiss." He sucked in gulps of air but still felt off balance. He jerked at the knot of his tie. She was driving him crazy.

"And afterward you acted like what happened was just another business arrangement to be worked out. You want to talk about what our next steps are, I'll tell you. Call Tanya for your good time and leave me alone."

The words were so ludicrous he laughed. "Will you stop being so stubborn? Stop acting like we can keep ignoring what's between us. I can't anymore. I won't."

Kim took two angry steps forward. Her hands still balled into fists. "This isn't an act. Holding onto my integrity is all I have left."

"Sleeping with me isn't taking your integrity."

"You only want to sleep with me. Then you'll throw me away. I've seen your game."

"I don't want to just sleep with you, Kim. I want to take care of you."

"You think I don't know what that means? I know how you take care of your mistresses. I've purchased the gifts, paid the rents, and covered the car payments. I'm not going to be one of your possessions. You won't buy me."

He tossed his tie aside and closed the distance between them. "I don't want to buy you."

"Oh really." She crossed her arms over her chest. "Then tell me what you want. Tell me that you're ready to give me what you know I want. Tell me that you're ready to give me access to your heart. Tell me that I can trust you with my love."

The words were a punch to the solar plexus. Access to his heart. The idea was laughable, but he'd made that mistake before. There was nothing in his heart to give. Pride, determination, confidence, the will to win, that was all he knew. All he trusted. Family betrayed, friends betrayed, colleagues betrayed. Kim would betray him one day, too. When there was something she wanted more than him. Knowing that didn't stop him from wanting her for however long he could have her.

"That's what I thought." Hurt twined around her voice like a vine. She turned away and walked toward the door.

"You can trust me not to hurt you," he said. She stopped walking. A good sign to keep talking. "You know the difference between you and those lovers you bought gifts for? I respect you, Kim. I've worked beside you for two years and I see you. I see a woman that has had my back when no one else has. I can give you loyalty, commitment, and my promise to never take your love for granted."

"I can't believe that."

She moved forward. Isaac clasped her shoulders. "Yes, you can. I've seen the way Curtis takes for granted my mother and stepmother's love. He took advantage of the love Andre and I had for him. I've watched people manipulate others in the name of love." He turned her to face him. "I respect you too much to do that."

"I can't be the only strong one in this. You're afraid to let me in. That's the coward's way out." She tried to pull away.

He gripped her hip and pulled her soft curves flush against him. "Then work your way in."

Confusion clouded her hazel eyes. "What?"

"You've already possessed my mind. Who's to say you won't possess my heart?" The stiffness in her body eased. Isaac caressed the softness of her cheek with the back of his hand. "Make me believe in love again, Kim."

He wanted to kiss her with the same urgency he had earlier, but uncertainty lingered in her gaze. She was afraid to believe him. Fear made his heart pound. He couldn't believe he'd issued the challenge. He'd examine the reasons for doing so later. Regardless of the reason, he wouldn't withdraw. Having her now was worth any future pain.

When his lips touched hers gently, she didn't pull away. Relief swept over him. He coaxed her with soft, easing pulls on her lips until her body completely relaxed and her arms wrapped around his neck. The slow unraveling of her desire overwhelmed him until Isaac wanted nothing more than to feel every inch of Kim's skin against his. Be surrounded and engulfed in the softness of her.

Isaac lifted her and carried her to his desk. Kim's excited gasp played against his lips. He swept kisses across her lips, cheek, and jaw. Tasting the sweetness of her skin, knowing he'd be addicted to her flavor. Desire, need, and adoration burned fiercely in her beautiful eyes. His dick swelled to near painful hardness. His chest tightened, too. No one had ever looked at him like that before. His hands eased down thick thighs to the edge of her skirt. Slowly, he pushed the material up her legs.

Kim's breath hitched. The tip of her tongue darted out across her full lower lip. He leaned in and kissed her again.

"Take off your shirt," he ordered gently.

She nodded and her hand worked at the buttons of the soft pink blouse. A second later it was open, and she pulled the material off her arms and threw it onto the floor. Her bra, a tan lacy thing teased him with glimpses of the hard nipples he'd enjoyed earlier. The clasp in the front was a nuisance, however.

"Unhook the bra," he said.

Kim did, her full breasts spilling out. The toffee tips thrust forward with each of her ragged breaths. His mouth watered.

Isaac jerked on the waistband of her panties. Kim pressed her hands against the desk and lifted her bottom. The panties were off and over his shoulder in a blink. Isaac spread her legs and look a long look at the sweet pink treasure between her thighs.

Then his soft, sweet Kim ran her hand down her chest between her gorgeous breasts, down her nicely rounded stomach to the neatly trimmed patch of hair he admired and spread herself open. His balls tightened, and he feared he would explode right in that second.

"You've fucking possessed me," he murmured then cupped the back of her head and kissed her hard.

*

Exquisite ripples of pleasure ran through every fiber in Kim's body. She kissed Isaac with as much fierceness as he unleashed on her. Her fingers worked to get the buttons released on his shirt. Many of them popped. She groaned in frustration when she found a t-shirt underneath. Isaac leaned back, pulled off both shirts then kissed her again. His tongue eased in and out of her mouth, gliding across hers with bold, possessive strokes. She wanted to be possessed by him. His hand slipped between them and rubbed perfect circles across her swollen clit. Her head fell back. Isaac gently nipped and sucked along her throat. A firm hand pushed her back, and he took one breast in his hand, sucked hard on the tip, and two fingers of his other hand pushed into her sex.

"Oh, fuck, yes," she groaned out. Then the only noises she could make were quiet whimpers and moans of pleasure. Her hips pushed forward and moved to meet the perfectly timed thrusts of his fingers.

He left her breast and trailed his tongue down her stomach. Kim leaned back on her elbows. She couldn't force her body to do anything differently even if she'd wanted to. Not when his hand caressed her so perfectly. Her lids drooped to the barest slits.

Isaac ran his tongue across her sensitive nub with just the right amount of pressure. Not once stopping the motion of his hand. The pleasure, decadent and delightful. Kim cried out. One of her hands shot out and clutched the back of his head. A deep, encouraging sound came from him. He worked her body like a pro. Driving her wild with careful kisses, light licks, and soothing sucks. Her nails dug into his head, but he didn't seem to care. The more she moaned, twisted and cried out the more deliberate his caresses became. As if he could sense exactly what she liked then doing more of that. His lips surrounded her clit, there was a soft, warm pull, and then she exploded. Her vision blurred and her heart drummed against her ribcage.

The sound of his zipper preceded his pants falling to the floor. Then the dark blue boxer briefs were gone. Isaac's dick protruded long and thick from his body. Kim pushed up, grabbed his arms and jerked him forward. Their naked chests hit with a sexy slap.

"Fuck me," she growled.

"Gladly."

He pulled a condom from the coaster holder on his desk. Quickly put it on, then rammed into her. They both cried out, then swore and grabbed each other. Isaac had her hips in a death grip, and he took her with intense, deep thrusts. Kim spread her legs as wide as she could and pushed forward with each drive of his hips. Deep, he was so damn deep. She felt him everywhere. The depth of her need for him was a tug that grew tighter and harder with each stroke. Her body trembled around him. The aftereffects of her orgasm combined with the pleasure of their lovemaking and she knew she was going to go over again.

Her body convulsed around him. Isaac's eyes popped open. A triumphant grin spread across his handsome face. He kissed her, thrust deep then groaned with his own climax.

CHAPTER 19

Isaac went straight to the gym after work. He'd had a definite bounce in his step all day. Kim was his lover, and that was the one win he needed in the midst of all the things he needed to overcome. He'd wanted her to spend the night with him, but she'd insisted she needed to go home. He hadn't asked if she still planned to meet with Rodney. If there was one thing he was sure about with Kim, it was that she wouldn't play a man for a fool like that. Rodney was no longer a threat.

Cal took one look at him and grinned. "Finally got that woman out of your mind?"

Isaac shook his head. "Found a better option."

Cal laughed. "A little bit of that good stuff is a better option."

Isaac couldn't agree more. He still hadn't taken the time to figure out the future obstacle in his relationship with Kim. She wanted access to his heart. Wanted to trust him with her love. He'd had women love him before. Tanya had claimed to love him when he'd broken things off. He knew her feelings were one of the reasons she continued to come to his bed when he wanted her. He'd known he was taking advantage of her feelings, but he wouldn't do that to Kim. As for telling her to work her way in? In the absence of blinding passion, the words didn't bother him much. He refused to fall in love. Therefore he had nothing to fear.

The training session with Cal was as brutal as always. By the end of their hour, Isaac was sweaty, tired and sore, just like he liked.

"Come on," Cal said after they took off their gloves. "Let's do a quick run before we cool down."

Isaac nodded. Cal's idea of a quick run was a mile down the road and back. Nothing he couldn't do, but when Cal threw it in after a brutal workout, it was damn near torture.

"Why the hell did you add that to the end?" Isaac asked between pants when they returned. They stood in the parking lot. Isaac bent over and rested his hands on his knees while he tried to catch his breath.

"You seemed to have a little extra pep in your step. That meant I hadn't killed you enough," Cal said, breathing just as hard as Isaac.

Isaac tried to laugh between pants. "You're evil, man."

"I've trained you for almost two years. You should know that by now."

Isaac stood straight and wiped the sweat pouring down his face. "I thought we were friends."

"Friends don't let friends do weak-ass workouts at their gym."

Isaac laughed and stretched by pulling his right heel to his butt. "See if I hang out with you ever again."

Cal chuckled. "Hey, I had fun when you came to the club with us after the fight. We don't hang out much outside of the gym, but if you ever feel like catching a drink give me a call."

Isaac dropped his foot and stretched the other leg.

You have no friends. Kim's words when she said he appeared too cold. Even if he hadn't seen Kim that night, he had enjoyed hanging with Cal and the other fighters. Cal was the closest thing he had to a guy friend. Even before Andre left, his brother went to his best friend Jonathan almost as much as he came to Isaac. If not more. Maybe it was time to take Cal up on his offer.

He dropped his left foot and nodded. "I'll do that."

The gravel crunched behind them. They both turned to watch a car pull into the parking area. Isaac took one look at the driver and tensed.

Rodney. Cal lifted a hand to wave. Isaac entwined his fingers and stretched his arms out in front of him.

"Yo, Rodney, how's it going?" Cal called when Rodney got out of his car.

Rodney slung a gym bag over his shoulder and walked over to them. "Ready to get this workout in." He clasped hands with Cal then turned to Isaac. "Mr. Caldwell, I wanted to talk to you about earlier."

"We're not in the office," Isaac said. "You can call me by my first name."

"I wasn't sure after you threw me out."

Isaac stretched his chest by pulling his arms back. "Kim and I had some unfinished business."

Rodney's jaw tightened. "You know we're dating."

Isaac dropped his hands and shook out his arms. "We're dating." Cal threw Isaac a surprised glance which he ignored.

Rodney's head cocked to the side. "What you say?"

"I said you were dating. That's over with."

Rodney crossed his arms and shifted his weight. "Says who?"

"I say. If you don't believe me, ask Kim."

Rodney went still. A flash of a challenge lit his eyes as comprehension hit. "She deserves better."

Isaac lifted his shoulders in a cocky shrug. "I say she's chosen better."

"You'll dog her out. Just like you've done the three or four other women you've slept with at the company."

Isaac cracked his knuckles. Calvin took a step forward and threw Isaac a warning look. Isaac dropped his hands. "I recommend you worry about what's happening in collections. Stay away from the executive offices, and keep Kim out of your mind. If that's a problem, then let me know. I'd hate to lose a talent like yours because your ego was bruised over a woman."

Rodney clenched his teeth. He hoisted his gym bag higher on his shoulder. "Kim will realize who the better choice is, but you know what? You can have her. I thought she was smarter than that. I don't sit around waiting for a rich man's seconds."

He brushed past them and toward the gym's entrance. Isaac turned to follow. No one was questioning Kim's intelligence in front of him. She was his to look out for, and jealous assholes like Rodney weren't using their frail egos to demean her.

Cal clasped Isaac's shoulder and stopped him from following. "You want to fight him then do it in my ring, not in my parking lot like a couple of thugs."

Isaac shook off Cal's hand, but he didn't follow Rodney inside. Kim must have possessed his mind. He was not the man to start fights in a parking lot.

"Rodney's a good dude," Cal said.

Isaac glanced at Cal. "I'm better."

Cal held up his hands. "Whatever. Just don't bring that shit to my gym unless you're ready to strap on gloves."

"One more word out of him about Kim, and I'll do just that."

They finished stretching, then Isaac went inside to grab his things before leaving. He felt the daggers of Rodney's gaze the entire time but ignored him. His cell phone rang when he got to his car. Andre's number. They hadn't talked since the day he'd accused Andre of bailing on him and the company.

"Andre, hey," he answered.

"What are you doing this weekend?"

"Working, why?" He always worked on the weekends. Andre knew that. Andre used to always work on the weekends, too. Back when his priorities were straight.

"You shouldn't be working on Saturday night."

"Why the hell not?" He unlocked the car doors and threw his gym bag in the passenger seat before sliding in the drivers.

"Because Mikayla and I will be in Columbia. We're going to dinner at Renee's place. I thought you'd like to come."

"What makes you think that? I don't want to have dinner at Renee's."

Renee Caldwell was their cousin. Both he and Andre had staunchly avoided their Uncle Philip's side of the family for years. Andre even spent years in a petty fight with Renee's brother Ryan. Mostly at the urging of Curtis. Now Andre was married to Renee's best friend, and Renee was dating Andre's best friend which made the relationship between the Renee and Andre cordial. More like friendly if they were doing couples dinner parties.

"Look," Andre said. "I want you to come to dinner."

Isaac put the car in reverse and backed out of the parking space. "Why? You'll have Jonathan there."

"Jonathan isn't my brother."

"So?"

"So, you asked when the last time I came to Greenville was. Well, I'm not coming to Greenville, but I'll be an hour and a half away, and I'd like to see my brother."

"Look, I know our last conversation was weird, but you don't have to get all touchy feely with me. You've come to South Carolina and just gotten together with Jonathan before. It's no big deal."

"Well, it's a big deal to me. You're my brother. We were close, and we vowed not to become what dad and Uncle Philip are."

"We won't." He didn't agree with Andre's choices, but that didn't mean he would ever turn on his brother the way Curtis had turned on Philip.

"Then don't turn on me now. Come to the damn dinner. Hang out with your brother. Take a break for once."

Isaac took a deep breath as he eased into traffic. Maybe Andre felt the difference in their relationship, too and realized the bond they'd tried to keep was weakening. He'd rather do anything than spend an evening with his cousin Renee, but he did miss Andre. He hadn't really hung out with his brother since his wedding, and even that was a brief visit.

"Is Ryan going to be there?" He really didn't want to deal with Renee's drama king of a brother.

"No."

Isaac exhaled in relief. "Fine. But next time you've got to come to Greenville."

"Deal."

*

Kim sat in the den watching television when her mom came to sit beside her. "Momma said she thinks something's going on with you and your boss."

Kim groaned and rolled her eyes. "Ask Grandma why she sent him to my room instead of the bathroom." She had no doubt Ruby intentionally told Isaac the wrong room. Her mom chuckled instead of questioning, which meant she'd admitted as much to Jackie. "She's always trying to hook someone up."

"What about Rodney? Your sister said he was cool."

Damn, she didn't want to think about Rodney. He'd texted her a few minutes ago.

You fell for the Caldwell charm too, huh.

She hadn't responded, even though her first instinct was to text back and tell him to mind his own damn business. She had to work with Rodney. He'd figure out she was with Isaac, so she'd view it as an easy way out of the "it's me not you" breakup speech.

"Rodney is cool. Isaac is just...who I'm with at the moment."

Jackie's brow furled. "You said he's emotionally stunted and only wants women for one thing."

She wasn't sure that had changed. Despite what he'd said. "I was wrong, Ma."

"You seemed sure. What's up? Is he blackmailing or pressuring you?"

Kim turned to her mom and shook her head. "No, ma, really? He's a decent guy. You just need to talk to him."

"I don't know if I like this. Kim, are you—"

"I'm okay, Ma. Everything is fine. I'm just going for what I want, okay. Ask Nakita. She'll tell you I've been fighting my feelings for Isaac for a long time."

Jackie reached over and ran a hand over Kim's hair the same way she did when Kim was a kid. "You worry about us too much. That worrying is what almost got you into trouble."

Kim squeezed her eyes shut. She pulled away from her mother's touch. "I'm not going to do anything stupid. We'll find a way to get the down payment."

"I didn't want you to know I was laid off. I wouldn't have told you if you weren't here when I got home. I figured if I could find a new job before you found out, then I wouldn't have to tell you."

"I can handle bad news."

"But you shouldn't have to." She leaned back on the cushions of the couch.

There were footsteps at the door. Kim glanced up as Nakita came in. She was in a form-fitting burgundy dress that dipped low in the cleavage. Her name badge sat right on the edge of her plunging neckline.

She took one look at the two of them and frowned. "Are you worrying about money again?"

"No," Kim said. "I thought you had to work tonight."

Nakita shrugged. "They overscheduled again. When they asked if anyone wanted to go home, I said yes."

"Nakita, why would you throw away those hours?" Jackie scolded. She never turned down an opportunity to take overtime.

"Because I've got better things to do than make a lousy few bucks an hour talking on the phone to people about insurance coverage." She walked over and sat in the empty chair across from Jackie.

"What better things?" Kim asked.

Nakita raised a brow. "Better than sitting here listening to you worry about coming up with the down payment for the house. Especially when all of this can easily be solved. There are other ways to make a lot of money fast." She gave Kim a sly look. "Kim knows how."

Their mom glared. "We aren't going there."

"Why not?" Nakita asked. "It was fine for her before. What's different?"

"I didn't know."

"You didn't ask because you didn't want to know. Now we all act like everything never happened." Nakita leaned forward, her face serious and excited. "I saw Rebecca yesterday. She's looking for help—"

Kim jerked forward. Rebecca was back in town. Anger ripped through her. How dare she go to Nakita instead of coming to Kim? "No. She's scamming people and breaking the law."

Nakita rolled her eyes. "She knows how to do this. And this time no one will be on the fence ready to sell her out." Her voice was accusatory.

"Why are you so eager to live that life?" Kim asked. "It's not glamorous."

Nakita jumped up from her chair. "Because this life sucks. Instead of struggling to come up with a few thousand dollars, you can earn real money. Save Grandma's house easily."

Jackie shook her head. "She wouldn't want the house saved that way."

"Come on, Ma," Nakita said. "Men have used women for years. All Rebecca is doing is using them back."

Nakita sounded like she'd drunk the Rebecca Kool-Aid. Kim understood the allure. Easy money. Using men that would have taken advantage of her anyway. All reasons that seemed justifiable then, but not now. Nakita had the chance to do better. While Kim had already been down that road and had no desire to go there again, she refused to let Nakita fall into the trap.

Kim looked at Nakita. "Stay away from Rebecca. You aren't working for her. I'm doing all this extra work on the employee week. Maybe Isaac will give me an advance on my salary."

Nakita snorted. "That's what you're calling it now. Grandma told me there's something going on between you too."

Kim could shake her grandma right then. "Is Grandma here? I need to remind her to mind her own business."

Jackie shook her head. "BINGO at the senior center. Don't worry, she's not going to fall off the wagon."

Kim really hoped not. "I'll ask for the advance. We'll find a way legally."

TRUST ME WITH YOUR LOVE

She stared at Nakita.

Her sister stood and shrugged. "Fine. Be content as some rich man's secretary. I just know I'm not working at a call center for the rest of my life." She walked out of the den.

Jackie stood too. Concern filled her gaze. "Promise me you really like him and aren't sleeping with him for the advance."

She couldn't get mad at her mom for the statement. She'd done a lot worse before in the name of helping the family. "I'll invite him to dinner and you can see for yourself. This isn't like that."

Jackie smiled but didn't look relieved. "Okay. Now, let me go try and talk some sense into your damn sister."

Kim closed her eyes and laid out on the couch. Her brain hurt with thoughts of impending down payments, layoffs, and her sister's thirst for easy money.

Ask Isaac. The whisper of a thought slipped through her brain.

He'd take care of her. If she asked for an advance, he'd give it to her. His generosity would take the worry off of her mom and grandmother. Save the only safe place she'd known as a kid. This thing with Isaac was different than what she'd done before. She wanted Isaac. Was crazy about him. He wanted her and had even given a small glimmer of hope that he could love her. There was nothing wrong with going to him for help. Was there?

Nakita and Jackie's voices rose in the kitchen. Kim sighed, opened her eyes and slowly sat up. She got off the couch and went to intervene. This, all of this, was her problem, not Isaac's. She wouldn't even blur the lines of their relationship. Not if she hoped to convince Nakita to take another path.

CHAPTER 20

Kim tried to appear nonchalant when Isaac came into work the next morning. Yesterday had been so busy they hadn't had time to get caught up in the what-do-we-do-next hoopla from having sex. Today's schedule was relatively slow. On slow days Isaac typically spent the day playing catch up in his office. She'd did the same and checked in on him every so often before leaving the floor to handle other work. Which meant a long day of just the two of them in the office while she tried to figure out how to ask him to dinner at her house without making dinner with her family sound like something monumental.

He entered scrolling through his phone as usual. A serious expression on his face. His gray suit fit him perfectly. Kim remembered just how perfect his body was beneath the clothes and shifted in her seat.

He stopped at her desk. "Everything okay?"

She tried to smile. She'd treat dinner like a bandage. Rip the damn thing off quickly. "Everything is good. Ma just has a lot of...concerns."

He stopped scrolling through his phone and slipped it into his pocket. "Concerns?"

"About us. My grandmother figured out that you weren't in the bathroom the other day."

"That wasn't hard to figure out," he said with a half-smile. "Why is she concerned?"

"Here's the thing, I've spent two years insisting I wouldn't hook up with you. Now I am. It's kind of spontaneous to her."

His look said he understood the dilemma. "Couldn't you just tell her things naturally progressed?"

"That's not the only reason she's worried." Like a bandage. "I need to ask for an advance on my salary, and she's worried I'm sleeping with you to get you to say yes."

After arguing with Nakita for more than an hour about all the reasons not to work for Rebecca, then her grandmother coming home with a pocket full of money from BINGO and suggesting she could double her winnings at one of the new gaming houses, Kim decided asking Isaac for the advance was the path of least detrimental consequences.

Isaac did one slow blink. "Come again?"

Embarrassment heated her face. "She's worried that I'm—"

"I heard what you said. Why would she think you'd do that?"

Saying history repeating itself wasn't the right answer. "She's naturally pessimistic."

"Why do you need the advance?"

Kim relaxed a little. She could give him some of the truth. "The man who owns our house is selling it. My grandmother wants to buy it, but she doesn't have enough for a down payment. I'm helping her get the rest of the money."

"How much?"

"Five thousand."

"I can't give you the advance, but I'll give you the money."

It was Kim's turn to give a slow blink. "What?"

"I can't give you the advance. Not while I'm trying to win over board members. If they look into the company finances, doing you financial favors won't look good."

"Then how will you give me the money?"

"Out of my personal account," he said simply.

She shook her head and stood. "No. You can't do that."

"Why not? I told you I'd take care of you."

"And I told you I wouldn't be bought," she shot back.

He inhaled and exhaled deeply. She could almost hear him internally counting to ten to calm himself. "Then are you telling me what your mother fears is true? Are you sleeping with me for money?"

"No."

"Then I'm not buying you. I'm simply giving my woman some money." He lifted a hand when Kim opened her mouth. "Don't even try to say you're not my woman. I've still got the scratches on my back to prove otherwise."

Her face and body heated. His desk, the floor and the small conference table in his office could testify on his behalf. "I can't just take five thousand dollars from you."

Isaac put down his messenger bag and came around the desk. He placed a hand on her hip and eased her forward until their bodies touched. Kim pressed a hand to his chest. Not to push him away, but because she ached to touch him again. "What if someone comes in?"

He didn't let her go. "Are you embarrassed to be caught with me?"

The question caught her off guard. A week ago, she would have thought the answer would be yes. That she'd be worried about what people thought. Having Isaac call her his woman blew away any of her previous concerns. At least for now. "Of course not."

"Then who cares? Kim, let me do this for you. I won't have you thrown out of your home because you think it's crazy to take money from me."

"Only if you agree that I'll pay you back."

He took another deep breath. "If that makes you feel better, fine." He kissed her quickly before letting her go and strolling back to the other side of the desk. "There is something I wanted to ask you, too."

"You're loaning me a few thousand dollars. I think you can ask me anything."

"I'd originally turned down Bob's suggestion about me being in a long-term relationship as part of this takeover. Now that we're together, I think it will be good for the rebrand for people to see us together."

"You said we weren't some business arrangement." The accusation crept into her voice.

"We aren't. What I said the other night hasn't changed, but we both know this is also good for the company. I need to show that I'm capable of being in a real relationship. Everyone in this business knows the way Curtis treats people, including his family. I have to demonstrate that I'm capable of being in love."

Her unease grew as the idea that he still viewed them as a business arrangement crept in. "But you don't love me."

He met her eye with a hard stare. "I respect you which is even better. Outside of my family, you're the only person I trust. You're the only person I can rely on to help me. I hired you because of my attraction to you, but you pushing me away that night was the best thing for the company and us. I will show everyone that you're different from any other woman I've been connected with because you're the only woman I trust enough to help me save C.E.S. You know this company inside and out. You care about the employees. You work harder than anyone I know. To me, that's stronger than love."

The embers of hope flared to life in her chest. What Isaac described were the precursors to true emotion. He'd dared her to make him love her. Maybe he was close enough to doing just that, but because he'd seen nothing but Curtis as an example, he didn't realize his feelings.

And maybe you're a bit delusional.

"I'll do it."

A curt nod was his only indication of appreciating her agreement. "Don't worry about your mom. We'll convince her there is really something between us."

"At dinner tonight."

"Come again?"

"She wants you to come to dinner. Besides, if you're going to have to convince the board and others that you're crazy about me, dinner at my house is a way to do that."

He considered her words and finally the frown disappeared. "Fine. Dinner at your place tonight."

"You know my ma is going to scrutinize us."

"Don't worry about tonight. I've watched Andre with Mikayla, and you've occupied my thoughts more than any other woman. I think I can convince your mother that I'm crazy about you."

His phone buzzed. Isaac pulled it out of his pocket, gave her a curt nod then answered. He strode into his office without a backward glance. Kim sank back into her seat and stared at his office door. His admission about how much he thought about her was flattering, but she'd been a hustler before and knew what it was like. Right now, she had a feeling that she might have been played.

CHAPTER 21

Isaac had an errand to run after work, so Kim hadn't expected him to arrive at her house the same time she did. To her surprise, he pulled into the driveway right behind her. He got out of his car, flowers in one hand and a bottle of wine in the other. He'd ditched the suit jacket and tie but still looked handsome and overdressed in the light blue shirt and matching gray slacks.

Kim chuckled and eyed the gifts in his hand. "That was your errand?"

He held up the bottle of wine and walked over to her. "I couldn't come empty handed."

"You could have picked up a case of sodas or a pack of rolls from a grocery store. We don't drink wine with dinner."

He looked as if having a meal without wine was unheard of. "Why not?"

"We just don't. We'll have tea or water, but not wine. We don't really buy wine. Except when Ma wants Moscato or something on special occasions." Alcohol tended to trigger her grandmother's sense of invincibility when it came to internet gambling.

"I can't imagine a family dinner without wine."

"Spoken like someone who can barely tolerate family dinners."

"I can't deny that," he said. "Are you really ready to face your mother's scrutiny without having a glass of wine?"

Kim eyed the bottle and thought about the dozens of questions her mom was going to shoot at them. She took the bottle out of his hand. "You know, wine with dinner might not be a bad idea."

"That's what I thought." He took her hand in his. "Shall we?"

Her heart did a little skip. She liked his hand clasping hers. If only he knew convincing her mother of her feelings would be easy. Hiding a two-year crush was hard to do when you lived with people. Convincing her ma Isaac wasn't using her as part of a bigger elaborate plan would be harder. Mostly because a part of her suspected the same.

Kim led him into the house through the front door instead of coming through the carport as she normally would. Her mom and grandma would more than likely be in the kitchen, talking about whatever happened during the day and probably plotting their investigation of Kim and Isaac. No way was she walking in on that.

"We're here," she called out.

Three seconds of silence before the sound of chairs scraping across the kitchen floor greeted them. That and the smell of the tacos her grandmother said she was making for dinner. Her mom and grandma rushed from the kitchen to the living room. Automatically she tried to pull her hand from Isaac's, but he held firm. And, of course, that's exactly what her mom and grandma took in first.

Ruby hurried over and pulled Isaac into a big hug. "It's certainly great to see you again."

Isaac looked like a scared cat for a second before he relaxed and patted Ruby on the back. Kim bit her lower lip to suppress a smile. She should have warned him Ruby was a hugger when she wasn't brandishing a loaded water hose.

"Nice seeing you, too," Isaac said when they broke apart. "Have you had any more problems with your neighbor?"

Ruby rolled her eyes and waved a hand. "I'm getting my mail, so she got the hint. Thanks again for helping out that day. I wasn't being myself."

Both Kim and her mom snorted. Ruby glared at them then turned to Isaac and smiled.

Kim gestured toward her mom. "And this is my ma, Jackie Griffin."

"Sorry, we didn't get to talk much the other day. It had been a rough day at work," her mom said. "Kim has told me a lot about you."

"All good things I hope?" Isaac handed her mother the flowers. "For you."

Jackie's face brightened. "Ooh, fancy."

Kim lifted the wine. "He also brought wine."

"Really fancy. Well, I hope it goes well with tacos." Jackie took the bottle of wine from Kim. "Tonight, is a special occasion. We finally get to meet the man you swore you'd never end up with."

And here we go.

To his credit, Isaac didn't seem put off by her mom's words. "She told me the same thing."

"Did she?" Jackie asked. "Well, then why don't you tell me what you've done to change her mind?"

"Ma," Kim said in a warning tone. "Can we at least eat first?"

"Don't worry about it," Isaac said. "She's your mother. She has a right to know what's going on with us." He looked at Jackie. "A year ago, I wasn't the right man for your daughter. My head wasn't in the right place and she knew it. Add to that her being my employee and how any involvement between us could overshadow her hard work, and I understand why she turned me down for so long."

Jackie placed the bottle of wine on her hip and eyed Isaac, skeptically. "Then what changed?"

"I don't want another meaningless relationship." Isaac sounded completely sincere. "Your daughter told me what she wanted in a relationship two years ago, and it scared me. I don't have the best role models when it comes to love, which made me doubt my ability to be in a positive relationship. But the way I feel about Kim is different. She makes me want to try." He looked at Kim, his gaze confident and sure. "I want to be a better man for her."

Ruby sighed with adoration. If hearts could sigh, Kim's would be doing exactly that. Jackie's mask of skepticism softened slightly.

"How sweet," Jackie said

Kim tore her eyes away from Isaac. She didn't need him to see how much his words turned her into a hopeful romantic.

"Are we ready to eat?" she asked.

"In a few minutes." Jackie placed the flowers on the side table, pulled her cell phone out of her pocket, and checked the time. "Your sister is supposed to be here."

"Nakita's coming? Why?"

"I told her you were bringing company."

A triple team. She shouldn't be surprised. Nakita had urged Kim to hook up with Isaac from day one. Her sister would insist on a front row seat for this.

The front door opened, and Nakita breezed in with a big smile and inquisitive eyes. She came straight over to Kim and Isaac. "So, you're Isaac Caldwell."

"I am."

"Sorry I didn't get to talk to you at the club. I was preoccupied." Nakita winked at Kim. "What took you so long to cave to this?"

Kim took her hand from Isaac's and elbowed her sister.

Nakita rubbed her side. "Ow."

"Sorry," Kim said with a lack of sincerity.

"Let's eat," Jackie said.

Isaac was charming throughout dinner. The perfect example of what a great boyfriend should be. He reached for her hand. Smiled at her while telling stories. Complimented her grandmother on the cooking. For a moment, Kim wondered why she'd taken so long to say yes. Then the answer came to her.

If his goal was to convince people, he wasn't as cold and unfeeling as his father, then, of course, he would practice on her family. She knew he was practicing because he was too perfect. There was no way he could suddenly be this personable, sweet and charming. Not just because they were a couple. Guys didn't have magic switches that made them great.

Or maybe you're just being too cynical.

Her family insisted on "cleaning up" after dinner and ushered Kim and

Isaac into the living room. A blatant way of having an excuse to talk about them without being overheard.

"You're really good at this," Kim said when they were settled on the couch.

Jeopardy played on the television. Isaac's arm rested on the back of the couch. They sat close enough for her to smell his cologne and feel the heat from his body. She wanted to snuggle against his side. Then she wanted to reach beneath his shirt and run her hands along his chest. The downside of living with her family was not being able to drag Isaac to the bedroom like she wanted. She'd spent last night reliving their time in his office. He hadn't appeared as eager to repeat the experience. Did that mean he hadn't enjoyed himself?

Get out of your head, Kim!

"Good at what?" Isaac's hand on the back of the chair lightly nudged her shoulder.

Kim took the hint and moved closer to his side on the couch. "Pretending to be crazy about me. You almost convinced me." She tried to sound light-hearted.

He watched the television. "It's the perk of being a good businessman. You always have to know what face to put on for a meeting."

Kim's heart deflated like a tire with a nail dug into it. "Sure."

He nudged her again and this time made eye contact. "This face was easy because I'm already intrigued by you." His warm hand cupped the side of her face. "This isn't an act, Kim. It's not a business arrangement. You're mine." His thumb brushed her lower lip.

Kim's pulse raced and her skin prickled. "Your possession?"

He shook his head and met her gaze with an intense, honest stare. "My woman. My lover. My partner." His voice lowered to a seductive caress that flared her desire. He pressed his lips to hers.

She sighed like a foolish romantic and leaned into the kiss. He didn't push to deepen the kiss, but she felt the tension humming in his muscles as if holding back from devouring her was just as hard for him as it was for her. Kim shifted closer and gently flicked her tongue over his lower lip. Isaac tilted her head and kissed her harder. A throat cleared. Isaac's disappointed groan was so low she barely heard it. She opened her eyes and smiled at him. He took a deep breath then pulled back. They both turned to Jackie coming out of the kitchen.

"I apologize," Isaac said. "I forgot where we were for a second."

Jackie grinned as if it were no big deal. "I was young and in love once. I understand."

Nakita pushed past Jackie and plopped down onto the chair next to the couch. "Yes, they're the picture-perfect couple, aren't they?" Her voice dripped with sarcasm.

Isaac threw Kim a curious glance. She shook her head and rolled her eyes. Who knew what was into Nakita tonight?

"I think that's my cue to go." Isaac stood and Kim followed.

"You don't have to leave," Jackie nudged Nakita's shoulder, but her daughter just waved her off.

Isaac gave her mom a charming smile. "I promised my stepmother I'd stop by tonight," he said. "Dinner was great."

"I'll walk you out," Kim said.

Her mom and grandmother wished him well, hugged and kissed him and told him to come back again. Kim made sure to close the door behind her and Isaac. They stopped at the bottom of the stairs. The sky was the dark reds and oranges before sunset. A soft breeze fought away the worst of the evening heat.

Isaac nodded back toward the house. "I think that went well."

"It did."

"Come to my place tomorrow."

"What for?"

He took her face between his hands and kissed her. "To finish what we started on the couch in there."

Kim placed her hands on his waist. "You want to make out with me some more."

His lips played softly over hers. "I want to make love to you some more."

"Men and their one-track mind," she teased even though her body flared.

He answered by kissing her. The minutes rolled by as she was swept away by the power of his kiss. If he didn't leave soon, she'd rip off his clothes and try to sneak him back into her bedroom. She slowly ended the kiss. The rigid proof of his longing brushed her stomach. She bit her lip and moaned. Save this house then get her own place ASAP.

Isaac brushed his thumb over her lower lip. "You're on my mind a lot. And it's not only because of the sex." He kissed her again then stepped away. "I'll see you in the morning."

She watched him go with a mixture of emotions. What was she doing? Could she really make him love her? Was she a fool for even trying?

The front door opened, and Nakita came out. "So, Mr. Wonderful has left."

Kim sighed heavily. She spun on her heels and faced her sister. "Okay, Nakita, what's the deal?"

"What do you mean?"

"You've been hating on Isaac from the second you walked through the door. Why?"

Nakita's lips twisted in a smirk. "Because this is bullshit and you know it."

"What are you talking about?"

"You may have convinced Mom and Grandma that you two just naturally came together, but I know what's really going on." Nakita hopped down the steps and stood next to Kim.

Kim glared at her sister. "There's nothing going on. We are together. We fought it for years and decided to stop fighting. I thought out of everyone you'd be the happiest." Her voice sounded defensive, she shouldn't have to defend her feelings for Isaac.

"I'd be happy if you told the truth. Did he give you the advance?"

Kim ran a hand over her head and tugged the end of her ponytail through her fingers. "The advance has nothing to do with this."

"Sure, it doesn't. Old habits die hard. Just because you're getting a paycheck, doesn't change what you're doing. Don't turn your nose up at me if I decide to work with Rebecca."

"That's completely different. We're in a relationship. I'm not doing anything wrong."

Nakita only smirked. "Sounds like you're trying to convince yourself. Don't worry, sis." She patted Kim on the arm. "I don't cast stones. I'm all about making the paper. Any way you need to. It's like Rebecca said earlier, there's nothing wrong with taking what you need from a man. They've taken from us for centuries."

Nakita turned to go up the stairs. Kim grabbed her arm and spun her. "Earlier? Did you see her today?"

Nakita jerked from Kim's grasp. "I ran into her at the store. We talked for a few minutes." She didn't make eye contact. She was lying.

"Nakita, you said you'd stay away from her." Kim didn't care if she sounded like a scolding mother.

"Stop. Don't even come for me." Nakita pointed in the direction Isaac's car had left. "Not when we both know you're with him because he's loaded."

"I'm with him because I love him." Her mouth snapped shut. Her heart did five hundred mile an hour sprints in her chest. When had she fallen in love with Isaac? No, she'd been in love with him for a long time.

Despite Kim's internal revelation, Nakita gave a disbelieving snort. "Yeah, but does he love you?"

Kim couldn't answer. Nakita's smirk said *that's what I thought* before she went back in the house. Kim stared up at the darkening sky. When had things gotten so out of her control?

CHAPTER 22

Isaac met with Gloria Kelly the next afternoon in the lobby of the Hyatt Regency on Main Street. Gloria sat on the board, and even though Bob hadn't sent her his way, Isaac had been right in thinking she would help him get Curtis out.

"Your father knows the true identity of my daughter's father," the fifty-two-year-old former beauty queen had said when Isaac told her about his plans. Gloria possessed the same stature and poise that had won her titles in her youth. Her stylishly cropped short blonde hair, fit body and impeccable style still made her one of the most beautiful women Isaac knew.

"My husband knows, but his parents do not. Their income gave us our start. I don't need them to know I turned to someone else in order to have the grandchild they wanted. Curtis threatened to reveal that."

"What's changed now?" Isaac had asked.

"My daughter turns eighteen in a few weeks. My in-laws no longer pose a threat to taking away her inheritance. Curtis can't hold that over me anymore."

Isaac wasn't surprised Curtis would compromise the future of a child in his quest for power. He'd only gotten Gloria and her husband to invest in C.E.S. recently which was why Isaac had believed Gloria's loyalty wouldn't run deep.

Gloria agreed he needed to clean up his image to help turn the perception of many about the company. When he'd told her about his plans for the employees, she'd been impressed but suggested more.

"You need to show you're different from your father. Everyone knows Curtis is heartless. You have to show people that you're at least capable of some type of compassion."

"What about proving to people that I'm in love?" he'd said. "My father isn't capable of that."

Gloria's eyes had turned shrewd. "It's one thing to come to the outside world and say you're in love, but another to convince people. Let's be honest, your father has been married for years, yet he brings prostitutes into the office."

Isaac hadn't been able to hide his surprise and he'd jerked back. "How do you know that?"

Gloria had only raised one arched brow. "People notice things."

"I'm not sleeping with prostitutes, nor do I plan to."

"Then convince everyone, including your family, that you're capable of love. If you can convince your father that you're really in love with this woman, then others will believe you."

"That's not necessary," he'd argued.

"You can't tell people you're stable and have your father call bullshit," Gloria countered. "Convince Curtis, and I'm with you."

Isaac had come straight to his father's home after the meeting. If he had time to think about what he was doing, he'd change his mind. He had no idea how to convince Curtis that he was suddenly in love with Kim. Then there was the question of whether or not to tell Kim about Gloria's recommendation. On one side not telling her was for the best. If she believed he had fallen, then that would make their newfound love even more plausible to Curtis. On the other side, he'd promised her he wouldn't take advantage of her emotions. He'd have to tell her, even though doing so might make her even more guarded about being in a relationship at all.

Robert, his dad's butler, answered the door. The sound of voices raised in anger greeted Isaac before he could ask if Curtis was home.

He stepped into the house. "What's going on?"

"Your mother is here," Roger said simply.

Isaac frowned. That shouldn't be a case for yelling. He'd accepted long ago that his mother was content to come back and be the mistress of the man who'd left her for his best friend's wife. Mostly by ignoring his parents' warped affair.

"Why are they arguing?" Isaac asked.

"That's not for me to say." Roger held his hand out in the direction of one of the front rooms.

He understood why Roger pretended not to know what was going on. His dad would punish any employee who gossiped about what happened in his home. So many unsavory things happened behind these walls.

Isaac followed the direction of the angry voices. He took a deep breath, centered himself and opened the door. His parents faced each other. Curtis held a glass of bourbon in his hand. Sweat covered his face and his tie hung loosely around his neck. Isaac's mother, Dawn Caldwell, looked just as frustrated. Tendrils of light brown hair hung loosely from the knot at the back of her head. Her simple but finely tailored off-white pants suit was wrinkled, and her hands were balled into fists.

"You have no say in what I do with my life, Curtis," Dawn yelled.

"Like hell, I don't. You're my—"

"Your what, Curtis? Your whore? I'm not going to be anymore. I've sat around and lived for you long enough. I refuse to be unhappy anymore. I won't let you disrespect me any longer."

Isaac walked into the room, but they didn't notice him. They were too busy glaring at each other. He moved closer. "Why are you two arguing?"

They both jumped. Curtis spilled some of the liquor in his glass. "Damn it, Isaac! What the hell are you sneaking around for?"

Dawn held a hand over her heart. "What are you doing here?"

"I came to talk to Curtis. I guess it's good you're here, too, because you need to hear this." He looked between the two. "But first I need to know why you're arguing?"

"Your father won't accept the fact that we're over."

Isaac couldn't hold back a doubtful grunt. How many times had he heard that over the years? His mother always came right back after Curtis waved money and promises that he still loved her. Isaac had long stopped hoping his mother would come to her senses and realize Curtis only wanted to prove he could keep her on a leash.

"I'm serious this time," she said and held up her left hand. "I'm getting married."

Isaac stared at the ring. He tried to sort out how he felt about that. Sure, he hoped she'd found the good sense to move on, but why did she have to wait until an engagement to realize Curtis was only using her? "Is this a joke?"

She threw up her hands. "I should have known not to expect happiness from you. Andre is the only one who cares."

The jab hurt. Dawn also preferred Andre. The oldest son. The perfect son.

"Of course, he doesn't care," Curtis said in a nasty voice. "He knows you're lying out of your ass."

"Why can't you accept that I'm done with you?"

"Because you belong to me. Always have. Always will."

"She doesn't belong to you," Isaac said in a blade-sharp tone. Curtis drew up. His mother's jaw dropped. "You don't own her, Andre, or anyone else in this family. I don't know how many times we have to tell you that before you believe it."

"Is that what you came over here for?" Curtis's voice was hard. "To go against me like your mother and brother?"

If only he realized how close to the truth he was. "No one is going against you for wanting to live their own lives. We all want to be happy." He looked at his mother. "We deserve happiness."

Dawn crossed to him and took his hand. "This is no joke. His name is Wayland Joiner. We met about a year ago and have been dating. He asked me to marry him, and I said yes." She looked back at Curtis. "I stopped coming to see you around the time I met him. You can't say you're surprised."

"Then why did you come here to tell me?" Curtis demanded.

"Because I wanted to see the look on your face. To see if you would even care. Maybe it's stupid, but I thought you'd really realize that you lost me. Instead, you did exactly what I expected. Threw a tantrum and tried to tell me what I can't do. Your hatefulness has ruined this family."

Curtis pointed a finger in her direction. "My ways have kept this family comfortable. I don't regret a single decision."

"And I regret ever coming back into your wicked arms," she replied.

Curtis's laugh was nasty and caustic. "You didn't complain while you were there." He glared at Isaac. "Might as well get your bad news too."

"Why do you think I came here with bad news?"

"Because we both know you don't come over here for my fatherly affection. You only come to tell me what I'm doing wrong at C.E.S. What is it this time? I'm letting you have that damn employee week."

"Not without trying to ruin it first."

"You fixed it. Got that cute little piece of ass working for you to put together a committee."

Isaac shook away his mother's hand and faced Curtis with a glare. "Don't you ever talk about Kim that way."

Curtis's brows rose. "That's a lot of bass in your voice for a secretary."

"Kim isn't just my administrative assistant."

Curtis took a gulp of the bourbon then smirked. "What? You've finally screwed her. Took you long enough."

Dawn threw up her hands and paced to the fireplace. "You're disgusting."

Curtis laughed. "Don't look so offended. It's no secret Isaac hires his secretaries based on their cup size."

"Kim isn't like that," Isaac defended. "She knows the employee's needs, and she cares about C.E.S." He swallowed and took a fortifying breath. "It's why I love her."

Curtis dropped his glass. His mother gasped. Hopefully, that meant his declaration sounded sincere.

"What are you talking about, boy?"

"Kim and I are together. I wanted you to know before we started making public appearances. I don't want you to think this is just some bit of fun. It's serious."

All the laughter in Curtis's face was gone. "What the hell does this mean?"

"It means I'm in a serious relationship."

"I don't give a damn about any of that. What does this mean? Are you pulling an Andre? Are you leaving the company, too?" A bit of panic wove its way into his voice.

Isaac shook his head. "No, but I am asking that you show Kim some respect. She isn't just a fling. We're serious."

Curtis narrowed his eyes and studied Isaac. "What brought this on?"

"It's been brewing for a long time. I finally convinced her that I'm sincere."

"And you're not leaving the business?"

"We're both happy and only want to do what's best for C.E.S."

Curtis's shoulders relaxed. "Fine. Sleep with your secretary. Fancy yourself in love. As long as you aren't planning to betray me the way your brother did."

"This isn't betrayal. It's about doing what I need to do." The truth in a way. Pretending to be in love helped his plan. There was nothing wrong with that. He and Kim had already decided to be together. Some lies were needed in order to win the ultimate prize.

Curtis snorted and glared at him and his mother. "Everyone wants to be in love. What the hell did love ever do for anyone? A damn overrated emotion." He kicked the fallen glass. "Don't come crawling back to me when he leaves you."

Dawn squared her shoulders. "I won't be back."

Curtis rolled his eyes then stalked out of the door. They stood there in silence for several minutes.

Isaac peered at his mother. "Are you happy?"

"Finally, I am." The tension left her body and she smiled. "I know Andre had a quick, small wedding because he didn't want your father and me in the same room. That's when it hit me that Curtis and I were ruining any chance at rebuilding our relationship with you boys."

"Andre wanted you there," Isaac said. But inviting her and not Curtis would have only increased Curtis's rage. So, Andre had a small wedding at his lake house. Isaac was the only member of the family there.

"I understand his reasoning. Curtis would have only ruined the day. Me being there would have only increased this revenge plot your dad has out for him." She crossed the room to him. "Andre is in love and would do anything to make Mikayla happy."

"He would."

"Do you feel the same about this Kim woman?"

"I will take care of her." Make her happy? That was another story.

His mother's soft brown eyes looked worried. "I don't know what you're up to, Isaac, but be careful."

"I'm doing what needs to be done," he said stiffly.

"And this Kim woman? Does she know you're not really in love with her?"

Isaac sat in stunned silence for a few seconds. "How do you know that?"

"Because I've seen love. Wayland shows me love. When I had dinner with Andre and Mikayla, I saw their love. You aren't in love with her."

"I want her. She wants me. We both want what's best for C.E.S."

His mother's smile was sad. "What's best for C.E.S. may not be best for you." She took his hand. "If there is even a chance you can love this woman, take it. I want you to be happy Isaac."

He'd seen love. His mother's love for Curtis made her his mistress after he left her. Andre's love pulled him away from the company. They could have love. He wanted no part of love. He wanted loyalty, respect, and trust. Those were the things that mattered.

Isaac slipped his hand from her. "I love C.E.S. When I save it, I will be happy."

CHAPTER 23

Kim arrived at Isaac's condo a little before seven. He answered quickly after she rang the bell, still in the dress shirt and suit pants he'd worn to work. The tie was missing and the top buttons of the shirt were undone revealing an expanse of sexy dark skin. He held a beer in one hand. Frown lines bordered his mouth. She wanted to unbutton the rest of his shirt, run her hands over his chest, and kiss the frown off his lips.

"Right on time." He took a step back. "Come in."

Kim entered and Isaac closed the door behind her before leading her farther into the condo. This was the first time she'd been to his home. His place gave off the same cool sophistication that personified him. Brick walls, exposed piping, and sleek but comfortable furniture.

"Do you want anything to drink?" he asked.

"No." Her voice came out high and tight. She cleared her throat. "I'm good." He glanced at her. Kim hoped her smile didn't reveal the butterflies fluttering in her stomach. She licked her lips and broke eye contact under the premise of taking in his place. Being here, in his home, with nothing related to C.E.S. between them was surreal.

He took her to the living area. A large flat screen television was attached as if by magic to one of the walls. She didn't see any wires running to the device. A light gray sofa and darker accent chairs were arranged in front of the television. The living area connected to a spacious kitchen. Tall windows gave spectacular views of the city.

Isaac pointed to the couch. Guess that was her invitation to sit. He walked over to the windows and stared out. He quietly sipped his beer and the silence stretched.

Kim shifted nervously on the couch. "Are you okay?"

"Why would you ask?" Isaac slowly turned and met her gaze.

Because she was sitting there expecting to finish what they'd started yesterday, but he stared out the window as if she weren't there. "You seem distracted."

"Never better. I've got another board member willing to help. That's the most important thing." He took another sip, crossed the room and pointed to a sheet of paper on the coffee table. "A list of social functions I have to attend. Look it over and let me know which ones you can go to. The most important are the ones where board members will be in attendance." He casually paced in front of the coffee table.

Kim stared at the paper then back at Isaac. She let out a heavy breath. Her anticipation releasing on the slow exhale. There was definitely something going on with him. She stood, walked around the coffee table, and stopped him mid-pace. She took his beer and set it on the table. "What's wrong?"

His stance shifted, hands on hips and legs spread. A defensive posture. "I'm asking you to come with me to a few events. Why do you assume something is wrong?"

"I've worked with you for two years. I can tell when you're distracted."

"Oh really?" He didn't sound amused.

"Yes, really. You don't deal with emotions. Any of them. Anger, frustration, happiness, excitement. It's why people think you're cold. You become detached. Don't do that with me. Talk to me. Relax."

Isaac's heated look made her breath hitch. A tendril of electricity zapped over her. "Are you going to help me relax?" His voice lost the note of distraction and lowered to toe curling intimacy. He took a step forward.

The words felt like a cue. He'd invited her over for sex, not to talk. Sex could be a gateway to emotional intimacy. He talked more when he wasn't in defense mode. *Work your way in.*

She placed her hand on his hard chest. Isaac's heart beat steadily beneath her touch, whereas hers was on overdrive. "I can help you with that."

Kim slowly licked her lips. His gaze dipped to her lips. His nostrils flared. She liked the way he responded when she did that. Desire, the one emotion he had no problem showing, darkened his eyes. Kim slipped one hand between his legs and pressed against him.

The tension in his face melted away and strong hands rested on her hips. She kept eye contact and traced the neckline of her blouse before easing the top two buttons open. His fingers flexed. His dick stiffened beneath her palm. Kim slipped open a third button, revealing the dark lace of her bra. Isaac drew in a deep breath.

She eased her hand up his chest and over his shoulder to the back of his neck. She tilted her head back and gently pulled his downward. Her lips brushed his. "I'm here to make you feel better."

She kissed him and gently massaged the growing thickness of his erection. She ran her tongue over the seam of his lips in an effort to deepen the kiss. Isaac broke away and gently pushed her back.

He turned away from her and ran a hand over his head. Embarrassment singed her cheeks. "What did I do wrong?"

"Is that what you think I want? For you to come through the door, rip off your clothes, and jump into bed with me?" His voice, his body, radiated tension.

Kim flinched and crossed her arms. Anger flared. "I'm sorry, but isn't that what you invited me over for?"

He snatched up the beer and paced toward the kitchen. "You're not my whore, Kim. Don't treat me like a john."

The words punched through her defenses. She felt seventeen again. Standing in a cheap hotel room with a guy who wanted her to moan louder, earn what he was paying her for. Angry tears burned her eyes. "To hell with you." Her voice trembled. She jerked her purse from the couch and stomped toward the door.

Isaac quick footsteps proceeded his hand wrapped around her upper arm. "Stop. Please." Regret filled his tone.

Kim froze. She sucked in several breaths and tried to get her emotions under control. This was Isaac. Not that guy. She wasn't his whore. *But does he see you as his partner and lover?*

Isaac pulled her closer until the heat of him caressed her back. "I need to tell you something."

The absolute worst words a man could say after interrupting an intimate moment and insulting her. She took several deep breaths. Slammed the door shut on the old, hurtful memories, then turned and met his eye. "What is it?" She managed to sound calm. She tried not to jump to the worst conclusion: he'd finally slept with her, and the shine had worn off.

The serious expression he wore before giving bad news to the board covered his face. "I met with Gloria Kelly today. She's with me. She even agrees that taking over the company will be easier if I show how I'm different from Curtis. She reiterated what Bob suggested about softening my image with a relationship. When I told her I was seeing someone, she went a step further. She thinks I need to convince people that I'm capable of falling in love. Including my father."

Dread pumped through her blood. "What are you getting at?"

"I agreed with her and told Curtis and my mother that I was in love with you." His voice was emotionless, which meant he was in defense mode again.

The words should have sent her heart soaring. If only he hadn't spoken them with as much passion as someone ordering sliced cheese at a deli. "You what?"

"I know this sounds crazy, but think about it. You said yourself you didn't want the people at C.E.S. to think you're just another Tanya. If I do this, then they won't think that."

Kim pulled away from him, stalked across the room and tossed her purse back on the couch. She spun back to glare at him. "You want me to be okay with you pretending like you're in love with me? Then what, Isaac?

You just drop the act after you've saved C.E.S. This newfound love you have for me will just disappear into thin air."

He slipped a hand into his pocket. "You're talking like we're ending after I push out Curtis." His tone said she was being ridiculous.

"Because that's what this sounds like. The more you talk, the more I'm starting to think you only spouted out all of that stuff about not being able to get me out of your mind and me *possessing* you were just part of your game plan." She stalked back to him and balled her hand into a fist to keep from pushing him. "You planned to go along with Bob's suggestion all along, but instead of telling me I was going to be your fake girlfriend to help soften your image you played me."

"Played you?" he said incredulously. "You think I would lie about this? Okay, here's another lie." He held up three fingers. "It took me three months to sleep with another woman after you turned me down. Not because I didn't want to, but because I couldn't." He stepped forward. "No other woman could get me up because you were the only woman I wanted."

Kim stuttered for a second. "You can't be serious?"

"Oh, I'm fucking serious. Andre witnessed one of the results. I got so damn drunk on one of our business trips thinking alcohol would make things better. It didn't." He pushed past her and went to get his beer off the counter before taking a long swallow.

Kim tried to wrap her mind around his confession. Tried to determine if he was once again playing her. "You've slept with Tanya."

"Mind over matter. You'd made it clear we weren't sleeping together. I couldn't go on as a monk."

Kim wanted to throw something at him. "That's supposed to make me feel better?"

Isaac threw out his arms as if he didn't know what else to do. "It's supposed to make you understand that I have a hard time getting you, and my need for you, out of my mind. I'm only telling you this now because I promised you that I wouldn't take advantage of your emotions. Do you think I hadn't considered how much easier not telling you would be? To let you believe I'd fallen hard for you. To watch you fall in love with me? I told you I respect you, and I do. That's why I'm telling you now." The frustration in his tone left the more he talked. Sincerity crept into his voice.

A smidgeon of tension left Kim. Not telling her would have been easier. She would have fallen for the game harder than a kid's first training wheel free bike ride and had the emotional bruises and cuts to show for it afterward. "That still doesn't explain why you pushed me away and called me a whore." Her voice tightened on the last word.

"I'm sorry. That was a poor choice of words." He rubbed his temple. "Curtis…he's bringing prostitutes into the office."

Kim sucked in a breath. Thought of seeing Rebecca in the elevator. Did he mean Rebecca? If so, would he eventually connect what Rebecca does to what she'd once done? Her hands turned clammy. "Are you sure?" she asked cautiously.

"I caught him with one." Disgust laced Isaac's tone. "Kim, I never want you, or anyone else to believe, I'm using you in that way. You're important to me. Regardless of how we move forward, remember that." He met her eyes with a steady, honest gaze. "I'm not Curtis. Whatever we choose to do moving forward is about us. Not just about me."

The rest of her anger faded. Without anger, she felt unsure. A little scared. He didn't say Rebecca, but that didn't mean Rebecca wasn't going for Curtis. "What does this mean for us?"

He shrugged and for the first time looked as uncertain as she felt. "I don't know. My mother's already insinuated I'm going to hurt you."

He walked to the couch and sat. Kim hesitated a second, then sat next to him. "Why did she say that?"

"Because Curtis has hurt her, and she can't help but see him in me."

She didn't know much about Isaac's mother. She rarely called the office since Andre quit. Isaac mentioned her even less than he talked about her.

"My dad left her for his best friend's wife. Afterward, he told her he still loved her, and she believed him. She was his mistress for the past several years."

"Why would she go back to him?" There was no way she would have been able to forgive that type of betrayal.

"Because she loved him," he said bitterly. "At first my stepmother stayed because she loved Curtis. Later she stayed because she was comfortable."

"That had to have been horrible for you."

He blinked. "Horrible for me?"

"Watching your parents split only to have them come back together in that way. It had to be confusing for you and your brother."

"Andre got angry. He took our mother's side in every fight. Which made Curtis fight harder to win him back. He promised Andre everything. Gave him whatever he wanted. I think that's even why he groomed Andre to take over the business."

"Whose side did you take?"

Isaac shook his head and leaned back on the couch. "Neither. I was angry at both of them. Curtis for disrespecting my mother, and her for running back to him for his scraps. I didn't bother to hide my anger. All the while hoping Curtis would realize how much he'd hurt me, our family by what he did. I pulled away, and they let me."

"They fought for Andre's affections and forgot about you?"

His smile was rueful. "Don't make it sound so sad. It wasn't. Andre is the oldest. He was always the favorite. I know what my parents expect from me. My dad wants loyalty. My mom wants me to respect her. I give them both when I can. Surprisingly, I grew close to my stepmother. She found me one day, angry because Andre had left to stay with my mom and Curtis did everything in his power to bribe him back. I couldn't understand why Curtis couldn't be happy to still have me there. Cynthia told me to stop wishing for Curtis's love. Stop wishing for anyone's love. She told me to find something that mattered to me and fight for that."

"You chose the business," she said softly. The one thing he still only relied on. That's why he didn't want anyone's love, he didn't expect love.

"I don't need access to my parents' affection, but the money my dad made could keep me comfortable. So, I asked Curtis for a part time job at C.E.S. After I had realized C.E.S. was my legacy, I decided to ensure its success. At first, the plan was to do that with Andre. Just because he's moved on doesn't mean my plans had to change."

"What about that will make you happy?"

He took her hand in his. His smile was resigned. "Owning C.E.S. outright will make me very happy."

"But Isaac—"

He shook his head. "I don't need love. I'm happy with my life. More so now that you're in it. The only thing that will make me happier is stopping Curtis from ruining the company."

She didn't believe him. He didn't realize it, but Isaac liked taking care of people, even if he didn't view it that way. He didn't offer the women he dated love, but he always looked out for their needs. He was hands off personally with employees, but any time he heard about someone on the staff having a problem he instructed her to send assistance. Helping people and fixing problems made him happy.

"I'm giving you an out," he said. "I don't want you to feel like I'm using you. If you really would prefer to be with someone like *Rodney*—" he said with a curl of his lip "—then fine."

"I thought you didn't want to let me go."

He would let her go if she really wanted out, and she'd be another person to reject his affections. Despite not saying he loved her, she knew he cared. He needed someone to take care of him. Someone to love him and put him first for once. Maybe they wouldn't last forever. Maybe she'd never work her way in and make him love her. Until the relationship ran its course, she could be the person there for him.

"I don't, but I won't take advantage of you. I also can't ignore Gloria and Bob's advice. Can you handle being with me? Convincing everyone we're in love, but knowing I won't love you?"

Those words sounded like a challenge. *Work your way in.* Kim slid across his lap and straddled him. She ran her fingers across the side of his face. "I don't want Rodney, and I'm here because I want to be here. I know who you are, Isaac. I want to help you, but I also want to be with you. Whatever it takes."

The heat of his palms as his hands slid up her thighs to hold her hips spread through her body. "Are you sure?" He watched her closely.

Kim nodded. "Positive." She kissed him.

Isaac's arms wrapped around her. One hand clasped the back of her head, the other rested in the center of her back. He kissed her slowly. Between tender kisses and soft caresses, Kim removed Isaac's shirt and he peeled away her blouse and bra. Then they were skin to skin. The softness of her breasts pressed against the sculpted muscles of his chest. The fervor behind the kiss grew. Their breathing became harsher, louder as their need for more built. Strong arms embraced her tighter locking her to him as if he'd never want to let her go. Kim squeezed him. Hoped he realized she would always be there for him to hold. Her hips undulated back and forth over the hard ridge of his dick. Pleasure swelled with each sensual sway of her hips. Her hands gripped him harder, her kiss turned more urgent.

"Shhh," Isaac said against her lips. "Let me enjoy you."

His hand cupped her breast. He eased back, resumed their languid pace. She matched his tempo, savored the feel and taste of him. She trailed her lips over his, down his neck, and across wide shoulders. Committed to memory each ripple of muscle, sharp inhalation, and low groan of pleasure. The seconds turned to minutes, and gradually the kisses, caresses, and breathing became, deeper, harder. Isaac pushed her back and lifted one full breast. His soft lips closed over the hard tip. Kim gasped at the delicious feel.

She reached for the waistband of his pants. Isaac pulled on the button of her slacks. "Why aren't you wearing a skirt?" he said in a husky voice.

Kim jumped up and took off the pants and underwear in a flash. Her gaze never left Isaac's as he pushed his pants and underwear down and pulled a condom out of his pocket before kicking them aside. He slipped on the condom and his large hand wrapped around his long dick. Dark eyes watched her as if he were just as amazed that they were together. Kim's chest tightened with a myriad of emotions. She quickly straddled his hips before she let those feelings show.

She rocked her hips, and the slickness of her core glided across the thick length of him. The pleasure so decadent and delicious that her eyes rolled back in her head. Isaac moaned and gripped her hips. His head fell back. Kim clasped the side of his face with one hand. Forced his head back up. Their gazes connected. She lifted her hips, took him in her hand and slowly lowered and took each exquisite inch of him. His fingers dug almost painfully into her hips. She didn't care if she bruised tomorrow. This was worth the marks. Her teeth bit her lower lip, her lids drooped as her body sang from the incredible pleasure, but she didn't look away.

His gaze changed. Not just lust or need shone back, but something else. Something deeper, and much more than the pleasure of sex. Kim rotated her hips and his eyes rolled back in his head. A small smile of satisfaction touched her lips. She would work her way in.

She loved him slow and thoroughly. Making sure every part of him was surrounded by her. She felt him swell after each movement. His head fell forward and he took her nipple between his teeth and nipped lightly. Her hips bucked. She cried out and she held his head to her breast. His hips lifted and he met her downward thrusts with his own hard pumps. He left her breast and kissed her lips. His arms wrapped around her and held her tight.

Isaac's lips brushed her ear, and he whispered, "I'm not letting you go."

The orgasm tore a cry out of her that echoed in the room. Her heart pumped frantically with the love she couldn't vocalize. Not yet.

CHAPTER 24

The blaring of the alarm clock woke Isaac the next morning. He kept his eyes closed and groped around until his hand slapped down on the clock. He took a deep breath to center himself and smelled Kim's perfume. The night before flooded his memory. Had it really been that good?

Yes. Better.

Kim stretched and sighed next to him. Her soft ass pushing into him before she snuggled deeper into the covers. Isaac slowly turned his head from where he lay on his back toward her direction. Kim was buried so deep into the bed that only the top of her head was visible. The covers rose steadily with her deep breaths.

He had the urge to start his morning off right, the way any normal couple in love would. Except they weren't a normal couple. He liked Kim. Would even admit he cared for her, but he couldn't love her. Not allowing himself to love may be a coward's way out, as she put it, but he refused to go through another rejection from someone he loved. He couldn't let emotions pull him away from what was ultimately more important. He wasn't like Andre. He wouldn't give up everything and start over because of a woman.

He pushed the covers aside and got out of the bed. He lifted his hands over his head, stretched, and glanced at the clock. If Kim needed to go home before going to work, then she would need to leave soon. But he couldn't force himself to wake her just yet. She looked damn good in his bed.

Isaac set the alarm clock to go off in another ten minutes. She could sleep for a little while longer. He walked into the bathroom, went through the normal motions and got into the shower. He'd just started washing his upper body when the door to the bathroom opened and Kim strolled in.

She wore one of his undershirts, which meant she'd gone through his drawers. The thought didn't annoy him because she looked too damn delicious in the sleeveless tank. Her hair was a tangled mess around her face and shoulders. She rubbed her eyes and yawned. When she dropped her hands, she placed them on the backs of her hips and stretched. The hard tips of her breasts pressed against the thin material of the shirt. Isaac dropped the soap.

"Do you have an extra toothbrush?" She looked at him through the glass shower, and her full lips parted before appreciation filled her hazel eyes.

The hot water had steamed up the panel, but she could get a good enough look at him. They may have spent the night getting familiar with each other's bodies, but the way she openly ogled him made his cheeks burn hot enough to boil the water coming out of his shower.

"Uhh…no. I don't typically have company."

He never had company. Any woman who stayed either left in the night or first thing in the morning. He hadn't done the morning routine with anyone else. Kim being the first woman he did that with seemed right.

She shrugged and turned to the sink. "You've got Listerine. That'll work for now." She crossed to the sink and unscrewed the cap.

"Don't you have to get home and change?"

She held up a finger while she swished the mouthwash around. She gargled then leaned over to rinse. The back of the t-shirt barely covered her goodies as she bent over the sink. Isaac ran his tongue over his lower lip.

All too soon, she straightened, faced him and grinned. "This is my notice that I'm going to be late for work today." She opened one of the drawers next to the sink.

"What are you doing?"

"Looking for a brush." She pulled out a brush. "Aha. This might work." She winked then strolled out of the bathroom while brushing her hair.

Isaac stood there for several seconds. Was she really planning to take her time getting out of there? She seemed comfortable. She acted like they were a normal couple in love, like the type he'd imagined earlier. He should put a stop to that before she expected him to get emotionally involved. But the memory of her in his t-shirt in his bathroom after spending the night next to her was too good. One day wouldn't hurt.

Isaac showered, shaved, brushed his teeth and took his time getting dressed. Kim hadn't come back into the bedroom or bathroom. He alternated between thinking if she had left that could be a good thing and hoping she hadn't.

The rich smell of coffee greeted him when he left the bedroom. Kim stood in the kitchen, still looking fantastic in the t-shirt. The brush worked well enough because her hair was now tamed in a loose French braid he had an urge to undo. She scrolled through her cell phone while coffee filled the pot.

"I thought you left," he said.

She frowned at her phone. "Scott wants to schedule a meeting with you at two. He sent over the latest numbers from the accounts. Curtis also sent an email to the board members saying plans are moving forward to buy out your brother's company."

Isaac grabbed his cell phone off the counter and opened his emails. He scanned the email from Curtis and cursed. "I should have known he'd retaliate after my mom's announcement. He's always worse when he's angry."

"Scott's numbers will prove how foolish it'll be to try and take over any company." Kim typed out a few things. "I'm setting up the meeting with Scott. You should also invite Patricia from Finance. The next board meeting is next week. Have them prepare a report that isn't scrubbed on the company's earnings. It'll be hard for Curtis to get the board to approve the venture if the money isn't looking good."

"And it'll give me the ammunition I need to get more members to support me in pushing him out."

She put her phone down and nodded. "Exactly." She turned and opened the cabinet right above the coffee machine. "Want a cup?"

"How did you know where those were?"

"I found them while I looked for the supplies to make coffee," she said as if the answer were obvious.

He liked her half naked in his kitchen. He liked waking up with her in the bed. He even kind liked her barging in while he showered, but she couldn't just go through his stuff. He didn't have anything to hide, but if he had something to hide, he didn't need her digging up his secrets to use against him later.

"You're making yourself very comfortable in my place," he said coolly.

"I'm the woman you told your parents you love. If they ever see us here together, then I need to look like I'm comfortable here." Her voice was matter-of-fact, practical.

He blinked and then admitted, "That makes sense."

She crossed to the fridge and pulled out a gallon of milk then went to the pantry and grabbed the container of cereal. "Also, we've got to get some of the foods I like in here. And I definitely don't like bran flakes." She scrunched up her nose. "I was really hoping that you had a hidden stash of Fruity Pebbles or Lucky Charms in there."

Isaac leaned his hands against the kitchen island. "Why?"

"Because you're so serious and straight-laced in everything." She poured the cereal into a bowl and topped it with milk. "I'm waiting to find your secret hidden guilty pleasure."

"I don't have one."

She grinned at him. The smile sent something rippling through his chest. "Everyone has a guilty pleasure," she said. "There's got to be something silly that you indulge in."

"Search all you want. My focus has, and always will be, the company. I don't have time for guilty pleasures."

She rolled her eyes before going back to the coffee. He followed the sweet sway of her hips. There were some pretty good perks to having her around in the morning. Seeing Kim walk around in his t-shirts daily wouldn't be a bad thing. What type of pajamas did she wear? Cute frilly things with lace and satin, a plain cotton nightgown, camisoles, and underwear? Any one of those would work for him.

"Then I'll have to find you a guilty pleasure." Kim came back and placed a cup of coffee in front of him.

Isaac ignored the coffee and came around the counter, wrapped an arm around her waist and pulled her against him. Her body was warm and soft against his. "I think I've already found it." He kissed the side of her neck. "Stay again tonight."

Kim reached back and palmed his cheek. Her face turned enough for him to see her smile. "Ask nicely."

He cupped one full breast and gently pinched her nipple. She sucked in a breath. His other hand lifted the short hem of the shirt to lightly brush the inside of her thigh. "Please."

She nodded quickly. "Okay."

Isaac kissed the side of her neck. "Good." He let her go and picked up the coffee cup.

When Kim faced him, he was more than happy to notice the tips of her breasts were once again hard beneath the shirt. "Do you have any suggestions on how we reveal to the staff that we're a couple? I know that was a concern of yours."

She ran a hand over her hair and tugged on the end of the braid. "You're not just going to announce it?"

Isaac leaned against the counter. "I also thought about what you said. I don't want people to think we just had sex on my desk one night and now we're together."

"That's kind of what happened." She grinned and poured herself a cup of coffee.

"Doesn't mean everyone has to know that."

"People around C.E.S notice the little things that you wouldn't think they would. Don't start treating me any differently. The employees know you respect me. Don't start treating me like Tanya or any of your other mistresses."

Isaac's back straightened. "How do I treat them?"

Kim rolled her eyes. "You let her touch you like she owns you. You came out of your office with her lipstick on your collar."

He put down the mug and met her gaze dead on. "She tried to kiss me. I jerked away and she missed. Tanya and I are through."

Kim cupped the mug in her hands, took a sip, and nodded. "You need to make that clear to everyone. Her hands are always on your arm, shoulder or back whenever she's in a room."

"Done. Anything else."

She shook her head. "No, except, maybe show that you pay attention to the things I like. People may notice if you don't know my favorite candy or something like that."

"Easy. Mike and Ikes."

She appeared stunned. "You know that?"

"Of course. You get them when you're working on a hard project and to treat yourself after a good day. You don't like chocolate, but you are okay with caramels."

"Oh." She tugged on the end of her braid again. "My favorite movie?"

"The Lion King. You've got a miniature Simba on your desk. You and your sister watch it at least once a year during your one Friday a month movie night. You want to see the show on Broadway one day. I plan to be the one to take you."

Kim's long lashes fluttered as she blinked several times. "How do you know all of that?"

Isaac put down his mug and crossed the room. He placed his hands on the counter on either side of her. "You're not the only observant one in the office. I don't think anyone will doubt the fact that I play close attention to you."

He held her gaze, a little afraid of the realization that he already displayed some of the habits of a man falling in love.

"I think you've got it," Kim said in a rush. She put her coffee mug down. "I should go home now. Don't want my boss yelling at me for being late."

Isaac didn't move. "If Curtis finds out I'm trying to push him out and that you're helping me, he'll try to hurt you." Because Curtis came for anything and anyone who threatened him. "I won't let him get to you. I won't let anyone hurt you."

Kim's lips lifted in a small smile. She raised her hand to the side of his face, her warm touch gentle and comforting. He couldn't remember the last time a touch had comforted him. She raised her chin just slightly and as if on autopilot, his head lowered until his lips touched hers.

Her lips were so soft. He savored the feel of them, the gentle press of her breasts against his chest, and the quickening of her breath. His hand lifted to the base of her neck. The heaviness of her braid brushed the back of his hand. He didn't try to deepen the kiss even though a restless anticipation to push harder, kiss her more fully thrummed through him. His need for her felt almost desperate.

Kim pulled away at that second. As if she knew she could make him crave her. "Who's going to protect me from you?" she whispered.

He had no good answer for that. He clasped her waist and lifted her. Kim's legs wrapped around him. Perfect. He pressed a kiss to her neck. "We'll both be late for work this morning. Just this one time."

She grinned and he took her into the bedroom.

CHAPTER 25

Kim headed straight for Rebecca's place after work. Nakita said she was back in town and more than enough time had passed. She had to do something to get out of Rebecca's debt and keep her away from her job and her family. She wasn't going to sit back and wait for Rebecca to come calling. No, she was getting this mess over and done with.

Rebecca still lived with her mom in the apartments managed by the Housing Authority Kim had grown up in. Kim had rarely gone back there since moving across town to her grandmother's place, but she kept in contact with one or two of her former neighbors through social media and Nakita. A sense of nostalgia hit her when she pulled into the apartment complex.

The two-story brick apartments had been built in the eighties. They were laid out in a square. In the middle of the square, a one-story brick building served as the community center with a playground next to it. The playground hadn't changed at all. Kids played on the same metal swing set, slide, and monkey bars with the sharp edges she'd played on. A few teenagers huddled around a metal picnic table. Flash back ten years and she would have been one of the teens at that table.

Kim parked in front of one of the apartments in the back. She reached for the car door, then stopped and glanced down at her suit and pulled off the boxy jacket. She wore a pastel pink button up top that had come from the "old and miserable section" according to Nakita. She couldn't do much about that.

With a heavy sigh of determination, Kim opened the door and got out of the car. The building held four apartments, two on the bottom and two on the top. Rebecca lived in the top right apartment. The heavy beat of bass music came from the downstairs apartment.

Her heels echoed against the steps. The sounds of arguments from the apartment on the left could be heard over the bass from downstairs. Kim smiled. Some things never changed.

Her smile faded as she stared at the number 3 on Rebecca's door then knocked. There was a time when she would have just opened the door and announced her arrival. She and Rebecca had once been that close. Now she was no longer welcome to enter a place that had been like a second home to her. The realization stung.

A few seconds later, the door opened. Rebecca took one look at Kim and her lips twisted into a frown. "I heard you've been looking for me."

"I won't play this game you've started. You covered the job that was meant for me and suffered for it. I want to help you."

Rebecca slowly shifted her stance and crossed her arms. "You came here to say you'll help me?"

"Yes."

"You're going to take a million from your job?" Rebecca said doubtfully. Kim shook her head. "No. I won't do that."

Rebecca rolled her eyes and turned back toward the door. Kim reached for her. Rebecca jerked her shoulder away and whirled to face her, her body tense and ready for a fight.

Kim held up a hand. "I can't risk my job. No matter how much I want to help you."

"Then how the hell are you going to help me? What's six years of my life is worth to you?"

"Rebecca…"

"No." Rebecca stepped close. "Look me in the eye and tell me six years of my life isn't worth a million dollars? Tell me that if you were the one in that cell and I was the one out here, you wouldn't think that's what your lost time was worth?"

"I can't say that. I don't know how I'd feel, but I wouldn't come out and ask you to put yourself at risk."

Rebecca scoffed. She turned away and tossed her hand. "You always tried to act like you were so much better. Save that shit for someone else. I know you're not. I know what you'll do for money."

Kim's face burned. Her stomach churned with disgust. "I learned from my mistakes. There's nothing wrong with that. I decided to prevent a downward spiral."

"You decided to turn your back on us."

"We started out tricking a few guys out of money. That was stupid enough. I couldn't go further. I hate what happened to you, but I also told you not to go along with Benji. You almost killed that guy because he didn't want to pay."

Rebecca crossed her arms over her chest. "I thought we were best friends. You left me there."

"I asked you to leave with me. You should have left when I did, and I regret not fighting harder to make you leave, but I don't regret not becoming one of Benji's whores."

Rebecca flipped her hair over her shoulders. "We'd gone too far to turn around."

"When something doesn't feel right, it's never too late to say no."

Rebecca snorted. "You backed out and you see what happened? That's why you don't renege on a promise or a job. The guy wanted you and when he didn't get you things got fucked up. Now you want to help out six years too late. Then help me. Take the million from the company."

"No. I will help in other ways. You're out. There has to be things you need. The offer to help find you a job still stands."

"Charity." Rebecca damn near spat the word. "You want to give me your ugly suits and old makeup and be a reference on my resume."

Kim gritted her teeth. "I want to help you get back on your feet. Help you get out of Benji's debt."

Rebecca straightened then took an eager step forward. "I want you to do another job with me."

A chill went across Kim's spine. "I'm not working for him."

"You don't have to. Benji lets me handle my own deals."

"For how much of a cut?" Kim didn't bother to hide her disgust.

Rebecca's face hardened. "You came here to offer your help. I'm asking for one job."

The thought of going back to her old life made Kim's skin crawl. There was no telling how Rebecca would try pull her in, and she didn't trust Rebecca to not try and set her up.

"If I say no?"

"Your sister likes making money."

Kim's eyes narrowed. "I told you to keep her out of our thing."

Rebecca's lips lifted in a vindictive smile. "I've heard your boss likes ordering up women."

Kim took a step forward. "Leave Curtis and everyone else and C.E.S. out of this." Kim didn't care about Curtis getting hustled, but if Rebecca got close to him, she'd use the position to make Kim's life miserable. "This is between us."

"Then accept my offer." Rebecca's voice was hard. "One job or a million dollars. You decide what's easier."

Kim didn't have much to debate. If she didn't do something to get Rebecca off her back, she would do everything in her power to lure Nakita into the business with promises of easy money. Things were finally working out with Isaac. No matter how much she despised Curtis, he was Isaac's father, and she wouldn't let him get hustled by her old friend. She needed out of Rebecca's debt and in a hurry.

"Fine. One job."

"That's what I thought." Rebecca's smile made Kim feel like she'd agreed to sell her first-born child.

"When?"

"I'll let you know when."

Irritation pinched and prodded at Kim. "I need this over with." Before Isaac had the chance to find out about what she'd once done. She wouldn't give him a reason to doubt her.

Rebecca smirked and opened the door to the apartment. "Don't worry. I'll be calling you soon enough."

CHAPTER 26

Isaac placed his hand on the small of Kim's back as he walked her to the front of Renee's home. Renee lived in one of the subdivisions built by Caldwell Development, the company her father started, and she and her brother Ryan worked for. Pink flowers filled the planters next to the door, and a Welcome sign decorated with flowers and bees hung on the door giving the place a cute and quaint appeal. Two words he never would have associated with Renee. Cold superiority were the words that usually came to mind.

He rang the bell and smiled at Kim. She looked fantastic in a pair of beige pants and a dark blue sleeveless blouse. Her hair hung loose and brushed her shoulders. He ran his hand up her back and touched the edges of the soft strands. He was glad she didn't dress like this at the office. He'd get nothing done.

"Anything I should know?" Kim asked.

"I'm here because Andre asked me to be. Not because I'm particularly fond of Renee."

She gave him a questioning look. The door opened before she could ask anything else. Renee answered. Her short hair had grown out of the shorter cut she typically wore into a mid-length bob. She dressed impeccably, as usual, and the scent of delicious food wafted out of the door. A welcoming smile that didn't quite meet her eyes graced her lips. He wasn't offended. They'd spent most of their lives feuding. Now, here he was coming over for a couple's date night. A few years ago, he never would have imagined that happening.

"Isaac, hi," Renee said in a light tone. "Come on in."

They entered and Renee held out her hand to Kim. "I'm Renee."

"Kim Griffin." Kim shook her hand.

Renee took Kim's purse, hung it in the closet next to the door then led them further into the house. Andre sat on the couch, and Mikayla was in his lap with one arm around his neck. Andre's friend and Renee's fiancé Jonathan relaxed in a chair next to them. They were laughing and talking like comfortable old friends.

Andre looked up. He and Andre were of similar height and build. Andre seemed a lot more relaxed now than he had when he worked for C.E.S. His brother's smile didn't dim, but a hint of uncertainty flashed in his eyes when they bounced to Kim. He tapped Mikayla on the back and she moved so that he could stand.

"Isaac, glad you made it." Andre gave him a stiff, awkward hug.

Isaac lightly tapped his brother on the back and quickly pulled back. He hadn't seen him in months. They talked, but the close relationship they'd once shared wasn't there anymore.

Isaac placed his hand on Kim's lower back and stepped closer to her. "You remember Kim."

The question returned to Andre's eyes. "I do. Kim, it's good to see you again."

"Likewise." Kim nodded.

"So, you two are…" Andre's voice drifted off.

"Dating," Isaac said easily.

Andre's raised brow asked a dozen questions. "Dating? I didn't know that."

"You haven't really been around. There's a lot that you don't know." He kept his tone calm.

What might have been hurt flashed in Andre's eyes. "Apparently. How long has this been going on?"

"Long enough," Isaac replied.

Mikayla hurried to Andre's side and slipped an arm around his waist. He'd always thought Mikayla was cute with her clear cocoa complexion, friendly eyes and curvaceous figure. She was nothing like the polished beauties his brother used to date, but he couldn't quite imagine Andre with anyone else. "Andre quit interrogating your brother. Hey, I'm Mikayla. It's nice to meet you." She held her hand out to Kim.

Kim's shoulders relaxed as she shook Mikayla's hand. Mikayla introduced Kim to Jonathan, who greeted Kim with a charming smile. His blue-grey eyes were filled with interest as they bounced between Isaac and Kim, but he didn't turn on the flirty routine he typically did whenever he met women. He'd like to think that was because Renee threatened to hack off his balls, but according to Andre, Jonathan was head over heels in love with their cousin. Andre tried to catch Isaac's eye while Kim spoke to Jonathan and Renee, but Isaac pretended not to notice. He didn't owe Andre an explanation.

The six of them settled in around Renee's living room. He and Kim took the love seat. Only their hands touched where they rested between them.

Renee settled on the arm of the chair Jonathan sat in. Mikayla nestled into the crook of Andre's arm on the couch. He wanted to sneer at their ease with each other, their obvious affection and lack of concern of one day being betrayed by the person they loved. He couldn't. They weren't afraid in their relationships, and he'd never been one to sneer at bravery.

The conversation started with a recap of a recent trip Andre, Mikayla, Renee, and Jonathan had taken to the Biltmore House in Asheville. Isaac hadn't known about the trip. He reminded himself that he and Andre didn't update each other on everything they did in their free time. He shouldn't feel left out.

The rationalization still felt hollow.

"We had such a great time," Mikayla said. "Isaac, you and Kim should come next time."

"I've never been to the Biltmore House," Kim said.

Isaac leaned back and crossed one ankle over the other knee. "If I had known, we could have met you all there."

An awkward pause. Jonathan coughed and changed the subject. "Andre, did you try that new fishing rod I told you about?"

Andre nodded. "I bought one the other week and tried it out in the lake behind the house. Caught a few bass. It'll come in handy for the fishing trip."

Isaac's head tilted to the side. "Fishing trip?"

Andre's smile dimmed. "There's this bass tournament. Jonathan and I decided to try our hand at it."

"You bass fish now?" Isaac couldn't keep the surprise from his voice.

"I'm just getting into it," Andre answered.

"Blame me," Jonathan said. "He met me at Lake Keowee a couple weeks ago and tried it. After he had caught a few, he was hooked. I'm surprised you caught any with that sad reel you had."

Andre laughed. "My reel wasn't sad. It just wasn't fancy as yours."

"You were at Lake Keowee a few weeks ago," Isaac asked in a neutral tone. "I didn't know that."

Lake Keowee was less than an hour away from Isaac. He couldn't rationalize why his brother wouldn't have reached out to him.

Andre's laughter died and he shifted. "Last minute. I was just there for a few hours."

"You know what?" Jonathan said. "Why don't you come on the fishing trip?"

"I don't fish." Isaac said at the same time that Andre said, "He doesn't fish."

Second awkward silence of the night. Mikayla and Renee exchanged a look. Kim shifted closer. Out of comfort or pity, he didn't know. He appreciated the comfort.

Renee broke the silence. "Have you all watched that new medical drama on Netflix?"

Kim sat forward. "No, which one? I need a new show to binge."

"I didn't think I'd like it. Mikayla recommended it."

Mikayla nodded. "I got hooked. Andre tried to avoid it, but as soon as Jonathan said it was good, he watched." She rolled her eyes and the ladies laughed.

"Is it good?" Kim asked.

"It had me up until two in the morning," Andre answered.

Renee waved a hand. "Hold up, not just you. You had us up until two. Calling Jonathan every darn episode to ask what would happen next."

Isaac cocked his head to the side. "Midnight conversations with the BFF. How cute."

Third awkward silence. Andre glared at him. Isaac returned the glare with a cool gaze. While he busted his ass trying to keep Curtis in control and C.E.S. afloat, Andre was having late night phone calls about a damn television show with his friend. Renee suggested they go to the dining room and eat. Which they did.

Isaac stopped counting awkward silences. The food looked great. Some fancy prepared meal Renee had ordered from some new, local source products restaurant. He ate but didn't really taste. He'd known his brother needed the break from the family to "make his life with Mikayla work." Witnessing how he'd completely thrown away all connections with his family to start a new, perfect life with Mikayla, Jonathan and Renee of all people made betrayal and anger simmer in his midsection.

Andre had been the one person he could count on. The one person who'd been in his corner through all of their dad's bullshit. He'd missed working with him, complaining about Curtis, and making plans to build C.E.S. with him. He'd thought, that on some level, Andre missed him too. He'd assumed Andre would realize they made a good team. He'd held onto a minor hope that once Curtis was gone, Andre would come back to C.E.S. That hope shriveled and died as Isaac talked about fishing trips, couple's visits, and the near daily contact with Jonathan. He'd been crazy to think Andre was coming back. Andre had neatly excised Isaac from his life with the sure-handedness of a brain surgeon. Just like he'd excised Curtis.

Isaac's hands clenched into fists. Kim placed her hand on his knee. He glanced at her while the *four amigos* yacked about some other fun-filled adventure.

"Are you okay?" Kim whispered.

No one should have heard, but Andre's attention snapped to them. "Isaac, you cool?"

He forced a smile. "All good. Just enjoying the stories."

Andre didn't look convinced. Renee, the perfect hostess, turned the conversation elsewhere. Dinner finally ended. Renee took Mikayla to see some new dress and dragged Kim along to be friendly. Jonathan stepped out for a phone call, which left Isaac and Andre alone.

"What's the deal?" Andre asked.

There wasn't any accusation in his brother's words. A little bit of concern if Isaac wanted to be honest with himself. The question still made him bristle.

"The deal? There is no deal."

"You were borderline rude during dinner."

Isaac pointed at himself in disbelief. "*I* was rude? You know what's rude? Being less than an hour from your brother and not calling."

Andre's jaw tightened. "We were fishing. You're not into that."

"Not the point."

"Look. I know I haven't been around, but Dad makes everything difficult."

Isaac took a step back and touched his chest. "You think I don't know that? I work with the man daily. I'm trying to stop him from stealing your company, but what do I get in return? Not a damn thing except a brother who's forgotten every member of his family."

"It's not like that."

"Then tell me what it's like."

Andre rubbed his eyes. "I'm tired of the games." He dropped his hands and looked tired. "You know that. Our family is toxic. I don't want that for Mikayla and me."

"I'm toxic?" Years of hiding the pain of their father's insults kept him from lashing out, but that didn't keep the disbelief from entering his voice.

Andre pointed to the stairs. "You're here with Kim Griffin."

"So?"

"Isaac, I was there when you hired her. You're just sleeping with her. Using her until you grow bored."

"That's not what's going on."

"Oh, really? I'm supposed to believe you're actually in a relationship now?"

He scowled at his brother. "Why the hell is that so hard to believe?"

"Look me in the eye and tell me that you're crazy about her."

Isaac glared at Andre. A year ago, he would have confessed that he did feel something for Kim. That he actually wondered if he could love her and ask Andre how he'd known he could love Mikayla. Today, he didn't trust Andre enough to confide in him.

"Exactly," Andre said with a disgusted twist of his lip.

"Look. We're together. She isn't just someone I'm sleeping with. I need her."

"For what?"

Isaac took a deep breath and rubbed his hand over his mouth. "I told you I'm trying to get rid of Curtis. I'm rebranding the company image.

Including mine."

"You're pretending to be in a relationship?" Andre said as if Isaac just claimed he could fly to the moon.

Isaac tamped down his frustration and spoke calmly. "I'm showing the board members and our clients that I'm not like Curtis. I'm being a stable leader. Kim is helping me. She wants to protect C.E.S., too."

"This is exactly what I'm talking about. This is why I had to get out. The games, the lies. I don't want that anymore."

"You're high and mighty now. Remember Angelica? You were prepared to marry her for the same reasons."

Andre would have married a woman Curtis chose just to improve his image. Now he had the audacity to question Isaac's motives?

"Do you remember where that left me? Finding Angelica in the closet with Ryan?" he replied, referring to Renee's twin brother. "Don't get caught up in something that isn't worth it for the business."

"Just because you gave up on the family, doesn't mean I will. C.E.S. is all I have. It's pretty fucking obvious I don't have a brother anymore."

"Don't say that. You don't have to stay. Leave Dad and his bitterness behind. I did. I'm happier."

"You didn't just leave Dad. You left me behind. You abandoned me to the business. I'm not walking away from everything I worked for to live on a lake and go bass fishing." Contempt crept into his voice.

Andre's face hardened. "There's nothing wrong with the life I chose. I still run a company. I just don't have the drama that comes with being a part of his family."

"His family?" Isaac asked incredulously. He pointed and Andre. "This is your family."

"Not anymore," Andre snapped.

Kim, Mikayla, and Renee came down the stairs. They stopped and stared at them. Mikayla went to Andre's side, her brows drawn together.

Isaac looked Andre up and down. "To hell with you." He stalked to the door and held out his hand toward Kim. "We're leaving."

She came over and clasped his hand in both of hers. He gripped hers tightly. Without another word, they walked out without looking back.

*

Kim didn't say much on the ride to the hotel. Isaac had gotten a room in Columbia. On the drive down he'd said he'd expected to have dinner at Renee's, hang out with Andre afterward, and maybe have breakfast with Andre and Mikayla in the morning. None of that would happen now.

When she'd asked what happened with Andre the only answer she'd gotten was "nothing." The word made her want to hit him. Nothing wouldn't make him grip the steering wheel, walk stiffly to their room, or send him straight to the mini bar. He opened a bottle of beer and nearly downed the entire thing. He stared out the large windows in their upper floor room.

Kim walked up behind him and placed a hand on his arm. "Isaac?"

He shook her hand away. "Not now."

"What's bothering you?"

He faced her. "At the moment, you."

Kim jerked the beer from his hand. "Back at you, asshole."

"Did you call me an asshole?"

"Yes, and I'm going to call you a lot of other names if you don't stop pouting like a damn kid and talk to me."

"This is why I don't do relationships," he muttered before stomping to the fridge and pulling out another bottle of beer. He uncapped the top and kept going into the adjoining bedroom.

Oh no. He was not about to just dismiss her. If he wanted to be a jerk, then she'd get her own room instead of dealing with this shit.

She marched to the door and froze. He'd kicked off his shoes. His navy button up shirt was untucked from his tan slacks. He lay on the bed, legs bent over the side. One hand massaged the bridge of his nose, while the fingers of his other drummed against the beer bottle. Her anger seeped out of her. He was really upset. No, he looked like he was hurt. Isaac didn't get overly emotional about anything. Whatever happened with Andre must have been bad.

She slipped off her shoes and went to him. She stood between his legs.

Isaac's hand moved from his nose to massage his temple. "I'm not arguing with you anymore."

"I'm not here to argue."

She took off her shirt and pants. Isaac eased to a sitting position and silently watched her. Anger and hurt lingered in his eyes. She reached for the front hook of her bra and slowly released her breasts. Isaac's nostrils flared. Desire wrestled with the other emotions in his gaze. When she stood there in nothing but her panties, desire won. Her nipples tightened. A slick tingle spread between her legs.

She traced a finger down the side of his face. He gripped her wrist firmly, but not painfully.

"I don't need to be handled tonight."

Kim grabbed his chin and jerked his face up. "I don't want to handle you. I want you to fuck me."

Need flared bright and hot like a torch in his dark eyes. "Pity sex doesn't interest me."

"This is clear-your-mind sex. Get it right."

A dry, humorless laugh. "Oh, really?" he asked. His fingers slipped into the side of her underwear. "You're not even…" His fingers found her entrance and dipped into the early evidence of her desire.

Kim gasped and clutched his shoulder. She parted her legs. "Not. What?"

The firm pads of his fingers eased back and forth over her increasingly slick folds. "Damn, you're wet." Surprise filled the hushed words.

"Just the thought of being with you makes me wet."

He tossed the beer to the floor and flipped her onto her back on the bed. Dark eyes studied her face before his head lowered and he kissed her. His hands were everywhere. Lingering along her side, squeezing her breasts, edging along her neck. Kim's anticipation swelled with each tender caress. She didn't want caresses. She wanted him in her.

Her hands jerked open the button of his pants. Isaac lifted away to lose them and his shirt. Her legs spread welcoming him back. His kisses and caresses were more intense this time. Pulling her closer against him. Kissing her until she was breathless. Making her beg and clutch desperately at him. He made her yearn for him, and in turn, she sensed he needed her, too. Long fingers pulled her underwear to the side and, in one swift push, he filled her.

"Yes, Isaac, yes, yes, yes," she moaned. Her legs cinched around his waist.

Isaac supported his weight on one hand, the other took her hip in a demanding hold. He drove into her. Just when she knew she would explode, his hips slowed. He pressed his forehead to hers. Their gazes locked. "If you leave me…" he didn't finish the statement, but worry flashed over his features.

She cupped the side of his face. "I'm not going anywhere."

He kissed her hard and his hips pushed deep. He claimed her body and soul with slow, steady strokes. Kim's lips parted with silent gasps. She brushed his lower lip with her thumb. Isaac turned and kissed her palm. The jerk of his orgasm triggered her own. The heaviness of his weight collapsed on her. Wrapping her arms around him tightly she squeezed him close. They remained entangled in each other long afterward. Their breaths mingled.

"I like clear-your-mind sex," he said between pants.

Her lips curved in a smile. "So, do I."

Isaac rolled onto his side but kept her in his arms until she was cradled against him.

"He said we're not his family anymore," Isaac said in an emotionless voice.

She didn't have to guess who the 'he' was. "Just your father?"

"All of us."

Kim bit her lower lip. Isaac had been close with his brother before

Andre left the company. She'd assumed they'd remained close after Andre married and started a new company. That assumption had been dashed at dinner tonight. She'd sensed the bitter disappointment in Isaac after each revelation of Andre's new life. "Are you sure that's what he meant?"

"Absolutely. I knew he needed a break from Curtis, but apparently, he needed a break from everyone. Including me. We fought so hard to not be like Curtis and Uncle Philip. Curtis always said one day we'd split. That one of us would turn our back on the other the way he believes Philip did him. I hate to admit that Curtis was right, but he was. Andre turned his back on me. I'm in this alone."

Kim placed her hand on his chest, right over the steady beat of his heart. "You're not alone. I've got your back. I'm in this with you, and I won't leave you hanging."

"I don't deserve this from you."

Maybe he didn't. Anything lasting with him would be an uphill struggle. She didn't fear struggle. "You've gone too long thinking you didn't deserve to have someone fight in your corner. I know taking down your father isn't easy for you. You shouldn't have to face this without knowing someone has your back."

"Why?" he said as if he couldn't grasp the idea of having someone completely on his side.

"Because I'm your woman, Isaac. I'm here to lighten the load, listen when you need me too, and tell you when you're being an asshole. I'm here to help, not make things more difficult."

A few seconds of silence descended while he studied her, his expression unreadable. Then he took a long, slow breath. His eyes cleared and he kissed her slowly. "You've got me thinking too much. I think I need to clear my head some more."

Kim grinned against his lips. "Then let's give you something good to think about."

CHAPTER 27

Isaac was reviewing the latest reports from public relations when an email reminder popped up on his computer. *Dinner at Gloria's.* Shit! He'd forgotten about that. The entire week had gone by in a blur. Between working on a new proposal and reviewing the new ad campaign, he'd barely had time to think.

When he did stop and think, the only thing on his mind was Kim and their night together in Columbia. He refused to think about the fight with Andre. He chose to focus on the positive. Kim's commitment.

She said she was there for him. He'd liked hearing that. He liked hearing that a lot.

He got up from his desk and walked out of his office to Kim's space. She'd been busy this week too with the plans for the employee luncheon the following week. He'd given her his opinion when she'd asked for it, but otherwise stepped back and let her get things done. They hadn't spent the night together since Columbia. He missed her.

"Kim, I need a favor," he said.

She continued typing on her computer but nodded. "What do you need?"

"For you to come with me to dinner at Gloria's tonight."

Kim stopped typing and looked up at him. "Tonight?"

"Yes. I forgot she mentioned it earlier in the week. She's having a few people over, including a few board members. I only need one more vote on my side. I may also be able to convince a few of the other people there to invest in C.E.S."

"You need more investors?"

"It'll help after I take over. Getting control over the board is most important, but it wouldn't hurt to also bring more money to the table."

She ran her fingers across the keyboard. "Are you sure you need me there?"

"Need, no. Want, yes. I can talk with the board members and convince them on my own. You know the direction we need to take the company for the employee's benefits and can relay that better than I can. Plus, I'd like to have you with me. Not just to show them that I'm in a relationship, either."

She bit her lower lip and glanced away. Not a great sign. "What's wrong?"

She shook her head. "Nothing. I'd love to come…" She held up a hand before he could reply. "Except I already made plans with my sister."

A quick mental calculation and he remembered. "The last Friday of the month. Can't you reschedule?"

"We do this every month. It's our thing. I can't just cancel on her with no real notice. I hope you understand."

He tapped his phone in his hands. "You're dumping me for a movie?" That was a first.

"I know it sounds silly, but it's more than that. We've done this for years. She'll be upset if I break the tradition."

Disappointment filled his chest. The heavy weight of the emotion surprised him. "Don't worry about it. I think I can handle the thing with Gloria."

"Are you sure?"

No, but he wasn't going to ruin her relationship with her sister. "I've gotten this far on my own. One dinner party won't kill me."

She winced slightly. "Isaac, any other night and I'd be there."

He smiled, but his lips felt stiff. "It's fine. I don't want you and your sister to argue. Go be with her. Next week all of the board will be around for employee appreciation week. That's when it really matters."

"I'm sorry."

"Don't be." He returned to his office and tried to ignore the letdown of another evening without Kim.

*

Isaac didn't mention the dinner for the rest of the day, but the disappointment on his face stuck with Kim. She'd flipped back and forth between going with him and canceling movie night, to ignoring his disappointment and keeping the family tradition. She was still unsure about her decision when she arrived at Nakita's apartment at seven p.m.

Her sister swung open the door. The pink of her Hello Kitty pajamas was as bright as her grin. "I've got *Love Jones* and *27 Dresses*. You can—" she took a good look at Kim and frowned. "—pick."

Kim ran a hand over her black cocktail dress. "Can I get a rain check?"

"Seriously? You're bailing on movie night?"

"I have to. Isaac has this dinner and it's really important—"

"You're bailing on me for a john?"

Kim grimaced and clenched her teeth. "He's not a john, Nakita. We're dating."

"You're not dating. You're sleeping with him. I don't know why—"

"Because we're together."

"But I know it's not because he suddenly had an epiphany and realized you were the only woman for him," Nakita said with a mocking twist to her lips.

"Nakita, don't be a hater. You know I tried to pretend like I didn't care about Isaac. I'm not pretending anymore. You told me to stop lying to myself. Why can't you be happy for me?"

"Because the third Friday of the month is our Friday. Don't you remember when you promised those Fridays to me?"

The night of the month when she didn't go out with Rebecca and leave Nakita at home alone while their mom worked late. The one night they pretended like there really were decent men like those in the movies and fantasize about finding a guy like that.

"I don't have to fantasize anymore," Kim said. "I found a decent guy."

Nakita crossed her arms over her chest. "Now you think he's in love. You said yourself he wasn't the type."

"I was wrong." She really hoped she was wrong. "Come on, Nakita. We both knew these nights wouldn't last forever."

"Whatever. I know you too well, Kim. Just a few weeks ago you insisted you'd never be with him. Now you've got a raise and can suddenly save Grandma's house. Now you're bailing on our night to be with him. He pays well."

Kim's hand twitched. She closed her eyes and took a deep breath. "I don't have to listen to this. You're jealous, and you're hating. I'm out."

"Go do your job." Nakita slammed the door in Kim's face.

The conversation replayed in her mind on the way to Isaac's place. She hoped she wasn't being hustled. Isaac respected her, cared about her, maybe even would love her one day. He wasn't using her to soften his image. He couldn't fake the connection she felt. Their night in Columbia marked a shift in their relationship. He would trust her, and when he trusted her, he would love her.

She glanced at her watch and hoped he hadn't left early for Gloria's. A few seconds had passed before the lock clicked and he opened the door. He wore a dark sports coat over navy pants. His hair was freshly cut and the light that brightened his eyes blew away all her concerns that he didn't feel something for her.

"You're here," he said as if he couldn't believe his luck.

Kim held out her arms. "Surprise."

"Your sister didn't mind?"

She waved away the words. "She understood. Tonight, is important. I want to be there for you."

He pulled her into the apartment and into his embrace. His arms were firm around her and he kissed the side of her neck. "We're going to be perfect tonight, and I'm going to get the board votes I need."

A spark of disappointment flared when he automatically went straight to talking about the board decision instead of her choosing to be with him. Baby steps. He would have to take baby steps. That excitement in his eyes was for her, not for board votes. She would stick with that.

She leaned back and smiled at him. "Let's get you those votes."

CHAPTER 28

The first official C.E.S. employee picnic was a success. Despite a few people who would complain even if they won a million dollars, there was nothing but laughter and smiling faces as employees and their families sat around the Paladin Plateau at the Greenville Drive baseball stadium, eating, conversing, and waiting for the game to start.

Several board members had shown up—Gloria, Doug, and Bob Livingston along with a few more Isaac had talked with at Gloria's party. Kim had made certain every board member got an invitation, including Curtis.

Kim scanned the crowd of employees for Isaac. He sat at a picnic table with some of the truck drivers from collection services. He'd been with them for the past twenty minutes. Even though their relationship wasn't really a secret, she hadn't wanted to flaunt it at the picnic and kept a respectable distance between them. Something that had proved more difficult than she expected.

She made her way toward Isaac to let him know they could start toward their seats but stopped with she heard her name called. She turned to Fanta. Rodney stood with her. Kim's smile tightened. She hadn't talked to Rodney since his cryptic text message. He sent someone else to help on the planning committee and stopped his trips to the executive suits when he had a meeting downtown. Not that she minded avoiding any awkward encounters.

She couldn't avoid him forever and made her way to Fanta. "Everything is going great, huh?"

Fanta nodded. "Better than that. We were just talking about how much fun everyone is having."

Kim met Rodney's gaze. He didn't scowl at her, but his eyes were flat and guarded. "What about you? Are you having a good time?"

"I am," he said in a tone as flat and unsavory as his gaze. "It's the first time I've been to a game."

"Really?"

"Not that much of a baseball fan. Honestly, I didn't think I'd enjoy the day, but I was proven wrong."

"I'm glad that you're enjoying yourself. We really wanted to show appreciation to all the employees."

His gaze sharpened. "We? You speaking for management now?"

Kim kept the smile pinned to her face. "We, as in the committee. We all worked hard to pull this together, Fanta included."

Fanta didn't acknowledge the tension between Kim and Rodney. "We did work hard. I'm thankful Mr. Caldwell finally decided to do something for the employees."

"He wants to ensure the company remains strong inside and out," Kim said. "This is just the first of many changes he hopes to implement to make C.E.S. prosper."

"He tells you all of his plans now?" Rodney asked.

"Not all of them, just some of his visions for the future."

"That's some real sexy pillow talk, huh. Talks of his vision to make more millions to keep you happy. It's not like everyone doesn't know you two are sleeping together. There's a wager in Collections about how long you'll hold out compared to the others."

Kim put a hand on her hip and glared. "Did you start the wager?"

"I didn't. I tried to stop it, but, you know, sometimes you can't stop people from making bad decisions." He walked away.

"He's a jerk. Don't pay him any attention," Fanta said.

Kim rubbed her temple when she really wanted to take off her shoe and beat Rodney with it. "He's a jealous jerk."

"Well, you did toss him aside really quick for Mr. Caldwell."

"I didn't toss him aside. We weren't really together."

"Come on. You knew he was into you. Everyone knew he was into you. Then you went on a few dates."

"A few dates doesn't mean much."

"Girl, please. He told one of the guys he was really feeling you. He was hurt when you broke things off. He really likes you."

"That still doesn't give him a reason to be a jerk. He should man up and find someone else."

Fanta's gaze darted over Kim's shoulder and her eyes widened. Her happy, relaxed demeanor shifted. She stepped back, crossed her arms and stifled her smile. There was only one person who made employees withdraw that way. Kim turned and faced Curtis Caldwell.

Curtis's smile did not reach his eyes. "Maybe he'll find someone as happy as you apparently make my son," he said.

She didn't take the bait. "Hello, Mr. Caldwell. I'm glad you could make it to the picnic."

"I didn't come for the picnic. I came to talk to you." He gave Fanta a smile laced with poison. "Walk away now."

Fanta hurried away. Kim clasped her hands and tried not to show how much he made her skin crawl. "How can I help you, Mr. Caldwell?"

"Let me know how much it'll cost to get you to tell me what Isaac is up to."

She was temporarily stunned. She waited for him to say more. Instead, he stared at her with deadly serious eyes.

"Isaac isn't up to anything."

"What has he promised you? I know it has to be something big. You've avoided my son for the longest and now, all of a sudden, I'm supposed to believe you're crazy about him. Come on, Kim, we're both smarter than that."

"I am crazy about him."

"You're good at pretending like you're crazy about a man. That's how you and your friends used to rack up extra money when you were a kid, right? Leading men away from bars, gas stations, and grocery stores, taking them back to a hotel room and robbing them." He leaned in. "Sometimes doing a little more."

The pit of her stomach fell into her feet. "I don't know what—"

"What I'm talking about? Save me the lies. I know all about your past and what you used to do. I know you're a hustler and prostitute."

Kim flinched and glanced around to see if anyone had overheard him.

"Don't worry. I don't care about your past. I know Isaac wouldn't dare be serious about you. Not with your past."

Panic choked the breath out of her. Curtis was right. He wouldn't stay with her if he knew about her past. He'd never trust her.

An opportunistic grin spread over Curtis's face. "Ahh, I see. He doesn't know about your history working the streets."

"I didn't work the streets. I did what I needed to do to get by."

"What every hooker says. This is how I know you're doing the same now. I know your grandma's home is for sale. I know that if you can't come up with the money, you'll lose the place. I also know that your mother lost her job recently and money is getting really tight. In comes Isaac with the perfect plan. Give you a few thousand dollars for a down payment and you pretend to be his perfect hostess. He can prove to the board he's not an asshole like me. Am I right so far?"

Kim couldn't speak. "That's not what's going on. We are—"

Curtis's laugh was low and full of pity. "Oh, don't tell me. You think he really cares. That there's actually a chance for you. I guess he didn't tell you his part of the plan. Isaac and his brother are just like me. This move is straight out of my family playbook. Except he doesn't realize that his perfect woman is a ho."

She met his hateful gaze with a glare. "If you call me that one more time, I will slap that smug smirk off your face," she said between clenched teeth.

His brows rose in a delighted gesture. "Ah…there's the fight in you. Fine, I won't use those words, but we both know what you did and we both know Isaac won't be able to trust someone like you. He's got issues with trust."

Curtis wouldn't come to her with what he knew unless he had a reason. He hadn't told Isaac about her past which meant hurting Isaac wasn't his ultimate motive. "What do you want?"

"For you to tell me what Isaac's plans are. You tell me and not only will I give you the money you need, I'll get your mother back her job."

She watched his face for signs of deceit, but for once, he looked genuine. Calculating and cold, but genuine. "How can you do that?"

"Because I know her boss. He owes me a great deal of money." He said a little too gleefully. "Tell me what Isaac is doing and she'll be back to work by the end of the week with a raise."

She wanted her mom to get her job back, but not at the expense of owing Curtis a favor. "Isaac isn't up to anything."

"If he's trying to push me out, it won't work. I've got too much dirt on any board member that would think about voting me out. He'll have to buy them out, and he'll need everything to do that. I know how much he has. It isn't enough to purchase their shares and give you whatever money he provided. He lied about being able to help you. Probably to get you in his bed." Curtis spoke in the same cool, no-nonsense voice that Isaac used in the boardroom. That bothered her more than his delight in her misery because that meant he was confident in his observations.

"He wouldn't lie to me." She couldn't hide the doubt in her tone.

"Yes, he would. He's just like me. He's wanted you from the moment you started working for him. Now he's got you with promises but no guarantees. I will make this hard for him. He will lose and end up broke. Your best bet is with me." Curtis's eyes went cold. "Now, how much will it take? I'm not afraid to give you more than he could ever offer you."

Kim's mind raced. She tried to think clearly. Had Isaac played her for a fool? Made promises to get what he wanted—the company and her? Had she read more into their relationship than there really was?

She met Curtis's eyes. He didn't look at her with a smirk or the nasty gleam of victory. Instead, the look he leveled her with was one of shame. Like she was the poor fool who'd fallen for the biggest con out there.

"How much, Kim?" Curtis asked.

"I—"

"Is everything okay over here?" Isaac stepped up to them.

Kim started. She put a hand over her racing heart. "You startled me."

She met his gaze. The anger simmering there left no doubt that he'd overheard Curtis's question. "That's usually a sign of a guilty conscience."

"You have nothing to worry about there, son," Curtis said. "Kim knows what's right and what's fishy. Isn't that right, Kim?" He winked. Kim's stomach heaved. "I think it's time for the ballgame." Curtis glanced at his watch. "I'll go enjoy some of the company of my employees. Pretend to care and make them feel secure in their jobs." He strolled off.

Isaac turned to her immediately after Curtis was out of earshot. "Are you going to accept his offer?"

"Of course not," she said.

"But you considered it."

"I listened to him. I wouldn't sell you out like that."

He didn't look convinced. "Come on, let's go watch the game."

CHAPTER 29

"I wouldn't sell you out like that."

The words burned in Isaac's brain. A low, hot simmer at the edge of his reason. Every time Curtis smirked at him and Kim with that conniving gleam in his eye was like a spray of gasoline. How many times had he heard something similar?

Everyone had the capability to be disloyal. Curtis, Andre, his mother and stepmother, even the board members he was trying to sway were only connected to C.E.S. because Curtis had identified their lies and broken commitments. Kim's situation wasn't desperate, but taking more money from someone else didn't require desperation, only greed. If Curtis made her believe he'd give her more than Isaac promised, would she go for that?

His subconscious said he knew her. She wasn't the type of person to sell him out. Unless Curtis made her situation desperate. If Curtis wanted Kim to cave, he'd make her life a living hell until she had no choice.

When the game entered the seventh inning stretch, Curtis announced he was leaving. Isaac followed him out. Neither spoke until Curtis stopped near the exit. "Go ahead, son, make whatever threats you plan to make."

"Why do you assume I'm going to threaten you?"

"I went through this spill with your brother. Let me guess. Leave Kim out of this. Stay away from her or else." Curtis gave a loose wave of his hand, his tone indifferent.

The words were kindling to Isaac's seething anger. He forced the anger to the side. Emotion only prodded Curtis more. "She has nothing to tell you," Isaac said calmly. "There is no big secret."

"You must think I'm stupid, boy. I know you're trying to take over the company."

Years of confrontations with Curtis were the only thing that kept Isaac from showing his surprise. "I'm not trying to take over the company."

"I know that you've been meeting with Gloria, Bob, and Doug behind my back. I also know they've approached some of the other board members. One of whom told me there's been chatter of voting me out. Sounds a lot like a hostile takeover is in the works."

This is why he didn't trust easily. Of the three, Doug was most likely the one to get word back to Curtis. Still, he wasn't going to admit to anything unless he was truly beat. "I'm meeting with board members to talk them out of your idea of taking over Andre's company. It'll kill us when we really need to be concentrating on keeping the contracts we have and getting new ones."

Curtis narrowed his eyes. "Your brother deserves to pay for walking away from this family."

"I don't agree with Andre's decision to ignore the family any more than you, but not at the expense of everyone working their asses off every day for C.E.S." Isaac pointed back toward the stadium. "That's what's most important to me. I'm making sure the board doesn't approve any foolish revenge schemes."

"And that's all you were doing with them?"

"Yes. There were no other ulterior motives."

"Then you'll have no problems knowing that I plan to make offers to buy out Gloria, Doug and Bob's shares on the board."

Isaac's plans exploded and settled into ash at his feet. He ran the mental calculations over and over but got the same thing. He'd have to take all of his savings to buy out the board members. To make matters worse, he didn't have the added capital of years of dirt that Curtis no doubt would use to buy out board members at a steal.

"You are?" Isaac's world had wavered, but his voice didn't.

"Yes. You see, even if you weren't planning a takeover, the idea that you might made me look into what it would take to buy them out. To give myself full control over the board and their decisions. I can offer them much more than just the cost of their shares, and they can walk away without any more obligations to me."

More money and no obligation to Curtis? That was a hell of a better deal than what Isaac could offer. "Have you approached them?"

"Not yet, but I will early next week. So, all of your efforts to convince them to not buy out Andre's company are wasted. We're doing this."

"You're willing to risk bankruptcy in order to get back at Andre? Willing to play with the livelihoods of all our employees?"

Anger made Curtis's eyes look almost crazy. "I will destroy your brother for going against me. Just like I'll destroy you if do the same. Face it, Isaac. You're beat." Curtis grinned and took a few steps back. "Don't worry about Kim. I'll let you feel like you're protecting her from me. It'll make it all the more enjoyable when your admiration of her turns to disgust."

"That won't happen."

Curtis wore the sick smile of someone who had a secret that could destroy your world. "You really believe that, don't you?" He walked away without waiting for a response.

The sound of footsteps approached. "Everything okay?" Kim asked. She took one look at him and frowned. "What's going on?"

His mind whirled with the next steps. He'd have to liquidate assets fast. Meet with Gloria and Bob in the next few days. Find out what it would take to buy out the rest. Where the hell was Curtis getting his extra money from?

"My dad is going to make an offer for the shares Doug, Gloria and others on the board own." Despite his earlier worry that she'd accept Curtis's bribe, Kim was the only person who could help him think this through.

"He's going to buy them out." She looked just as shocked as he felt.

"To avoid a takeover and to keep me from stopping plans to buy Andre's company. He's going to make his offer early next week."

Kim stepped closer and placed her hand on his arm. "What are we going to do?"

He met her gaze and some of his worry faded. We. He took a deep breath. In that instant, he knew he shouldn't have doubted her. "I've got to come up with the funds by the end of the week and buy them out before he does."

"Can you?"

"I can." There was a spark of hope in her eye he was about to dash. "But it means I can't give you the money for the down payment." At least not until after he had control of C.E.S.

Disappointment flashed in her hazel eyes. He waited for the anger to come next. For her to accuse him of using her like Curtis said.

She inhaled deeply and squared her shoulders. "I understand. We can't let your father ruin C.E.S. Don't worry about the house."

For a second he couldn't think of a response. "You're not mad?"

"Isaac, I didn't feel right taking the money from you in the first place. Wait. Did you think I'd get mad?" Her hand slipped away from his arm.

Isaac took her hand in his. "I thought you would listen to Curtis."

Her body stiffened. "Do I need to believe what he said?"

"I've told you the truth every step of the way."

Her fingers tightened around his hand. "Then trust me to do the same."

He studied her for any signs of deceit. Saw none. The cool breeze of trust doused the fires of anger. He trusted her. The admission made him feel like he stood on a raft in the middle of a hurricane.

Isaac squeezed her hand. "I do."

CHAPTER 30

The next morning, the smell of bacon, coffee and soul music woke Kim. Her eyes popped open. Dread spread ugly tendrils through her. Grandma only cooked huge breakfasts when she had bad news. Slowly, Kim got out of bed and slipped on her bathrobe. She opened her bedroom door at the same time as her mother. Jackie wore the same expression of concern.

"What happened?" Kim asked.

She'd gotten home late. After the baseball game, Fanta and a few others invited Kim to come hang out at one of the local bars. To her surprise, Isaac had agreed to tag along. He hadn't been the life of the party, but he had participated in the conversation and seemed to enjoy himself. Fanta and the other employees had been surprised by how down to earth he'd been.

Jackie shrugged and tied the belt of her fuzzy lavender robe. "I don't know. She wasn't here when I got home."

They exchanged another look. The years of worry and disappointment in her mom's gaze no doubt matched her own expression. Kim squared her shoulders and followed Jackie to the kitchen.

Ruby didn't notice when they stopped at the kitchen door. She was busy flipping pancakes. Bacon, sausage, grits, and hash browns were already made. A carton of orange juice sat on the counter. This was really bad.

"Mom, what's going on?" Jackie said in a soothing tone.

Ruby jumped and flipped a pancake on the floor. She slammed a hand over her chest. "Are you trying to make my heart explode?"

Kim wasn't going to let her deflect the conversation. "Grandma, what's all this?"

Ruby bent and picked up the dropped pancake. "I just wanted to make breakfast for my family. I haven't done that in a while." She tossed the pancake in the trash and dusted off her hands.

"Mom," Jackie said sharply.

Ruby sighed and turned off the stove. "I went to one of the new gambling houses last night."

Kim bit her lip to stop the curse. "And?"

Ruby faced them. She met Kim then Jackie's eye before looking away. "I lost."

Jackie crossed her arms. "How much?" Her voice shook.

Kim's body trembled. *Just a few hundred. Just a few hundred.* She crossed her fingers.

"I owe five grand."

Jackie stumbled and leaned against the wall. Kim sucked in a breath. "Five grand? How?"

"I hit the jackpot at BINGO. I won a thousand. I was hot, so I went to the BINGO parlor. It was crazy. I won another three." Ruby's voice tightened with the rush of excitement. "I was on a roll. I figured I could double it and save the house. We really wouldn't have to dip into your savings for the down payment. I was doing good at one of the video poker games. I kept going, sure I would hit the jackpot." Her shoulders slumped. "I lost."

"They let you leave without paying out?" Kim asked.

"Benji manages the place," Ruby said. "He gave me a month."

The breath whooshed out of Kim hard and fast. "Benji?"

Ruby nodded. "Your high school friend. He told me not to worry. He gave me time. We'll figure it out. We always figure it out. I'll go and win some more at BINGO."

"Stop it, Momma," Jackie snapped. "Just stop it."

"Don't freak out," Ruby said irritably. "Benji is Kim's friend. He won't send people out to hurt me. He'll give us time to pay him back. He isn't out to get me."

Kim nodded, but her world spun. "You're right, Grandma. He isn't out to get you." He was out to get Kim.

"See," Ruby said.

Jackie wasn't appeased. "I can't believe you put us in the situation. I don't have a job. We're about to lose the house. This was crazy and stupid."

"Don't call me stupid."

Jackie and Ruby argued. Kim turned and walked out of the kitchen. She went to her room and pulled out her cell phone. Her fingers felt like ice as she dialed the number. Time was up. She'd been offered one job and this was the calling card. Rebecca answered on the third ring.

"I need a job," Kim said.

Silence then a laugh. "Luckily I've got a big one coming that's perfect for you."

*

Isaac went for a jog the next morning. He thought about how things had changed between him and Kim, and more importantly, how that didn't bother him. He didn't believe she would take Curtis's money, and he felt more confident he could find a way to outmaneuver his dad with her help. By the time he jogged back to his building, he had some ideas to move forward and a smile on his face. He strolled down the hall to his condo. Andre sat on the floor outside of his door scrolling through his cell phone. Isaac's steps slowed. His smile died. Andre looked up and stood.

Varying degrees of emotions rushed over Isaac. Anger, relief, satisfaction, amusement, happiness. He ignored each of them and went with indifference. Andre had made his feelings very clear.

"Did you have a fishing trip and decided to drop in afterward?" Isaac walked to his door and unlocked it.

He didn't invite Andre inside, but his brother's footsteps followed.

"I'm here to talk to you."

Isaac dropped his keys into the holder next to the door and went straight to the linen closet for a towel to wipe away his sweat then joined Andre in the kitchen. "I thought we were done talking."

"I will not let us end up like Dad and Philip."

Isaac pulled milk out of the fridge and walked over to the blender. "We won't end up like them. I don't want to spend the rest of my life seeking revenge and trying to undermine you."

"They fight because they hate each other. I don't want us to hate each other."

Isaac reached for the protein shake mix beside the blender and poured two scoops into the blender with the milk. "Is Mikayla the reason you're here? Did she sprinkle you with her goodness and optimism and force you to come make amends with the brother you don't want any connection with?"

"I'm not here because of Mikayla. I'm here because you're my brother and I fucked up."

Isaac's hand froze before pressing the button to blend the mix. He faced Andre and crossed his arm over his chest. "That's something I didn't expect to hear."

"I admit to my mistakes. Moving away from the family wasn't a mistake. It needed to happen for Mikayla and me to work out, but moving away didn't mean I had to turn my back on you."

"Then, why did you?"

"Because I didn't know how to separate you from dad and C.E.S. Walking away from C.E.S. was one of the hardest decisions I ever had to make. There isn't a day that goes by that I don't miss working there."

That was unexpected. "You have your new company now."

"I do, and I'm proud of what we're building, but it's not the company I've worked to grow since I was thirteen years old. I like the people I work with, but no matter how much I enjoy them, it's not the same as working with my brother every single day. Every time we talked, and you brought up the problems at C.E.S., I felt guilty and wanted to come back. Coming back meant dealing with Dad and being brought back into the feud that almost ruined my relationship with Mikayla. Instead of dealing with that, I cut all ties. My bad. I'm sorry."

"You could have told me what was up."

"I'm telling you now."

Isaac turned back to the blender and made his shake. He used the time to process what his brother said. The relief was overwhelming. Thinking Andre wanted nothing to do with him or the company had been a hard blow. One that hurt like hell. The pain and anger that had clenched him for two years eased. He would have hugged Andre, that is if either of them had been big on showing emotion.

He poured the shake into a glass then sat at the kitchen table. On the way, he crooked his head for Andre to follow.

"It's not the same since you left," Isaac admitted. "It's hard working without you there to back me up."

Andre sat with his legs stretched out before him. "I feel the same every time I try to make a point in one of our meetings. I find myself looking across the table for you to agree with me even though two years have passed."

Isaac smiled and nodded. "Same here."

"You want to know something interesting?"

"What?" Isaac took a sip of the chocolate shake.

"When Steve approached me about working with him at Harden Composting, I was ready to jump at the chance to get out from under dad's thumb. But I also realized adding a composting component to Caldwell Environmental Solutions would be beneficial. I had a feeling one day the two of us could merge the companies."

That didn't surprise Isaac. Andre had always wanted to expand the services C.E.S. offered. It's why they'd purchased a landfill where they could reclaim the methane gas and sell it to nearby industries right before Andre quit. "Why didn't you ever bring that up?"

"Dad. I won't merge with him at the head."

"I don't blame you."

"How's the push out coming?"

Isaac took a heavy breath. "He's on to me. He's planning to offer to buy out the board members. They accept, and they owe him nothing. To make an offer better than his, I need a lot more money than I have on hand."

"Shit! What are you going to do?"

"Go to the bank, finagle my way into a loan for the funds I need and make offers to the board members before he can."

"Don't do that."

Isaac frowned. "Why not? If he's gone, then we can merge the companies."

Andre met his eye. "Because I'll give you the money you need."

"Do you have it?"

"Good question," Andre said with a half-smile. "How much?"

Isaac told him the amount. Andre winced. His brows drew together and his eyes unfocused for a second. Isaac could almost hear the numbers crunching in his brother's brain.

"It'll be tough on Mikayla and me for a while, but we can do it."

"Are you sure? Do you need to talk to her?"

"This amount of money, I have to tell her, but I doubt she'll say no."

Excitement danced in Isaac's chest. "We'll go against him together."

Andre met his gaze. Determination all over his face. "It's what we both knew we'd have to do one day."

"This fallout is going to be big. Worse than anything he tried with Philip."

"Let him try. Dad's way isn't the only way. We're stronger together. That's what he always failed to realize." Andre held out his hand. "Deal?"

Isaac grinned and shook. "Hell, yes, that's a deal."

Andre nodded then he looked pensive. "About Kim."

"What about her?"

"I tried the relationship-for-the-business thing. It's not worth it. I wouldn't have been happy. I wouldn't have Mikayla. I know you think love is foolish, but I want you to be happy one day."

"Can you blame me for thinking love is foolish? Before you met Mikayla, the only example of love I had was the way Curtis used the emotion to manipulate everyone around him."

"That's all I knew, too. Things with Mikayla felt right. I know it sounds cliché, but when the woman is right, you'll know. Don't let him force you into a loveless future."

"If I stay with Kim, it won't be loveless." He felt exposed admitting as much. He stared down into the shake instead of meeting Andre's gaze.

Andre stilled. "What are you saying?"

Isaac shrugged to appear nonchalant but felt that silly smile come back. "I'm saying what I'm saying. Kim and I wouldn't have a loveless relationship."

Andre grinned. "If that's true, then I'm happy for both of you."

Isaac raised his glass. He appreciated Andre for not making a big deal out of his revelation or asking a ton of questions. "To revenge on our dad and finally being free to be happy."

Andre bumped his fist to Isaac's glass. "Let's crush him."

CHAPTER 31

Kim met Rebecca at the burger place on Woodruff Road where they used to go as teenagers with the rest of the crew. She hadn't come back since Rebecca went to jail. The memories were too difficult. She ordered a burger and shake even though she wasn't hungry and waited in one of the booths near the back.

Rebecca arrived late. She definitely made an entrance. Every man in the place couldn't stop drooling over her, thanks to the black bodysuit that hugged her curves. She wore large gold earrings and a cross necklace. Her hair was swept into a ponytail on one side at the base of her neck. Everything about her screamed sex.

Rebecca didn't order food. She walked over and slid into the booth along with a hint of perfume that smelled expensive. She eyed Kim critically. "Why do you try to hide your shape? You always had a figure that made men hand over their entire mortgage payment."

Kim fought the urge to tug on her clothes. She hadn't gone for sexy and wore a fitted pink T-shirt and jeans. "I don't hide. I just don't flaunt it either."

"Why? What's made you scared?"

"I'm not scared. I'm more than my body."

Rebecca scoffed and raised a brow. "Oh. That's it. You've got brains and a heart. You want to be loved for your great conversation and how nurturing you can be."

"There's nothing wrong with that."

Rebecca rolled her eyes. "Women like us don't get that."

"I'm not like you."

"Then why am I here?" Rebecca slid to the edge of the booth.

Kim's hand shot and took her arm. "Don't go." Rebecca watched her with cool fury. "I'm sorry."

"This is what hurts, Kim." Rebecca's voice was tight. "Now you think you're better than all of us. And you're not afraid to show just how much you hate us. How much we disgust you."

"You don't disgust me." She meant it. She didn't agree with Rebecca's choices. She wished her old friend realized there was more for her in the world. That she could have gotten out of jail and chosen something different. Rebecca's life saddened Kim but didn't disgust her.

"I saw it on your face when I said I was working with Benji again. You looked at me like I'm worse than dog crap on your shoe."

"Not you, Rebecca. Benji is terrible. He wanted to use us to make money. I didn't like how I felt afterward. I didn't want to go through life like that. I would've killed any hope for me to feel something for any man. I wasn't going to do that."

"Then why are you here today?"

Kim met Rebecca's eyes. "You know why I'm here."

Rebecca at least didn't pretend to play coy. "Your grandmother's debt."

"Did you know he was going to set her up like that?"

Rebecca shook her head. "He didn't set her up. At the end of the night, he realized your grandmother had lost so much. He stepped in and gave her more time."

"You say that like he did us some kind of favor."

"He did do her a favor. Bookies don't give due dates. If she weren't your grandmother, she would have been in trouble." Rebecca leaned back in the booth. "If you would've done what I asked you when I first got out, you would have the money."

Kim shook her head. "I can't steal from Isaac. He's doing too much to make sure we still have a company to work for."

A calculating look came into Rebecca's eyes. "Oh, he's Isaac now. A few weeks ago, he was Mr. Caldwell."

"We're close."

Rebecca smirked. "How close?"

"Close enough."

"Does he know about us working together?"

"No, and I plan to keep it that way," Kim replied with a hard stare.

Rebecca's head tilted to the side. "He doesn't know you're here trying to work for me? That's really dumb, Kim. If you're *close* with a man who owns such a big company, why are you coming to me for a couple Gs? Can't he just write you a check?"

"I have my reasons," Kim said. There was no way in hell she'd mention anything about the buyout to Rebecca.

"Not that close, huh? I thought you were a better lay than that."

Kim gritted her teeth. "This is my problem, not his. Drop the subject. I told you I'd do a job to make things even. I need the money. I'm here."

Rebecca pursed her lips. "I told Benji you called."

Kim's palms sweated. "And?"

"And he says if you work the gig he has coming up, your grandmother's debt is paid."

The entire situation sounded too good to be true. Which meant she wasn't going to like the gig. "Who is he hustling that would make him forgive five thousand?"

"Benji is doing big things now and he runs with big people. If you play nice, so will he."

Kim's skin crawled. "What's the job?"

Rebecca rested her elbows on the table and leaned forward. "Entertainment for a few businessmen in the area. They're holding a party, and they want to make sure everyone has a good time. We're holding an auction. Highest bidder gets the prize. If the prize knows what she's doing, then maybe she'll get a tip."

Kim leaned back and rubbed her arms. "You're auctioning women."

Rebecca shrugged. "And a few men. Just for a night. We're not selling them permanently or anything." She said the last part as if any part of a sex auction was cool. "These guys like to flaunt their money and spend it on beautiful people. Benji said he'd provide the ultimate prizes." Rebecca tilted her head to the side and studied Kim. "You're older than most of the girls, and you're trying to hide your assets, but you still have what it takes to make a guy interested. I don't think you'll bring in much, but if you know how to work it, then this can be a win-win for you. Your grandmother is clear and you earn a little side change."

The idea made Kim's stomach boil. "I can't do that."

Rebecca didn't even look surprised. "Fine. We'll get Nakita instead. I'm sure she won't let your grandmother's debts go unpaid."

Kim's hand balled into a fist. "Stay away from my sister."

"She knows about the auction and she's interested. I had a feeling you'd be too queasy for this. If you won't do it, she will. Plus, she's younger and eager."

"She's twenty-two."

"She's legal with a young face. Plenty of grown men's fantasy."

"That's disgusting."

"That's business."

The promise of more money if the men liked their "prize" would make Nakita drool. Kim couldn't let her sister do this, even though she felt sick to the stomach at the thought of doing it herself.

"How do I know this isn't a front for some human trafficking ring?"

"Because these men would be hurt if it got out they're bankrolling something like that. They just want the fun of bidding on beautiful men and women in a controlled environment. This is the third one Benji's held. A few of the girls have built up a name for themselves and the men really fight to win. They also like new faces. We make sure all the girls are legal. That way, even though we're discreet, if word got out that they'd slept with one of them, there's no chance of jail time. Everything is classy."

Kim snorted. There was nothing classy about this. No matter how awful it sounded, if Rebecca was right, at least she didn't have to worry about being permanently "sold" to someone. The night would be humiliating, and disgusting, but the potential to keep men like Benji from going after her grandmother meant Kim couldn't afford to be picky.

"How do I know Benji will keep his word?"

"Do you think I could even invite you if he hadn't already agreed to it? Benji wants you there. He's always wanted you to work for him." There was a hint of bitterness in Rebecca's words. Rebecca had always wanted Benji, and Benji had always tried to get Kim. "If you come and play nice, he'll give it to you."

"Why?"

"He always liked your grandmother." Rebecca gave her a self-satisfied smirk.

Say no, and her grandma got hurt. Or Nakita worked the auction. Sacrifice one night and everything would be done. She could move on. Isaac didn't have to know.

But if he found out you'd be another person he can't trust.

Kim shook her head. "No. Give me another job. I'll consider anything else. Not this."

The smirk left Rebecca's face. The hard look of a person ready to go in for the kill replaced it. "If you don't do this, we get your sister to do it. Benji will also call in your grandmother's debt."

"This was always about getting back at me."

"Don't think so highly of yourself. I was going to rob your house or blackmail you with pictures of you and some of our marks back in the day. Your grandmother gave us this great gift when she lost at the place Benji's running. Now I'll have even better stuff to hold over your head."

"I'll go to the police."

"We've got a lieutenant coming to the auction. He'll bury your complaint before it goes anywhere. And if he can't, then there's still the matter of your grandmother owing some angry people over five thousand dollars. Nakita will do anything to help. Just like you. And if you think about going to your boss slash lover the same holds true. We won't take cash on this. You work or you owe us."

Not for one second did she believe Benji hadn't known her grandmother would lose. The trap had been set and she'd been led right into it. One night. She could survive one night.

You know it's not that easy.

Kim pushed away the thought. She wasn't giving her grandmother up to bookies and she wasn't watching Nakita go down a dark path. "I need a list of the men who'll be there."

"Why?"

"I can't have my boss running into someone who saw me auctioned off."

"Wear a mask."

"I will, but I still need the list."

"Fine. Anything else, Your Majesty?" Rebecca mocked.

"You keep Nakita out of this. Don't even entertain letting her come." She took a deep breath and ignored the nausea building in her stomach. "I'll do   it."

CHAPTER 32

"Are you ready?"

Isaac turned away from the view of the city from his office window to Kim standing in the door. She looked a lot calmer than he felt. His stomach was a tangle of knots. With the help of Andre, Isaac had gone to Gloria, Doug, and Bob over the weekend and secured their shares. He had disclosed his dad's plan, but they all were still ready to get Curtis out of the company. Everything was going according to plan. He had the shares, the majority vote, and he could take over C.E.S. Still, he felt nervous.

"As ready as I'll ever be," he said and turned back to the window.

His door closed, then Kim's footsteps crossed the room toward him. "What's wrong?"

"The answer should be nothing. I'm getting what I worked for. I know this is the right thing to do for the company. I can't let my dad run this company into the ground. If I don't take over, that's exactly what he'll do."

"But you still feel a little guilty for taking over."

Isaac took a deep breath. "I would've preferred if he'd seen things my way. Let go of his need for revenge against Andre and worked with me to make C.E.S. prosperous again."

She placed her hand on his back and moved closer to him. The small bit of support loosened the knots in his stomach. "You're not doing this out of spite. You're doing it because it needs to be done."

"That's what I keep telling myself. That doesn't change the fact that I spent most of my life telling Curtis I wasn't against him. I did whatever I could to convince him I wasn't going to betray him. Now, I'm doing everything I said I wouldn't do. Once this is done, any chance of a relationship with my father is gone. And what surprises me, is that a small part of me is actually looking forward to pushing him out. Does that mean I'm just like him?"

"You're nothing like Curtis. Curtis does what he does because he likes hurting people. You're doing what needs to be done to avoid hurting your brother and the people who work for you. Forget the tantrum your dad will throw. His influence isn't as strong as it once was. He'll be pissed, but he can't get to you."

Isaac wrapped an arm around her shoulder and looked into her beautiful eyes. "That's what bothers me. He may not get to me, but he can get to the people I care about."

Her eyes widened. "Me? Believe me, I'm not on your dad's radar. Besides, I have no money or influence. There isn't much he could do to me."

"Never underestimate my dad. I know he's already dug into your past."

Kim stiffened in his arms. "What did he say?"

"That you're not as perfect as I think you are." She tried to pull away. Isaac turned and faced her. He put his hands on her shoulders so she couldn't walk away. "I don't care about anything he could possibly say. But I would prefer to hear everything from you first."

Her eyes remained wide and frightened for a second before she lowered her gaze. Her shoulders lifted and lowered with a sigh, and she looked at him again her eyes were calm. "Some friends and I used to run little street hustles back in high school."

"What kind of hustles?"

She licked her lips. He didn't stop her when she pulled away. "We'd con guys. At clubs or bars mostly. They'd hit on us, wouldn't care that we were underage, and when we got them back to a hotel, we'd snatch their money and run."

He took a slow, measured breath before asking. "What happened at the hotels?"

She swallowed hard. "We always went in twos. One would kiss and start getting undressed. The other would take any money. Then we'd tie the guy up and run. They always thought we were being kinky when we brought up bondage."

"What made you stop?" He asked slowly.

"A friend of mine wanted to do more. She got caught up and went to jail. That was my wake-up call. I stopped. Enrolled in community college and eventually landed this job."

The woman who'd approached her outside of C.E.S. The tension left his shoulders. "Why didn't you tell me before?"

She licked her lips and shifted her weight. "Because I'm a former petty criminal. That's not something you want the guy that you're crazy about to know. I didn't want you to think I didn't belong here. That you couldn't trust me because of what I'd done."

"Is that everything?"

She met his eye and faced him fully. "That's all."

He believed her. He didn't care about Kim's past. He was relieved to know they didn't have to overcome something worse.

He took her hand and pulled her into the circle of his arms. "My dad built this company on a lot more than petty theft. That's not enough to scare me away from this."

A chime from his computer, the reminder that the board meeting was about to start, interrupted them. He took a deep breath. "Now or never."

The unease in his stomach settled as he and Kim walked to the conference room. The other board members were already there. Isaac crossed the room to Bob and shook his hand.

"This will be a board meeting for the history books," Bob said.

"As long as there is a future for this company to have a history book to look back on."

The conference room door slammed open. Curtis stomped into the room. "What the hell is this?"

Isaac and Bob exchanged a glance before Isaac walked over to Curtis. "You're here just in time for a board meeting."

"Why are we having a board meeting today? Our next board meeting shouldn't be until next month."

"We're meeting today because there is important business we need to discuss." Isaac gestured toward the conference room table. "Please, have a seat."

Curtis's eyes narrowed. He glared at the other board members before slowly crossing the room and sitting at the head. "Important business, huh? This isn't another attempt to try and talk me out of buying your brother's company?"

"No, this is about me taking over the company." Isaac sat in the seat opposite his dad and stared him in the eye.

Curtis laughed. "Really, you're taking over? Please let me know how in the hell you expect to do that."

"I've purchased Gloria, Doug and Bob's shares in the company. Combined with my own shares, I am now the majority vote on this board." Saying the words felt good.

Curtis's amused expression morphed into one of quiet anger. "You can't do that. You don't have the funds. I know. I checked."

Isaac wasn't surprised that Curtis had looked into his finances. "I can, and I have."

"Who would dare give you anything? I own this town."

"Your influence isn't as strong as you think."

"Who dared to give you money?" Curtis nearly spat the words.

"The funding doesn't matter. I now have the majority vote. My first order of business is to remove you as the head of Caldwell Environmental Solutions."

Omar, a board member loyal to Curtis, sat up. "You can't remove your own father."

Isaac turned his hard stare to the naysayer. "I can, and I will."

"No. You. Won't." The fury-filled statement came from Curtis. "You don't have the balls to kick me out of my own company. The company I built for you and your brother…" His eyes widened. "He helped you do this, didn't he?"

"Andre and I were always stronger together."

"How can you stomach betraying me like this?" Curtis sounded legitimately surprised. "I thought you were the loyal one."

"I'm not betraying you. I'm standing for the people who work for this company. In the past two years, you've been so focused on trying to ruin Andre's life you made decisions that hurt C.E.S. Under your leadership, we've lost twelve accounts, two of them major. We're being undercut by smaller businesses that aren't trying to win by intimidation and fear. Not only that, we're losing good employees left and right. You may have built this company, but you're also breaking it down. I refuse to let you do it."

"You're no better than me."

The statement rolled right off Isaac. "I never claimed to be better than you. The only thing I will claim is having different priorities."

"I will ruin you." Curtis's said in a low, nasty tone.

"You can try," Isaac replied calmly. "I make a motion to remove Curtis Caldwell as the head of Caldwell Environmental Solutions. Is there a second?"

Curtis raised his chin and glared. Patrick Jordan, a board member whose loyalty had remained in question, nodded. "Second."

Isaac didn't take his eyes from his father. "All in favor."

There were a couple of "Ayes." "Any opposed?"

Omar was the only one who voted against the takeover. The entire exercise was a formality. He had the majority vote over all the board members. Isaac didn't need to do this, but it was better than automatically kicking out his father.

"The ayes have it," Isaac said. "Curtis, thank you for your service."

Curtis slapped his hand on the table. "Save your bullshit talk. You've deceived me. I'll never forget or forgive you. I will ruin you and everything you care about. You and your brother." Curtis glared at Bob, Gloria, and Doug. "Everyone who had anything to do with this."

He pushed his chair back and stormed out of the office. Isaac dismissed the meeting. He hadn't expected it to go well, but he hadn't expected so little fight from Curtis. He expected yells, maybe even a thrown punch. Curtis had handled this too well. Dread, icy and sharp, pierced his chest.

"That was too easy," Bob said, his words mirroring Isaac's thoughts.

"I know."

"We've got to take your father down in a bigger way."

"What else could we possibly do? He's out of C.E.S. I'm not going to do any physical violence against him."

"Your father has his hands in a lot of things. Some of those things aren't exactly legal."

"Tell me something I don't know."

Bob stepped closer and lowered his voice. "Bring those activities to light, and he'll really be out of the way."

Isaac shook his head. "I wanted him out of C.E.S. What he does on his own time isn't my business."

Bob sighed and held out his hand. "You say that now, but I'll be in touch soon. Once you hear me out, you'll agree to help."

He shook Bob's hand "I'm done playing games. My focus is C.E.S. now."

His focus was on his future. He glanced at Kim, and she gave him a reassuring smile. Professional and personal.

*

Kim leaned back into Isaac's chest as they sat on his couch watching television. She smiled at the sitcom showing two people trying to get through a blind date from hell. She would have laughed, but there was too much in her head. Isaac had listened to her confession and accepted what she said. He really did trust her, and she was about to deceive him.

One night. One lie. Then you can move on.

She tilted her head to see if he was paying attention to the television, but he stared across the room at nothing in particular. Worry darkened his eyes.

Kim placed her hand on his cheek. "Hey, babe, what's wrong?"

Isaac shook his head and tried to smile. "Nothing."

"You're staring off into space. There's something wrong. Are you still thinking about the board meeting?"

Isaac sighed and took her wrist in his hand. He kissed her palm then lowered their joined hands to his lap. "Not the board meeting, but something Bob said afterward."

"About turning your dad into the authorities?" The idea of Curtis being involved in criminal activities hadn't surprised her. Neither had Isaac refusing to further go after his father.

"I know Curtis has blackmailed people, but could he possibly be doing something so much worse that it would warrant me turning him over to the police?"

"What do you think?"

"I think the answer is yes. I have no idea how far his criminal ties go."

"He never tried to get you or Andre involved in anything?"

"Only schemes aimed to increase C.E.S.'s power. He made threats to expose a person's darkest secrets and scandals, but outside of blackmail and coercion, he's never done anything really bad."

"Depends on your circle. Blackmail and corruption can be considered pretty bad." Rebecca's blackmail was a heavy burden Kim hated to carry.

"You're thinking about that woman I saw you with," Isaac said. "The one who feels you owe her a debt. Is she blackmailing you?"

Her heart twisted with guilt and regret. She should tell him. Now was the best time to confess everything. He'd move hell and high water to save her and her grandmother. But that wouldn't fulfill her promise to Rebecca. If she backed out, Rebecca and Benji would go to Nakita. Then they'd still come for her grandmother. She had to get this one night over with, and her problems would be over.

"I paid her back. I don't have to worry about her," she said easily. She looked at their entwined hands. He would see the lie if she met his gaze. "But, yes, I know that blackmail can be a burden. Just knowing I owed her something, or that she could come to you with what I used to do and ruin my job, my life, was terrible."

Isaac lifted her chin with a finger. "If anyone comes to you and tries to use something you've done against you, come to me. I won't let anyone hurt you. I'll be the fire and the damn brimstone to anyone threatening you."

The cold strength in his words and fierce protection reflected in his gaze brought tears to her eyes. She kissed him before she confessed everything. Isaac was one man. He might be able to help her, but what about Nakita and her grandmother? They weren't his responsibility.

She pulled back and smiled. "I will. I know that you would do anything you could to help me, and I appreciate that."

"I'll help you keep your family's home. Now that the business is mine, I can work on improving next quarter's profits. I'll have my money back in no time, and the first thing I'm going to do is secure your home, especially since you don't want me to move you and your family into my place."

Kim relaxed and pushed aside thoughts of what would happen if Isaac knew about Saturday. "You say you want us living with you, but you haven't woken up to my grandmother singing in the shower at the top of her lungs or my mom trying another new dish she'll ultimately mess up."

Isaac's deep laugh was a balm to her ravaged nerves. He'd been so tense, so upset about the board meeting. Hearing him laugh was good. "Maybe you're right."

"I don't know what type of activities Curtis may be involved in, but you have to remember that if Bob thinks it's bad enough to land him in jail, then you should know. He may not be in charge of C.E.S. anymore, but he was here for years. You're better off knowing what you're fighting against than being in the dark."

"You think I should send him to jail?"

"I think you should talk to Bob and find out what he knows. Determine if the ramifications of whatever it is your dad is doing could hurt everything you're trying to build at C.E.S. and then make a decision."

"I've already kicked him out of the company."

"Would he give you the same consideration?" A low blow, but he needed to be hit with the reality of the situation.

Isaac tensed and leaned back. Then he swore and shook his head. "No. He'd love to see Andre and me in jail just so he could gloat. Then he'd dangle our jobs in our faces on the day we're released and take us back with the promise of further pain."

"If you know he'd hurt you like that, then why are you trying to protect him? Think about it, Isaac. Learn what he's doing and then make your decision."

He stood and pulled her up with him. Kim laughed as he led her out of the room. "What are you doing?"

"I need clear-my-head sex," he said as if he were talking about the fiscal reports. The naughty gleam in his eye sent a tremor of anticipation through her.

"I know just the thing for that."

Inside his bedroom, they undressed quickly. He made love with an intensity that stripped her of her ability to breathe at times. Each sweep of his hand over her breasts, brush of his tongue across her sex, and deep inhale of his scent unraveled the feelings she'd hidden for so long. After climaxing so hard she scratched grooves into his back, he didn't pull away. His movements slowed, and he brushed the hair away from her face. Kim cupped his cheek and started to smile, but he slid back in and her lips parted with a gasp instead.

He kissed her palm. Looked at her as if she were everything. Her heart tightened so much she couldn't ignore her feelings any longer. She loved him.

"Isaac." All of the emotions swirling inside her filled her voice.

His brows drew together and he cupped the side of her face. "What's wrong?"

"If I say it, I'm afraid you'll pull away."

Concern filled his eyes. "Say it."

She took a deep breath and steeled herself. Getting rejected in the middle of sex would be horrible, but he needed to know before she…

He needed to know he was all she cared about. "I love you."

His slow thrusts stopped. The groove between his brows deepened. She'd seen that look before. He was processing what she said and deciding the best way to respond. Then his face cleared.

"I think I love you, too." A whisper of awe filled in his voice.

Kim's arms wrapped around his neck and her legs cinched his waist. She rolled him over and made love to him so hard he couldn't speak. Afterward, they lay in each other's arms panting.

"Andre wants me to come up to his place this weekend," Isaac said. "Come with me?"

She opened her mouth to say yes. Reality popped her bubble. She already had plans. "I can't. I owe Nakita for bailing on her the other weekend to go with you to Gloria's dinner party. I promised we'd hang out on Saturday."

He kissed her forehead and pulled her tighter against him. "I won't pull you away from your sister again. I'll go and hang with Andre and then you can come back with me another weekend."

She hugged him tightly. Not wanting to let him go. Not wanting to think about losing what they'd built together if he ever found out. He'd leave her. *One night. Just get through one night.*

CHAPTER 33

Nakita slammed into Kim's bedroom with the force of a hurricane. Her eyes wide and body tense. "You're such a fucking hypocrite!"

Kim continued pulling the large rollers out of her hair. There was no need to pretend she didn't know what her sister meant. She wasn't even surprised Rebecca had told Nakita. She would want Kim's family to know what Kim had done for them.

"I'm doing this for everyone in this house," Kim replied calmly.

Nakita crossed her arms and tapped her foot. "No, you're not. You're doing this because you think I'm a baby and that I can't handle it. You pretended like you were too good for the lifestyle and that you don't care about money, when that's exactly what you're all about. You think I don't know how much Rebecca is paying you for this? She told me right before she kicked me to the curb."

Kim spun on her sister. "The thought of what I'm doing tonight makes me sick to my stomach. I've taken anti-nausea pills just to make it through the day. Tomorrow I'm going to hate myself and spend half the morning scrubbing off the contaminated feeling even though it'll never go away."

Kim's outburst wiped away Nakita's angry glare. A look of wary concern filled her eyes. "If you hate this so much, why are you doing it?"

"Because Grandma owes money at Benji's gambling house. He said he'd forgive her debt if I work tonight."

Nakita sank onto the bed. "I thought she stopped gambling."

"I thought so too."

"Then why won't you let me do this instead?"

"Because I don't want you to feel the way I'm going to feel tomorrow. Nakita, I love you. I want you to have the chance to have a great life. You don't need this baggage. You don't want to have to explain to the man you love what you once did just to pay the bills."

Nakita raised her chin. "If he loves me, he wouldn't care."

"That's a fairytale, and we both know it." Kim's hands trembled as she removed the last roller. *"I think I love you too."* That belief would fizzle and die if Isaac found out.

"You aren't telling Isaac?"

"No. I promised Rebecca one job, and this is it. I never want to be in this predicament again."

"We can find another way."

"Tell me how we're going to get five thousand dollars by the end of next week. Don't forget we need another five for the entire down payment. If you have a great idea, then I won't go tonight."

Nakita frowned and looked down at the floor. "What else is going on, Kim? I mean, just now you looked...scared." Nakita raised her gaze to Kim's. "You never used to look scared when we were younger."

"Because I never wanted you to know how scared I was. I was terrified that the guy we were trying to dupe would kill us. I've been hit, threatened with a gun. Sometimes we barely got out of those hotel rooms. That's why Rebecca and Benji thought we should just become prostitutes. You worried enough when I left. I knew that if you realized how frightened I was, you'd tell mom exactly what I was doing."

"She knew what you were doing," Nakita said softly.

"I know. That didn't make talking about it any easier."

"You have to stop sacrificing yourself for us."

"What am I supposed to do? Let Benji and his crew hurt Grandma? If it were just the house, I wouldn't go. We can find a new place and be happy. I know what they do to people who owe them money."

"Do you really think he'd do something terrible to Grandma?"

"Do you really want to find out?"

Nakita shook her head. Kim stood and went back to the mirror. She didn't bother to comb the curls from the rollers. She'd do that when she met Rebecca. Rebecca told her that they'd also decide what she'd wear and do her makeup. She made it sound like Kim was participating in a fashion show.

Get through the night. Just make it through the next twelve hours and everything will be alright.

She lifted her bag off the floor. Nakita's hand closed over Kim's. "Don't go. Let me do this."

Kim pulled away. "Everything will be over tomorrow. Don't worry about me. Just make sure mom and Grandma don't worry, either."

"Kim."

She ignored her sister and exited the room. She hurried down the hall, thankful Jackie and Ruby weren't home. She doubted she would be able to look her mom and grandma in the eye and lie about where she was going.

"Kim!" Nakita called.

Kim rushed out the front door. "Just twelve hours."

That's all she had to get through. She repeated the words to herself all the way to Rebecca's place.

Ten minutes in and Kim's gut instinct said something wasn't right. The entire situation was wrong by itself, but that wasn't what gave Kim an overwhelming sense of foreboding. There were nine other women and three men there. All in various stages of undress, while Rebecca barked directions to another woman helping one girl squeeze her body into a skintight green dress. The slim, dark-haired girl jamming her body into the dress didn't look a day over eighteen.

Kim glanced at every other person in the room. Most appeared to be in their early to mid-twenties, but there were a few that seemed like they should be getting ready for prom, not a sex auction.

"You look lost." A soft female voice came from Kim's side.

Kim turned and her unease grew. The girl had deep golden skin, and curly black hair pulled into a loose knot at the top of her head. A red silk robe draped over her body, stopping at mid-thigh and gaped at the top. The girl had her arms crossed tightly over her chest. Her dark eyes darted from Kim to the other people in the room.

"You look scared," Kim said. *And young.*

The girl shrugged. "I'm the big draw."

"What does that mean?"

Another shrug. "I'll go for the highest bid. Mister says I better go for the highest bid."

"Who's Mister?"

The girl's gaze darted back to Kim before a frown covered her face. "You must be lost. Mister personally picked everyone for this. What are you doing here? Are you here to bust us?"

Kim shook her head. Mister had to be Benji. She wanted to kill him for the fear in the girl's eyes. "No, I'm not here to bust you."

The tension in the girl slacked. "You can't get me home."

Kim leaned in. "Do you want to go home?"

The girl's gaze darted around the room again. She shuffled from foot to foot and sucked her lower lip through her teeth. She was terrified.

"How old are you?" Kim asked.

Another voice answered. "She's eighteen." Rebecca put her hands on the girl's shoulder and pulled her away from Kim. "Go do something with your makeup," she said in a sharp voice.

The girl nodded and scurried away. Kim frowned. "You said everyone here was of age."

"They are. This is her first night. She's nervous. That's all." Rebecca frowned at the others in the room then turned her scowl on Kim. "You know what? Let's go in another room. Besides, Benji wanted to see you first."

Rebecca turned and walked out before Kim could respond. Kim threw one more glance at the girl before following Rebecca. They went into the bedroom next door.

"The auction will be downstairs," Rebecca said. "You're the oldest, so you're going first."

Kim frowned. "I'm the oldest? I'm twenty-seven."

"Yeah, that's almost thirty. Men like young, pretty girls. Which is why you have to work extra hard."

"Who's Mister?"

Rebecca snorted. "The guy who put this thing together. He directs Benji's operation."

"I thought Benji was the head of this?"

"He was, but he didn't know how to make it grow. Now Mister is in charge. He came up with the idea for this."

"She said he picks the girls. He didn't pick me?"

Rebecca smirked. "Who says he didn't? You called me for a job, Benji co-signed because he wants you, but Mister made the final decision. He checked you out and he liked what he saw."

A cold feeling washed through Kim's veins. "He spied on me?"

A knock on the door interrupted Rebecca's reply. Benji walked in. Her stomach rolled. Tall, fat, and shiny were the three words that came to mind whenever she saw Benji. He was close to six feet tall, too overweight to be just be called thick, with sand-colored skin, curly hair and a love of anything flashy. He wore a silver shirt that was dark near the armpits and black jeans with a silver dragon printed on them. Too many silver, or platinum, chains surrounded his neck and every one of his fingers had a ring on it.

"I just stopped in to see what I'm paying for," Benji said in a voice that would make Mickey Mouse sound like a baritone singer. His appearance made many people underestimate him, but she'd seen enough of Benji's cruelness to know he wasn't a man to be trifled with.

"That's why you have me here?"

Benji's high pitched laugh made her skin tighten. "Oh, it's one of the reasons. You always thought you were too good for me back in the day. My original plan was to make you prove that what I'm offering to my clients is worth their time."

She swallowed back the bile that rose in her throat. "Oh, really?" Her voice remained steady even though her insides wanted to revolt.

"Except Mister wouldn't let me sample the merchandise. I'll pay for you," he made air quotes with his hands. "It's only my money coming back to me anyway. Then I'll spend the entire night making you regret running out on us."

She looked at Rebecca. "You said my grandmother's debt would be forgiven. Instead, this is just a way for him to get back at me."

Benji laughed again. "Oh, Ms. Ruby will be fine. *If* I'm happy in the morning. You always thought you were worth a few grand. Let's see if that's the case." He reached into his pocket and pulled out a handful of green material. "This is what you're wearing." He tossed the material at Kim.

She caught the thin fabric. Recognized a ridiculously skimpy bikini. The top would barely cover her breasts. The bottom was nothing more than a small triangle and straps.

"I don't expect to have to pay too much for my night with you. Not with all the young girls here. But, still, try to shake your ass a little for the other men's enjoyment." He smirked and walked to the door. "Rebecca, come on. Let's make sure everyone is ready."

Tears burned Kim's eyes as they walked out of the room. Air wouldn't fill her lungs. Her heart constricted to agonizing tightness. She couldn't do this. She ran to the door and jerked it open.

Rebecca stood on the other side, a cell phone in her hand. "I've got Reggie down at my gambling house on speed dial. Mister also runs that operations. You run, we call in her debt tonight."

"You are a bitch," Kim said through clenched teeth.

"And you're a whore. Now choose."

Kim slipped back into the room and closed the door. She fought tears as she took off her clothes and put on the bikini. She looked in the mirror and had to fight not to throw up. She might as well be naked.

What was Isaac doing at that moment? She wished with everything in her that she was with him at his brother's house. Wished that she would be able to go back to him, but she wouldn't. She wouldn't be the same after tonight, and this wasn't the type of secret she could keep from him. She'd have to quit C.E.S., leave him, and try to move on with her life.

The idea was like a dozen shards of glass tearing at her heart. She wouldn't think of him now, and she wouldn't think about the pain and regret she'd feel tomorrow. She had to go numb. She had to forget everything and just get through the night.

There was a knock and Rebecca walked in. "It's time."

Kim closed her eyes, took a deep breath, and remembered how she'd survived a night once before. She forced all feelings, all emotions, all sensations out of her body. She cleared her mind of everything until she was detached. "I'm ready."

Rebecca's grin was evil. "Mister walks down all the girls. Gives great intros and all that."

Kim didn't even respond. She didn't care. She just had to get through tonight. She looked at the floor and followed Rebecca out of the bedroom to the top of the stairs where a man's shoes came into her vision.

"Well, well, well. I guess my son isn't paying enough."

Kim's eyes shot up. Her world imploded. Every attempt at being numb dissipated at hearing Curtis Caldwell's evil voice. His dark eyes twinkled with glee and he held out his arm for her. "I might even put in a bid on you myself."

Kim stood frozen. Rebecca pushed her forward. "Mr. Cald—"

"Just Mister, please." He pulled her arm through his. He wore one of the suits he came to the office in. As if this were just another business day. "And if you even think about telling Isaac about this, I will call in your grandmother's debts immediately with no leniency."

"You will pay for this," Kim said in a calm tone that was no less fierce. She didn't know how, but she would get him for this.

"That's what they all say. I will ruin Isaac and everyone else that helped him. Today I'm starting with you."

He nudged her none too gently toward the top of the stairs. The only reason she didn't fall was because he jerked her back to his side. She tried to bring back the numbness. Tried to clear her mind, but she couldn't. She'd known she couldn't go back to Isaac after this. Now she knew he would hear about everything anyway. Even if she did tell him about his dad's involvement, he would know that she'd chosen this path instead of talking to him.

"We've got an oldie but goodie for you here tonight, boys," Curtis said through a microphone. She had no idea where that had come from.

"The oldest one here, but that just means she's wiser. Once you get a look at these curves, you'll definitely want to see what lessons she's learned."

Kim tuned him out. He led her down the stairs. Vaguely she realized there were dozens of men there. A lot more men than the women and men upstairs. Did that mean double bidding? Bile rose in her throat. She swallowed it down. Her arrival was met with catcalls and whistles. She didn't look at any of the men. She couldn't even paste a smile on her face.

"We'll start the bidding at a thousand dollars," Curtis said.

Benji made the first offer. Others chimed in. Pretty soon her cost had shot up to five thousand, Benji, the highest bidder.

"Do we have any more bidders?" Curtis asked. "Hearing none—"

"Ten thousand." A cool, angry, and familiar voice shot out.

Her head jerked to the left and her heart shriveled to embers as she met Isaac's furious glare.

CHAPTER 34

The only thing that could have surprised Isaac more than seeing Kim next to his father on those stairs would have been to walk in and find Jesus doing the electric slide with his apostles.

A jumble of circumstances had gotten Isaac there tonight. A phone call from Curtis inviting him to a house party with a cryptic promise to show him the truth about some things. That phone call was followed with one from Bob revealing he's been helping with an ongoing investigation into Curtis and his criminal connections. Bob knew Isaac had been invited and wanted to invite him to help in the takedown. Which led him here. Seeing the woman he loved auctioned off in his father's illegal prostitution ring.

The satisfaction gleaming in Curtis's eyes was deep. "We've got a bid for ten thousand. A bit much for her, but who am I to judge? Any other offers."

Isaac's blood seared his veins. He couldn't look at Kim but felt her stare. How could she do this to them? Did she want money that much? He understood her need to get the down payment for the house, but there were other ways. Maybe she didn't care. Maybe she'd wanted to be here.

The man who'd made an effort to win Kim earlier took a step forward. Curtis's smug gaze left Isaac. With a quick shake of his head, the other man stepped back, his body stiff and his expression angry as he glared at Isaac.

"Well, we have a winner," Curtis said.

A round of claps and jeers went up from the men in the room. Isaac walked to the end of the stairs. His stomach churned as he was slapped on the back and provided with graphic descriptions of what he could do to his prize.

When he stood in front of Curtis and Kim, he still couldn't look at her in that crazy excuse for a bikini. Curtis's smile was everything petty and vindictive in the world.

"Congratulations, son. Let this be the first of many upcoming disappointments," Curtis said.

Isaac didn't take the bait. "Does this mean I get to have sex with her?"

Curtis laughed. "What the hell else do you think we're doing in here?

Your girlfriend was the opener. It wasn't smart to spend all your money on her when there are so many better women to choose from."

"And you're auctioning all of them for sex?" Isaac asked, filling his voice with a disbelief he didn't feel. After Bob had filled him in on the various crimes Curtis was under investigation for, he wasn't surprised. His father had always been dirty. He just never wanted to believe how much so.

"Sex and whatever else the winner wants." Curtis shoved Kim forward.

She nearly fell off the top step. Isaac caught her then quickly set her to his side. He couldn't bear to have her against him, the pain of her betrayal too much. Curtis laughed.

"You're enjoying this, aren't you?" Isaac asked through gritted teeth.

"This is just the first step in my promise to destroy you and your brother."

"You'll never stop."

"You're either with me or you're against me, and I know you're against me."

Isaac nodded. "I am, but you won't be taking out your revenge on Andre or me anymore."

Rage filled Curtis's face. Before he could spew out whatever insults lay on his tongue, the doors flew open, and police flooded through. Curtis took in the cops and his eyes widened. He glared at Isaac. "You didn't!"

"Plan your downfall so completely? No. But I am helping."

The men tried to run, but the cops had the place surrounded. Two cops approached them, one handcuffed Curtis, the other reached for Kim. Isaac shook his head.

"No. She's part of the operation?"

The cop didn't look convinced. "I wasn't told any of the women here were in on this. I've got to take her in."

Curtis glared at Kim. "Whore. What's going to happen to your grandmother now? I'm going to make sure my one phone call handles that."

Isaac glared at his disgrace of a father. "Are you threatening her?"

The cop putting handcuffs on Curtis started reading him his rights, and Curtis didn't say anymore. He stared at Isaac with nothing but disgust. Had Curtis ever cared for him?

He turned to Kim. Fear filled her gaze, and she struggled against the handcuffs. "No, I've got to get home."

The cop didn't seem to care. "We all do. Come on, lady, don't make this any harder than it needs to be."

She turned wide frightened eyes on Isaac. "Isaac, please, please check on my grandmother. I'm only here because of her. Please make sure she's okay."

"I can't trust anything you say to me," he said.

The cop pulled her away. Tears streamed down her face. "Please, Isaac. Hate me all you want, but please check on her."

He turned away. Bob and the detective he'd met before this operation walked over. The house was still a madhouse as the men in attendance were arrested, and shouts rang out between the men and women upstairs.

"Good job," the investigator said. "I didn't expect him to confess to everything so quickly."

"Smugness made him blind. He wanted to get at me and didn't think past that," Isaac said.

Bob placed a hand on Isaac's shoulder. "I had no idea Kim would be here. Did you?"

Isaac shook his head. "I'm as shocked as you."

Kim's pleas rang through his head. He didn't want to believe anything was wrong with her grandmother. But the fear in her eyes and the tears. Even after everything, it tortured him. "Do you need me anymore?"

The investigator nodded. "Yes. I want to take your statement officially at the station. Let us get everyone rounded up here and then we'll do that. We've been watching your father and his accomplices for over a year. This is a major human trafficking bust. Hopefully, we'll save a lot of people from an unfortunate situation."

Isaac nodded because he had no words. Curtis deserved everything and more thrown at him for operating a human trafficking ring. Not just that. According to the investigator, Curtis had ties to gambling organizations, too. The time Curtis hadn't wanted to commit to C.E.S. had been spent building his crime organization.

The investigator walked away to talk with the other deputies. Bob talked about how this would go a long way in preventing Curtis from destroying C.E.S. Isaac couldn't focus on that either. He checked his watch and thought about Kim's frantic concern for her grandmother.

*

Isaac arrived at Kim's house close to midnight. He'd tried to check his impatience as he gave his official report at the station. The look of fear in Kim's eyes when she'd pleaded for him to check on her grandmother haunted him. Then there was the threat his dad had thrown to Kim. Curtis shouldn't have anything to do with Kim's family. Still, Isaac rushed from the station and broke every speeding law to get to Kim's place.

There were several cars at the house. He recognized the one her mother and grandmother shared and her sister's car. There was also a dark vehicle in the drive. The windows were tinted and something dark covered the license plate. There was little to distinguish the vehicle from any other in the city. The house was quiet, no lights or sounds. No sign of any life at all.

Trusting the uneasy feeling in his gut, Isaac reached into the console between the front seats and pulled out his Glock. He checked the sleeve and safety before getting out of the car. The gun went into his pocket. Hopefully, he wouldn't have to use it.

Isaac knocked on the door first. He listened for any sound of movement. Hearing none, he rang the bell and listened again.

No answer except for the barest muffled sound. Almost like a stifled shout.

Isaac slid his hand in his pocket. The other rang the bell several times and pounded on the door. "Ms. Ruby, it's Isaac. I need to talk to you!" he yelled loud enough to get the attention of the women inside. "It's important. Please, open the door."

He gave another round of bell ringing and knocks. Pretty soon Ms. Corrine's porch light came on across the street. Exactly what he'd hoped for. "Come on, ladies. I don't want to wake the neighborhood. Kim's in trouble. This is important!"

Finally, he could hear shuffling and quiet voices on the other side of the door. Isaac leaned closer to try and make out the words. He only heard the tones, one higher, the other low and angry. A male voice.

"Hold on, Isaac," Ms. Ruby said through the door, her voice wobbly. "I'm coming."

The one deadbolt on the door clicked. Ms. Ruby only cracked the door open enough for her to peek out. Her body was stiff, her eyes red and puffy.

"What is it, Isaac?" her voice was curt and shaky.

"Kim's been arrested," he said.

Her eyes widened. Her gaze darted to the side of the door for the barest of seconds. Then she stiffened and focused on him again. "For what?"

"I'll tell you on the way to the station. We need to go."

She looked toward the floor then turned her head toward the side of the door again. To whoever was holding her captive. "Umm, not tonight. If she did something wrong, then it'll do her good to spend a night in jail."

"She didn't do anything wrong. I think she was set up."

Ruby looked at him again. "Set up? Are you sure?"

"I am. That's why we need to go. We've got to get this straightened out." He used his head to motion to the door then mouthed, *One guy?*

She nodded. "Yes." She licked her lips. "We do need to get this straightened out, but I can't tonight."

Isaac held up a hand and gestured for her to take a step back. Then he held up one finger. "That's crazy." Two fingers. "You've got to come with me." Three fingers.

Ruby lunged back and Isaac kicked the door. The sound of a grunt preceded a crash into the wall behind. He rushed inside and pulled his gun from his pocket in one smooth motion.

A man with dark blonde hair and wearing dark clothes lunged at Isaac. Isaac didn't need the gun. The lunge was sloppy. He stepped out of the way and slammed the back of the Glock into the guy's head. The man fell into a loose lump on the floor.

"Did he have a weapon?" Isaac asked Ruby.

Ruby nodded. "He had a gun. It fell when you kicked in the door. He didn't expect that."

"Then he's even sloppier than I thought."

Isaac slipped his belt off and kneeled. He pulled the unconscious man's hands behind his back and used the belt to secure them. "Do you have duct tape? That'll hold him better than my belt until the cops arrive."

"I do. I'll get it." But she didn't move.

Isaac looked around. "Where are Jackie and Nakita?"

Tears streamed down Ruby's face. "In the kitchen."

Isaac's stomach dropped. He jumped up. He ran for the kitchen, Ruby right behind him. Isaac's fear solidified into rage. Nakita and Jackie were both on the floor. Jackie sported a black eye and Nakita's lip was split. Their hands were handcuffed to the handle on the stove.

Isaac went to them. "Did he say he had a key?" He checked their injuries. Despite their facial injuries, nothing looked broken.

Jackie shook her head. "No. He rang the bell. When I answered the door, he started flashing the gun and telling us to turn out the lights and get in the kitchen."

Ruby pulled the tape out of a drawer and ran back into the living room. The sound of the tape as she pulled it loose trailed behind her.

"What did he want?"

Nakita spoke this time. "He said if Kim didn't follow through he had to call in the hit on Grandma."

Rage stormed inside him. "Who called in the hit?"

"Someone called Mister." Nakita shook her head, tears filling her eyes. "It should have been me. I was supposed to go, but Kim wouldn't let me. She's always trying to take care of things for us. I told her to let me go instead."

"You didn't need to be there either," Isaac said.

"You know where she went?"

Isaac nodded. "The police raided the place. I helped. Everyone there went to jail. Including Kim."

"Jail? What happened?" Jackie jerked against the handcuffs.

Isaac glared at the restraints. He may have been able to get the guy who'd threatened them down, but he was useless with picking a lock. "She went to do another job for Rebecca."

Jackie's jaw hardened. "Why would she do that?"

"To pay off Grandma's debts," Nakita said.

Everything clicked. Curtis was the reason Kim had been at the auction, and her mom and sister were cuffed to a stove.

"Damn, Kim," Jackie said. "She can't keep doing this."

Ruby came into the kitchen. "This is my fault."

Isaac saw the guilt on her face. He shook his head and stood. "Not now. The time to feel guilty can come later. Once the police come for that bastard out there, we'll get Kim and figure out what needs to happen next."

Fury and guilt gnawed at Isaac. No matter how much he hated what Kim had done, his family was partially responsible.

CHAPTER 35

Kim rubbed her aching shoulders as the officer led her from the holding cell to another room. She never ever wanted to spend another night in jail. Not like she'd have much of a choice after these charges went through. The possibility of spending more time in jail wasn't the worst thing about the night before. No, the look on Isaac's face when he'd seen her there was way worse. The betrayal, anger, and disgust in his dark gaze were burned into her memory.

The officer stopped in front of one of the interrogation rooms. Kim recognized it from the night before. They'd taken statements from everyone who'd been in that place. She hadn't lied. There was no need to. She'd chosen to go there. No matter how good her reasons may have seemed at the time, the decision had been hers. Her mistake and now she had to pay for it.

Kim walked into the room. A man in a dark blue suit stood. He had dark eyes and a low-cut fade sprinkled with just enough gray to make him appear distinguished. She recognized him from somewhere, but couldn't figure out exactly where.

"Thank you," he said to the officer. "I'd like a few minutes with my client before we speak to the investigator." His deep voice rolled with authority.

Kim glanced from him to the officer then back again. Client? This guy oozed power, and from the diamond watch on his wrist, the expensive suit tailored to his large frame and the gold set pens spread out on the table, he was too expensive to be any court-appointed attorney.

The officer nodded and left the room. Kim eyed the man and took a step backward. She'd been played enough not to trust Mr. Overpriced Lawyer. With her luck, Curtis had sent him to further ruin her life. No one listened when she'd asked them to check on her family. Her one call to her mom hadn't been answered. Combine that with the fact that she'd spent the entire night in lockup, she was barely keeping the panic at bay. What had Curtis done to her grandmother?

"There's no need to be scared," the man said.

"I'm not scared." Her voice came out strong and didn't betray her lie. "What did you do to my grandmother?"

A line formed between the man's brows. "When I spoke with your grandmother earlier today, she was fine. A bit shaken, but completely healthy."

Kim hurried forward. "You spoke with her? Why is she shaken? What did you and Curtis do to her?"

"Why don't we sit down and talk?" He pulled out a chair.

"I'm not doing a damn thing until you tell me why you're here. He's already ruined my life, and he's threatened my grandmother's. What else could he possibly want? If it's for me to stay away from Isaac, fine. After last night, Isaac never wants to see me again anyway."

Fancy lawyer took his seat and leaned back comfortably, unbothered by her outburst. "First of all, if Isaac never wanted to see you again, he wouldn't have hired me to be your defense attorney. Second, I don't work for Curtis Caldwell. That man is the scum of the lowest order. I've defended some bad dudes, so take my word on that. Third, your life isn't ruined. If you sit down, take that chip off your shoulder and listen, I'll tell you how we're going to get you out of this."

That stunned her for a second. "Isaac hired you?"

"Called in a favor. I owe him one. I thought he'd call in his favor for something harder than this." He shrugged and pointed to the chair opposite of him.

Kim pulled out the chair on her end and followed suit. "Who are you?"

His eyes widened. "I haven't not been recognized in a long time. You hurt my feelings." He chuckled. "Guess that's good for the ego. I'm Bradley Rogers."

Her jaw dropped. "Big Bad Brad?"

"The one and only."

Kim snapped her mouth shut. Brad Rogers was one of the best defense attorneys in the state. If not the best. He'd successfully defended clients accused of everything from white collar offenses to crimes of passion. He'd recently gotten the acquittal of a man who'd shot the mayor of a small town in Spartanburg. The man accused the mayor, who'd been well respected and loved, of molesting his daughter.

"I can't afford you."

"Which is why Isaac called in the favor." Brad turned the papers in front of him to face Kim and slid them across the table. "I've already worked out the deal. All charges dropped if you testify to the blackmail that led you to the house last night. Also, testify to speaking with Sherry Davis about possibly being able to get her out of there."

"Who's Sherry Davis?"

"A sixteen-year-old. Her parents went to the police when she went missing. She was considered a runaway. She'd been caught up in the trafficking scheme that led to the auction last night. She said she spoke with you and thought you would be able to help her get out of there."

"She's sixteen?" Disgust filled Kim's voice.

Brad's eyes turned hard, his mouth formed a grim line. "Yes. Curtis Caldwell began funding the auctions. That was one part of the crime ring he was developing in the area. That and the gambling. He asked Rebecca to get you there that night. He also worked it so your grandmother would lose and you'd have few options. He called in the hit when things went bad last night."

Kim sat forward. "What happened?"

Brad's eyes turned sympathetic. "Just some threats. It was broken up and the police called. Everyone is fine."

"I didn't know about all that when I agreed to go."

"Doesn't change the fact that's what happened. The prosecution can make the case that Curtis used intimidation and blackmail to get women to participate. You testify for them and your charges are dropped."

"Are the other men and women getting this deal?"

"I don't work for them. You're my client, and I'm getting you out of this."

Kim shook her head and pushed the papers away. "No. I can't just walk away scot-free, and they suffer. That entire place wasn't right. They need help too."

Brad watched her for several seconds. "You're willing to risk charges for them?"

"I'm not willing to walk away with an expensive lawyer and a deal when you said yourself Curtis used manipulation and blackmail to get everyone there."

Brad nodded. "Fine. The experienced prostitutes are on their own, but I'll help the ones coerced there. I've already taken on Sherry's case. Might as well build up my pro bono work for the year."

"That was too easy," Kim said. She'd expected him to fight more.

"Like I said, Curtis Caldwell disgusts me. I was going to help them anyway." He slid the papers back to Kim. "But knowing you were willing to ignore this deal in order to help them answered a question I had."

"What question is that?"

"Why Isaac Caldwell cares enough about you to call in a favor from me."

*

An hour later Kim had signed the deal and learned her home would be under increased surveillance until they finished pulling in all of the players tied up in Curtis's scheme to become the newest crime boss in the area. When she finally was released and was greeted by her family, tears streamed down her face.

Kim ran to her grandmother and pulled her into a hug. "I was so worried about you. I thought...he said..." she couldn't finish the words.

Ruby pulled back and wiped the tears from Kim's face. "Shhh...everything is okay. Let's get out of here and we'll talk about everything at home."

Kim didn't argue. She wanted to get the hell away from the police station and wash off the stench of the night before. They filled her in on what happened after she'd been arrested. Isaac had listened to her. If he hadn't, things could have been terrible. He'd had no reason to care, but he'd saved her family by calling in the favor with Brad. She didn't deserve any of it. There was no way she could pay him back.

Kim headed straight for the shower when she got home. Alone, all of the fear, grief, and guilt she'd suppressed for the past few hours finally took over. Tears fell in a violent, cathartic torrent. When she got out of the shower, she felt slightly better. She had to thank Isaac, but she didn't know how she could possibly face him.

Her family sat around the table in the kitchen. They looked up when she came in. Ruby jumped up and poured Kim a cup of coffee. "Come sit down with us."

"No. I've got something I need to do, but first I need to talk to you all." She went to Ruby and took the coffee mug out of her hand. "Grandma, I love you, and I'll do whatever I can to help you keep this house, but I'm never putting myself in that situation again."

"I never wanted you to be in that situation," Ruby said.

"I know, and I still won't stand by and watch someone threaten or hurt you, but you've got to promise me that I won't have to worry about you again."

"I swear, not even Bingo for me anymore." Ruby's eyes glistened with tears. She took Kim's hands in her own. "I'm so sorry. I got caught up trying to help. It was like it wasn't real. I never expected things to get this bad. This family is the most important thing to me. We don't need this house. We'll be a family no matter where we go."

Jackie stood and came over. "We'll all make it work. You don't have to take care of the family anymore. Especially not in this way. I ignored it when you were younger, and I've never forgiven myself. If there are problems, we'll work it out together. No more looking the other way or ignoring the issue. Don't ever think you have to bail us out at your expense."

"I won't. Which is why I'm getting my own place." She shook her head and held up her hands when they started to argue. "I need to. It's time to cut the apron strings in both directions. I've been saving to get my own place but decided to use the money for the down payment. I need space, and you all do too. It's time for me to take care of me."

Ruby looked around the kitchen. "There are a lot of good memories here." She met Kim's gaze. "And a lot of bad. I think finding a new place and you getting your own is a good idea."

They hugged and talked for a few more minutes before Kim knew she had to go. "I've got to find Isaac and thank him for everything."

Nakita shifted in her seat at the table. "I didn't think you two really cared about each other. I'm sorry for doubting you."

"No need to be sorry. Besides, it doesn't matter anymore. After last night, we're done. I'll apologize and tell him I'm looking for another job."

Nakita frowned. "I don't think you're done. He's still in love with you."

"You didn't see the look in his eye. He hates me."

Ruby squeezed Kim's hand. "You didn't see how upset he was last night. He might be angry that you didn't tell him about your—our—problems, but he still cares. You can fix this."

Kim shook her head and picked up her keys off the counter. "Isaac is rebuilding his company image. After this blows up with Curtis, it'll be even harder. He doesn't need a former street hustler slash prostitute on his side while he does that. Even if it could be fixed, it's not worth the trouble."

"It is if you love him," Jackie said. "And, Kim, you do deserve to be loved."

"I know. Just not by him," she said before going out the door.

CHAPTER 36

Finding Isaac was easier said than done. Kim went to his place, the office, and even drove to Curtis's home. No luck. She had met the stepmother he liked so much. She'd been nice enough. Kim assumed she didn't know Kim would be testifying against her husband, so she'd quickly left before the conversation could get awkward. Curtis's absence made Kim hope he was still in a jail cell.

Isaac's phone went straight to voicemail. She almost called Andre but didn't want to get the family drama even more stirred up and cause Andre to worry. She didn't want to go back home, and she couldn't keep wondering the streets. She ended up at Falls Park. She'd walk, clear her mind and think about the endless employment possibilities for her after she left C.E.S. There had to be tons of companies willing to take her once the media storm of Curtis's trial died down. *Yeah right.*

She folded her arms tight over her chest and walked the park's trails. She had so much to be thankful for. Things could have been so much worse. Isaac had helped her when he had no reason to. He may have begun to love her, but the disgust in his eye when he'd seen her? She'd never forget that. Neither would he. She couldn't stomach the idea of seeing that on his face again, or worse, having him throw it in her face when he got mad later. They were done. Even though she was happy things had worked out, her heart ached with that realization.

A man stood next to one of the benches overlooking the falls. Kim had planned to sit there and brood. She'd earned the right to drown in self-pity. She didn't want to force conversation. She started to turn away but looked at the guy again and froze.

"Isaac?"

He faced her. The anger and disgust from last night wasn't on his face. His entire expression was emotionless. "What are you doing here?"

"Clearing my head." She took a few steps closer. "I've been looking for you. I need to thank you."

He frowned. "For what?"

"For what?" Her disbelief evident in her tone. How could he possibly

192

ask that? "For everything. You saved my family last night. You got me the best defense attorney in the area. I've got the chance to start over again when I don't deserve it."

"It's the least I can do."

"You didn't have to do anything." Kim sighed heavily and pushed her hair away from her face. "I'm sorry I didn't tell you about the auction. My grandmother owed money, and I didn't want her to be hurt. I felt like I had to do something. I thought that was the only way." The tears she'd thought were all gone sprang back.

He crossed the distance between them and pulled her against his hard chest. "Kim, stop. I put you in this position. If I hadn't asked you to help me take down Curtis, he wouldn't have come after your family."

As much as she wanted to stay in his embrace, she couldn't. She pushed back, but he kept his hands on her shoulders. "You don't understand. Last night wasn't the first time I've done something like that."

His brows drew together. The urge to look away ran deep, but she forced herself to look him in the eye. "I told you about running the little scams when I was younger, but it was more than that. Rebecca was being tempted by this pimp named Benji for us to come work with him. She said it would be better money. Faster money, and when the guys we were picking up became more aggressive, I thought it would be easier than trying to run. So, I agreed to do a job with them. It was the worst night of my life. The next time they asked I couldn't go through with it. I ran. The guy got mad and started hitting Rebecca. She used the bedside lamp in the hotel to beat him. The cops came, and Rebecca went to jail. That's why she said I owed her. I told her I'd do one job to make up for it."

Isaac's grip on her tightened. His brows formed a line over his confused eyes. "Why?"

"Because I've felt guilty. It was stupid and ridiculous, but I did. She wanted me to steal money from C.E.S. and I said no. Working one job was my way to make up for leaving her behind. I didn't think it would be…what last night was. I told her I wouldn't do it, but then they said they would call in my grandma's debts. Even though last night was bad, I don't want you to think it was the only time."

His hands loosened on her arms. "Is that why you were so against my offer to take care of you?"

She nodded. "I don't want to be someone's high-priced prostitute. I want the fairy tale, even if it's not real."

Isaac let her go. "You should have told me the truth."

Her heart twisted. "I didn't want you to know. I'm not proud of my past, but it's part of who I am."

He shook his head. "Do you know he had teenagers?" Isaac's nostrils flared and his eyes burned with rage. "He organized Benji's operation. He

193

set up illegal gambling houses using fake businesses he opened. He didn't care about C.E.S. anymore. The business was his cover. Curtis is the vilest type of person there is, and he knew he could get to you through me. Last night was my fault." His voice tightened. His eyes glistened, but he sucked in a breath and blinked rapidly.

She didn't care if he didn't want to touch her, she took his hand in his and forced him to look at her. "Don't take the blame. I should have told you. I promised I'd tell you."

"You did, and I can't lie. Knowing you went behind my back is going to take some time to get over."

"Which is why I'm resigning."

"What?" He sounded surprised.

How could he be shocked? The answer was obvious? "I can't stay there anymore."

"Because of what Curtis did to you?"

"Because I love you and I hurt you. I can't do that every day."

His eyes narrowed. "That's the dumbest thing I've ever heard."

"Excuse me?" She tried to drop his hand, but he held on tight.

"I love you, too, Kim. You're the first woman I ever told that to, and apparently, the emotion doesn't just go away overnight. We're in a fucked-up spot right now, but that doesn't mean we have to throw it all away."

The blood rushing in her ears drowned out the sound of the falls. "You want to stay together?"

He eased back and looked uncertain. "You don't?"

"You're trying to rebrand the company. Everyone is going to know what I did. Everyone is going to hear about my past. That's not the type of person you need at your side."

Isaac let out a breath and looked at her like she'd mixed up the financial reports instead of nearly ruining his image. "To hell with what I need. You get what needs to happen at C.E.S. better than anyone. You care about this company as much as me. Not only that, but you love me. Why would I not want you at my side?"

"Because I won't make it easier." She tried, unsuccessfully, to keep the hope from creeping into her voice.

He tapped his chest. "Do I look like a punk? Do you think I'm not able to fight, or that I take the easy way out? We'll do this together and be stronger afterward because we survived the shit storm that's coming. Your past may have some blemishes, but that has nothing on my family, what Curtis did to screw over his family, the business and so many other people. How can I possibly judge you when I've got his corruption on my hands?"

Kim stepped forward and placed her hand on his chest. "His corruption isn't yours. You had nothing to do with anything."

"But I've been approached to bring him down. To participate in

194

investigations, but I never listened. I tried to remain loyal to him when he never deserved my loyalty. Ignorance doesn't absolve me of his crimes." He placed a hand on the side of her face. His eyes were full of pain, love, and hope. "Kim, I need you by my side as we get through this."

"I didn't think you'd ever trust me again." Her voice broke. Her heart pulsed with the need to believe they weren't over. Not once the night before had she allowed herself to think they'd recover from this. Knowing they might, that they could persevere, was almost too much to process.

"You asked me if you could trust me with your heart. I should have warned you then the danger of putting your trust in my family. It's time to purge my family of all the deceit, mistrust, and anger. To do that, I've got to open myself up to healing and forgiveness. It'll take a while, but it's worth it. For you." He cupped her face in both hands and used his thumbs to brush away her tears.

Her hand on his chest balled into a fist over his heart. Her body shook with relief and her efforts to not break down into tears. "I love you so much. I'm so sorry."

"Enough with the apologies. Let's try not to go through anything like this again." Isaac pressed his forehead to hers. "Are you willing to work this out with me? Are you ready to weather this storm with me?"

She wrapped her arms around his waist. Her heart beat so hard she thought she'd explode. He loved her. He wanted a second chance. She would hold on, grab their future with both hands and never let go. "I'd weather any storm with you, Isaac."

EPILOGUE

The shit storm lasted months and was as messy and disgusting as Isaac had expected. Curtis was a sloppy crime lord, blinded by thoughts of grandeur, which made it easy for the prosecution to build a case against him. That and the fact that his poor treatment of even the people he'd demanded loyalty from meant their loyalty had only lasted through about five minutes of an interrogation.

The entire time Isaac never once spoke with Curtis. He didn't trust himself not to harm his dad if he saw him, and there was nothing he could say. Curtis was vile and repulsive. Any loyalty Isaac may have once had was gone. His loyalty was now on keeping C.E.S. going.

"I just got this quarter's numbers from finance," Kim said, walking into his office.

Isaac turned away from the window. His chest squeezed with love, and a little bit of sorrow. She held no ill will toward him for his father's part in her trouble, but he hadn't shaken his guilt. Kim's reputation had nearly been trashed. He'd defended her, and surprisingly a lot of the employees there had as well. Brad did his part to show she was another victim of Curtis's games, but that hadn't made it easier for her.

"What are they?" he asked. They'd suffered the last quarter with the announcement of the arrests and the shakeup at C.E.S. Lost a few more clients, gained a couple based off peoples' trust in Isaac's ability.

"We actually turned a profit." Kim looked up from the paper and smiled. "Not as big as they were four years ago, but profit is profit."

Isaac grinned and came around the desk to take her into his arms. She kissed him back with a fierce passion he knew he would never get tired of. As long as he lived, he'd never be able to show her how much he appreciated her being by his side. With every revelation of his dad's crimes, with each demand from the board to do better, with the heartbreak of the families who blamed C.E.S. for the abuses of the former leader, she'd been there. She'd helped him set up a foundation to help victims of human trafficking when he wanted to do something but wasn't sure what. It didn't make up for what his dad had done, but it was something. Kim was beautiful, smart and strong as hell. He'd fight anyone who said otherwise.

"Maybe now the board will trust me a little. They're nervous about the announcement to merge with Andre's company."

"Merging is better than a hostile takeover. It'll put C.E.S. at the lead in the state in large scale composting. Between that and the push to convert more landfill gas for industry use, you're finding other revenue streams besides waste hauling. It's the direction you and your brother wanted to take the company in the first place. This minor profit is just the start. They trust you, just like I trust you."

She started to pull away, but he held her. "Do you? I mean *really* trust me?"

"I do. I'll never keep something so important from you again." She looked unsure for a moment. "Do you trust me?"

He didn't have to think about the answer. "Completely."

"Even after…"

"Kim, that's over. The trial is coming, my dad will go to jail, and then we'll put that securely behind us. But just know that between you and me, there is no distrust, no anger."

She smiled, but her eyes shimmered with tears. "I love you so much, Isaac. I can't believe we're here."

"Does that mean you'll say yes?"

"To what?"

"Marrying me."

Her eyes widened. "Are you proposing? Right before a board meeting?"

He nodded. "I am. I know I should have prepared something fancy or romantic. You deserve a better proposal than this, but it's in my heart right now. I want you by my side for the rest of my life. There is no one else I love more. No one I trust more than you. Later, I'll take you to buy the gaudiest ring you want, and we'll say I gave it to you in front of the Eiffel Tower, but for now, I need to know. Will you marry me?"

She shook her head and tears glistened in her beautiful eyes. "I don't need a big ring or anything fancy. I just need you. Yes. I'll marry you."

If Isaac believed in fairy tales, he'd swear he had a fairy godmother sprinkling luck and cheer. Instead, he reveled in the joy of her answer. "You've just made me the happiest man."

She laughed. "All men say that."

"You're right. Okay, how about this? You've just ensured that I close the biggest deal of my life."

The love in her eyes warmed places he never thought would feel the heat of love, affection, or trust. When she smiled, he knew he could face anything ahead of them because he had the best partner, lover, and friend by his side.

ABOUT THE AUTHOR

If you enjoyed Trust Me With Your Love (or not) don't forget to leave a review. Want to keep up with all my latest releases, appearances and get special previews? Sign up for my mailing list on my website.

Synithia Williams has loved romance novels since reading her first one at the age of 13. It was only natural that she would begin penning her own romances soon after. It wasn't until 2010 that she began to actively pursue her publishing dreams. When she isn't writing, Synithia is working hard on water quality issues in the Midlands of South Carolina and taking care of her supportive husband and two sons. You can learn more about Synithia by visiting her website, www.synithiawilliams.com, where she blogs about writing, life and relationships.

Facebook: http://www.facebook.com/synithiarwilliams
Twitter: http://www.twitter.com/@SynithiaW

Other Books by Synithia Williams
Caldwell Family Series:
Show Me How to Love
Love Me As I Am
Trust Me With Your Love

Southern Love Series:
You Can't Plan Love
Worth the Wait
A Heart to Heal

Henderson Family Series:
Just My Type
Love's Replay
Making it Real
From One Night to Forever

Harlequin Kimani Titles:
A New York Kind of Love
A Malibu Kind of Romance
Full Court Seduction

Made in United States
Orlando, FL
27 January 2022

14099346R00119